BLACK LUCK

PROF CROFT BOOK 5

BRAD MAGNARELLA

THE PROF CROFT SERIES

PREQUELS
Book of Souls
Siren Call

MAIN SERIES
Demon Moon
Blood Deal
Purge City
Death Mage
Black Luck
Power Game
Druid Bond
Night Rune
Shadow Duel
Shadow Deep
Godly Wars
Angel Doom

SPIN-OFFS
Croft & Tabby
Croft & Wesson

MORE COMING!

1

The bolt that hit Quinton Weeks in the low back felt like a cattle prod. Swearing, he clamped the cramping muscle. His snow shovel, loaded with trash and debris, fell short of his cart in a plume of dust. He leaned against the cart and panted beneath the searing sun.

This is for the effing birds, he thought.

Quinton wasn't a stranger to work, but this was hard labor. His wasted muscles weren't used to it. By the time he pushed himself straight, the sweat from his face had fogged up his goggles again. He swore, shoved the goggles onto his forehead, and pulled down his respirator.

While he waited for the pain in his back to ease, he peered around the ruined landscape, inhaling its grit. On all sides, workers in helmets and orange vests were shoveling, welding, jack-hammering, and climbing in and out of big trucks. He felt like he was on another planet. But he was in Lower Manhattan, a couple of months after the war down here.

A war over what? Hell if Quinton knew. There had been

all sorts of rumors. The wildest being that it had involved werewolves and vampires. The mayor had even claimed a wizard played a role.

Quinton snorted. Anything to get reelected. New York was weird, but not quite that weird. He'd seen some wild stuff, sure. Big, lumbering mutants in the East Village. And only a couple months earlier, the city had rioted en masse. Over what? Again, he had no idea. He'd been too stoned.

But he needed money now. Badly. He'd gone on a massive substance binge that summer, and by the time he emerged he was out of food, two months behind on rent, and one day shy of turning thirty. Somewhere in there, his girlfriend had dumped him. He had to get it together.

The cleanup gig guaranteed him six months of work, but now he wasn't sure he was going to last. It wasn't just the back pain or the withdrawal, it was the culture of the place.

A Styrofoam cup nailed the side of his helmet, splashing coffee over him.

"Hey, sissy!" someone shouted. "No one's paying you to play pocket pool!"

Case in point.

Quinton turned to see a thick worker leaning out of the passenger window of an idling truck. The driver grinned past him. He'd run into these two before, a pair of junior site managers who got their kicks shoving around debris collectors like him. He'd learned to stay off their radar, to look busy whenever they came by, but the place was so damned noisy, he hadn't heard them roll up.

"Sthorry," Quinton said, replacing his goggles and respirator.

He'd tried to bite back the lisp, but he'd been born with a cleft pallet, and there wasn't much he could do about it. The two workers climbed out of the idling truck and swaggered toward him.

Quinton kept his eyes on his shovel.

"Oh, you're *sthorry*?" the passenger said. "Where'd they find you? Broadway and Forty-second?"

The two of them laughed. Quinton squinted over at them, grinning as if he was in on the joke, even though he'd heard it most of his life. Their eyes glinted cruelly. Quinton shifted his gaze. A couple of blocks to the north, workers were disman-tling the massive wall that had separated Lower Manhattan from the rest of the city. A crane lifted out a huge vertical section.

"What are you staring at?" the driver demanded.

Quinton returned to his work, shoveling up more debris. His back protested as he lifted the load toward the cart. But before it got there, the driver planted a large work boot against the cart's side and gave it a shove. The cart tipped over, spilling the couple hundred pounds of debris Quinton had spent the last half hour loading.

The passenger snorted a laugh. "Oops."

The driver leaned toward Quinton, his mouth set in a dangerous scowl. "You don't have that shit picked up in the next five, and you're off the job. I don't know how your pansy ass got signed in the first place. You don't belong."

Quinton had heard that last part most of his life too.

"All right," he said evenly, even though his bladder was on the verge of letting go. His back screamed as he righted the large yellow cart and began to refill it quickly. The two watched for a minute or so before growing bored and swag-gering back to their truck.

"Five minutes," the driver reminded him.

The truck rumbled off, the two in search of someone else

to dominate. Quinton relaxed slightly, but on the next shovel-ful, his back gave out and he collapsed to his knees. He stayed there for the next minute, forehead to the debris-covered street. Screw the job, screw the money—hell, screw living. He didn't need any of it anymore. It added up to one big nothing.

"Oh, I agree," a voice said.

Afraid the two assholes had returned, Quinton lurched upright. But when he looked around, he was alone. Anyway, the voice had sounded older, more refined—and strangely sympathetic.

"This is far beneath someone like you," the voice contin-ued. "Someone of your ... *importance*."

With the last word, a chilly current ran over Quinton like hundreds of fingertips. His back stopped throbbing. He looked around some more, the broken glass that covered the ruined landscape sparkling sharply in the sun. Still no one. The voice was too clear for him to be imagining it. He paused. Was he losing his mind? He'd done some hard stuff that summer, like—

"What do you want for yourself?" the voice interrupted.

"Who are you?" Quinton demanded. "Why can't I see you?"

"I'm a friend," the voice replied smoothly. "Look beneath your left hand."

Quinton jerked the hand away from the pile. If there was a face down there, he was going to scream. At first he saw only dusty rubble and garbage, but something glinted up at him. He pulled his glove off, pinched the glinting object between a finger and thumb, and drew it out.

It was a silver necklace.

"You didn't happen upon me by accident. You are a Chosen One. Wear it, and I will open you to your true potential. I'll fulfill your wishes. You'll possess power you never dreamed possible."

A Chosen One? That sounded like New Age bullshit, but Quinton was still trying to get his head around the idea that a necklace appeared to be talking to him. He held it at arm's length.

"Would you rather stay here and scoop filth for the next six months?" the voice asked. "Be harassed by ogres?"

No, Quinton decided. No, he wouldn't. And what did he have to lose? Either his brain was damaged and he was hearing voices, in which case nothing would happen when he wore the necklace, and he would resume his miserable life. Or something might actually happen.

A hope Quinton hadn't felt in years kicked inside him. Tugging off the other glove, he fastened the necklace at his grimy nape. When the voice spoke again, it felt like someone talking into both of his ears at the same time.

"There," the voice said. "Doesn't that feel better?"

As Quinton stood, cold energy pulsed from the silver. Something was happening, but he couldn't tell what. All he knew was that the hopelessness that had being crushing down on his soul like a trash compactor seemed to have backed off. He felt scared and excited at the same time.

"It does," he admitted. "But who are you?"

"I am called Damien, and I have work for you."

The pulses deepened until they vibrated through Quinton's body. He felt larger, stronger, his worries of just minutes before a million miles away. A few drugs had made him feel that way in the past, but over time the effects had become fragile and fleeting. Gone too soon.

But this felt like a permanent state. It was as if something that already belonged to him was waking up from a long sleep, coming back to life. He loved Damien for arousing it. But he feared, too, that Damien could squelch it just as quickly, dropping him back into the gutter.

"Yes, anything," Quinton said anxiously.

"Gather your four most trusted friends."

Quinton considered that. Did he even have four friends he trusted?

"You did not happen on me by accident," Damien said. "And neither did you happen on them. Your whole life has been building toward this moment. You, Quinton, are central to the *Plan*." He said the word as though it were capitalized. That was the way Quinton heard it anyway.

He nodded. "When should I gather them?"

He felt Damien's lips break into a grin. For some reason, the thought of pleasing Damien filled Quinton with a wild joy.

"Why not now?" Damien said. "You're going to build an Ark."

"Yes," Quinton said, not knowing what Damien meant but at the same time sensing its importance.

He peered around. The array of burly workers suddenly looked puny and stupid. He felt an urge to crush them all beneath his boot. Instead, he used his boot to snap his leaning shovel in half. He then chucked away his safety equipment and strode from his trash cart. Two blocks later, he was kicking past the cordon.

"Hey, where do you think you're going?" one of the site managers called.

"Thith is for the fucking birds," Quinton called back, grinning too hard to notice his lisp.

"Yes," Damien agreed in his head. "For the birds."

2

Ten months later

I banged on the apartment door again, louder.

"Hello?" I shouted. "Anyone home?"

I looked at my cane, which had tugged me to Harlem and then up to the tenth-floor unit at 8:40 on a Friday morning. The hologram back at my apartment had started flashing about twenty-five minutes earlier. For the distance, I had arrived here in good time—assuming I was standing at the right address. It had only been two months since I'd burst into a wrong apartment, invoking a shield in time to spare myself a shotgun blast to the face.

Now my cane jerked and knocked against the door twice as if to say, *Yes, Everson—nether creature ahead!*

"All right, all right. Just wanted to be sure."

I dispelled the hunting spell and whispered, *"Protezione."*

My cane relaxed and then stiffened with new energy. An orb of light swelled from the cane's opal and grew to encompass me. With another Word, I shaped the light until it conformed to my figure. I'd been working on that last skill for the past several months and grinned now at being able to maintain the shield's form with only minimal concentration.

I tried the doorknob while gathering a force invocation. Surprisingly, the knob turned in my grasp. The battered door creaked open about a foot before stopping cold. Something was blocking it. Swelling my light out, I beheld a dim hallway. Loaded boxes were stacked floor to ceiling. By their dusty condition, they weren't going to be unpacked anytime soon.

Great, I thought, *a hoarder.*

The only thing I hated worse than going underground was being in confined spaces. Especially with nether creatures afoot. Grunting, I put my shoulder into the door and forced it open another few inches until I could squeeze inside. I checked all around before fixing my gaze ahead.

"Hello?" I called again.

I drew my sword from the cane as I advanced sideways between the towering heaps of boxes. The runes my father had inscribed in the blade's steel and silver pulsed with power.

"Anyone home?"

Though I'd answered hundreds of calls over the years, I never knew what I was walking into. Sure, the MO was predictable enough. Amateur conjurer comes into the possession of a spell book or enchanted item, decides to call up something—either for kicks or from the mistaken notion that benevolent, wish-granting beings actually exist—and then performs enough of the ritualistic steps correctly to summon ... something.

The *something* was always the question mark. Best case, a shallow nether creature that scurried or flapped around for a few minutes before evaporating back to its realm, the energy that called it forth too weak to sustain it. Worst case, something from deeper down that was much more adept at survival—usually by devouring the summoner's blood and/or vital organs before widening its search.

In the last year, with the Order still laboring to repair the tears left behind by the Whisperer, I'd been encountering more of the second.

I sniffed. It would have taken a werewolf's nose to discern anything amid the riot of odors, but I did manage to pick up the tangy scent of a recent conjuring. I eyed the open doorways off the corridor. Beyond the final door on the right, something was throwing shadows. Something big. The play of shadows was accompanied by scuffing, and soon muttering.

The conjurer?

"Hello?" I called.

A box near the bathroom fell to the floor behind me. I spun as more boxes toppled over. A creature the size of a pool noodle had emerged from hiding and was now racing along the wall on centipede legs. Where its head should have been, a pincer mouth opened and closed amid a mass of writhing tendrils.

"A scrabbler," I muttered.

Fortunately, they weren't particularly smart. I shrank back to give it the impression I was cowering. When the scrabbler was almost to me, it twisted, front legs peeling from the wall, and lunged. I met the mouth with the thrust of my sword. The blade disappeared down its throat. The scrabbler's tendrils grasped at my hand before jerking back, surprised by my crackling shield.

"Disfare!" I shouted.

Energy coursed down my blade, and the creature exploded in giant gobs of phlegm.

One and done, I thought, but I was bothered. A scrabbler didn't grow to that size without feeding.

I turned back toward the far room, where something continued to mutter and scuff around. I stole forward. As I passed the first bedroom off the hallway, I braced for the sight of a half-eaten conjurer. Instead, I found a space so packed with junk that roaches would have had a hard time navigating.

I pulled the door closed and sealed it with a locking spell. It was rare an amateur conjurer managed to call up more than one or two creatures at a go, but I didn't want any surprises.

Inside the next bedroom, a narrow path led to a queen-sized mattress and cluttered nightstand. Densely packed racks of women's clothes ringed the room. The bed was empty except for a scatter of spells books. My gaze locked on the title of one of them: an English translation of the *Khafji Scrolls.* That's where the spell had come from. I was in the process of foot-shoving an armoire back to close and seal the door when a row of dresses on the far wall began to shudder.

"Please be a cat."

But the three creatures that emerged were neither furry nor feline. They raced out on finger-like legs. Razor-sharp tails whipped back and forth, one of them making tatters of a purple dress.

Riddlers.

Guided by my heat aura, they launched at my face. With a jab of my staff and an uttered Word, I snagged them in mid air with a light orb. They scurried over one another, tails lashing. I shrank the orb until the riddlers were jammed together, the fleshy mouths on the undersides of their bodies snapping at their confinement. My brow tensed as I pushed more energy into the orb. The energy that sustained the three creatures pushed back, but I overpowered it as one by one the horrid creatures bulged and then popped out of existence.

I exhaled and deposited the phlegmy residue in a wastebasket beside the bed. Sealing the door as I left, I turned toward the final room.

Now for the Big Daddy.

Because there was no way now that the conjurer was still alive.

As I sidled up to the doorway, I wracked my brain for a class of creature on par with scrabblers and riddlers that could be so large. Either the thing had been conjured without triggering the Order's detecting wards, giving it time to grow, or it was from even farther down than the others.

Either way, a part of me anticipated the challenge.

The Order had promised to continue my training as soon as a teacher became available, but a full year had gone by without that happening. That hadn't stopped me from getting a head start, though. I was proud of the progress I'd made since we'd repelled Dhuul, the Whisperer. Creatures I'd once struggled to put down—such as scrabblers and riddlers— now barely made me sweat. I'd suffered no major injuries, and I wasn't having to depend on my luck quotient.

All right, I wasn't having to depend on my luck quotient *as much*. With more training and experience, I hoped it would become a dim memory.

As the blade my father had forged glinted in the dim corridor, I thought about the kind of mage he had been:

supremely powerful and wise. Not someone who depended on luck.

So let's send the Big Daddy packing without the quotient, hm?

I pressed my back to the wall beside the doorway. Sword and staff clenched in either hand, I peeked inside.

"The hell?" I muttered.

3

I wasn't looking at a Big Daddy. More like a plus-sized mama.

For a few more moments, I could only stare. The elderly black woman shuffling around the small kitchen on an aluminum walker clutched a can opener and a can of dog food in the same hand. A pile of gray hair stood from her head, while a pink bathrobe wrapped her ample body.

Was this the amateur conjurer? It had to be. The only habitable bedroom in the unit had contained spell books. But the woman shouldn't have been alive, much less tottering around her kitchen. I watched her drop the can opener into a crowded sink and then, muttering, dig a metal spoon from beneath a pile of plates. She smacked the spoon against the side of the can three times.

"Come and get your breakfast!" she called, her voice strong and maternal.

When she stooped down to shovel the dog food into the last of a row of plastic bowls, the explanation hit me in the gut. Dogs. She'd had dogs. And she was alive because the nether creatures had found them first.

I peered back down the corridor, half expecting to see more of the creatures skittering into view. I needed to get the old woman to safety. I took a step into the kitchen and cleared my throat.

"Ma'am?"

She had finished plopping the food into the bowl, and now she evened out the portions. "I know you don't like it when your food dries out," she called, "and this is all you're getting this morning!"

Damn. I was not looking forward to breaking the news to her.

"Excuse me? Ma'am?" I said louder, sheathing my sword so I wouldn't appear threatening. My shield continued to hum softly around me.

The woman cocked her head, then labored to straighten her bent back.

"I'm Everson Croft," I all but shouted. "I heard you had an infestation. I'm here to help."

She finally turned enough to notice me. I held up a hand to show her I was harmless. She leaned forward, eyes squinting past a pair of thick glasses with smudged lenses. "Said you're here about an infection?" she asked. "What infection? I don't know anything about an infection."

"No, no. An *infestation*."

She shook her head in annoyance and jammed a thick finger into her right ear. She twisted the finger one way and then the other until a hearing aid began to whine. Grumbling, she turned it back down.

"All right. Come again?"

"An infestation," I repeated. "You know ... critters that shouldn't be here."

She pursed her lower lip and shook her head. "Don't know about any of those. Only ones here besides me are my babies." She shouted past me, "You all coming?"

"Yeah ... about them—shit!"

I hadn't spotted the creature crawling over the top of the cabinets until it leapt down. It landed on the floor between us with a clack and snapped its claws at me. It could have been a lobster, except for the tendrils writhing from its mouth. Its name flashed through my mind: *a clawdad*. Though smaller than the other creatures, it was no less deadly. The woman grunted in what sounded like alarm, causing the creature to scuttle around and jump at her.

With no time to call up a force invocation, I swung my cane like a golf club. I would have liked to think I'd acted on honed reflexes, but my luck quotient had called the shot. Ever since learning I possessed a more active quotient than most magic-users, I'd become increasingly attuned to it. It manifested as a subtle tingling in my gut right before it kicked in. And I'd just felt it.

My cane met the clawdad's hard exoskeleton mid-jump with a crack. The creature tumbled through the air and smashed into a pantry.

"Stay back!" I shouted over my shoulder.

Canned food rolled from the pantry as I drew my sword and advanced. The woman behind me was trapped, which meant that whatever happened, I couldn't let the clawdad get past me. A bag of flour fell out next and burst across the floor as the clawdad scuttled around the shelves.

The woman shouted excitedly.

If I could spot the creature, I could trap it like I'd done the riddlers and squeeze it out of existence. I would then perform a final search of the apartment for any remaining creatures and incinerate the offending spell book. I'd leave the other books. Better for the woman to think she could cast from them than to have her go out looking for more.

In the pantry, the clawdad went still.

"Illuminare," I whispered. It only took a moment for the light from my opal to expose the creature. It was in the back, trying to hide beneath a pile of mac and cheese boxes.

Game over, you little—

Sparks flew from my shield as something came down on the back of my head. *Another one?* But when I spun, I found the woman standing at her walker behind me. At some point she'd swapped the spoon for a rolling pin. She reared back the rolling pin to strike again.

I threw my arms up. "Are you crazy?"

"Don't you hurt Buster!"

The rolling pin descended with another crack and shower of sparks.

"B-Buster?" I stammered, backing away. "Lady, that's not your dog!"

I stole a glance over my shoulder. Great, the clawdad was no longer in the pantry. I looked wildly around the kitchen.

"Who said anything about a dog?" She waved the rolling pin over her head.

I staggered back another step, almost tripping over the bag of flour. That's when I spotted the clawdad. In the confusion, it had circled the cluttered kitchen and was coming up behind the woman.

"Look out!" I shouted.

She followed my gaze, then lowered the pin.

"There you are, you little rascal." She reached a hand toward it.

Oh God, she's half blind, and she thinks that thing's her puppy.

I squinted as I tried to extend my shield's protection to encompass her. I was sure I would be too slow, that the next sound would be the creature's claw crunching through her fingers.

I *was* too slow, but in the instant before the shield took form around her, the old woman scratched the clawdad's head—and the clawdad let her. The creature skipped back, surprised by the shield.

"Mama's right here," the woman said in her maternal voice. "Oh yes she is."

As the old woman faced me again, her rolling pin in striking position, the clawdad peered at me from behind her legs.

"Ma'am, do you know what that thing is?"

"'Course I do," she snapped back. "I'm not blind." She peered past me. "Now where are my other babies?"

That's when the full understanding hit me.

Not only had she conjured the creatures, but she'd been raising them as house pets. I opened my wizard's senses. No supernatural aura around her. The woman was as mortal as they came.

I dropped my gaze to the small clawdad. It must have been the creature most recently conjured. How the wards had missed the others, I wasn't sure. I'd have to check them out.

The woman saw me watching her and her creature warily from across the kitchen. "He's harmless," she said, then added with a sigh, "and looks like the only one that's gonna get breakfast this morning."

She tossed the rolling pin toward the sink and pulled a

knife from a chopping block. I drew back, but the knife wasn't meant for me. As she turned toward the food bowls, the clawdad leapt up and down. I dropped the woman's protection to see what would happen, ready to throw it back in place the instant the clawdad turned aggressive. But it only scurried around her feet like a puppy anticipating a treat.

The old woman opened the fridge door, pulled a small blood-transfusion bag from a stack of them, and inserted the tip of the knife into the tube. She twisted the knife while holding the bag over the bowls.

"There you go," she said as blood dribbled onto the chunks of dog food. The clawdad squealed and rushed forward. It set upon the bowl, heaping the dog food past its writhing tendrils.

I counted the food bowls. Five. Which meant this was the final creature.

I thought about spearing the clawdad while it and the woman were distracted. But when I caught the loving look in the woman's eyes, I found myself notching my sword back in the cane. The woman released a soft chuckle and placed the empty transfusion bag in the trash. When our eyes met again, she squinted slightly as though trying to place me.

"How long have you been raising these things?" I asked.

She squinted at me another moment, this time mouthing my name. Her eyes widened behind her glasses. "Say, aren't you that boy who helped the mayor last year? The wizard?"

My role in the mayor's eradication program was no secret, but in a metropolis where the churn of headlines was endless, my name and face had all but faded into the archives. It had been months since anyone had recognized me in public.

"Yeah...?" I replied.

Her mouth broke into a huge smile. "Well, why didn't you say so? I'm one of your biggest fans."

"You are?"

"Have a seat over here and let me fix you up some coffee." She shuffled to a small circular table heaped with newspapers, kitchenware, and other odds and ends, shook a chair to empty it of a magazine stack, and beckoned for me to sit. The clawdad, which had finished eating, scurried up the woman's robe and perched on her shoulder. It held up its claws at me in warning.

"Be nice, Buster," the woman said. Then to me, "Go on."

I eyed the clawdad as it chattered. I couldn't leave here without destroying it.

"Go on," the woman repeated, nodding for me to sit.

"Thanks..." I said, and took a seat.

This should be interesting.

"YOU ASKED HOW LONG I'VE BEEN RAISING MY BABIES?" THE woman said as she fussed with a coffee maker. "Buster's a new arrival, but I've had the others going back six months."

I'd angled my chair so I was facing her broad back. The clawdad continued to watch me from the woman's shoulder.

"Six months, huh?"

She must have heard the distaste in my voice. "I know they're not much to look at, but they're the best pets I've ever owned. Loving, loyal. Make good watch dogs, too. Had an attempted break-in a couple months back." The woman chuckled. "One of my babies buried a hook so deep inside the man's butt cheek, you could've heard him scream clear to the two hundreds."

I smiled in fake appreciation. I was still puzzling over how the woman continued to breathe with five lethal nether creatures for housemates. And had she called them *loving?*

"I'm surprised they didn't try sinking anything into *you*," she finished, then peered over a shoulder. "Don't know why they're being so timid all of a sudden. You all coming?"

I swallowed. Euthanizing Buster was going to be hard enough without the woman knowing what I'd done to her other babies. I changed the subject. "You know, I never got your name."

"You can call me Mae."

"What got you into conjuring, Mae?"

"You did."

I stared at her. "Me?"

"That's right." Mae chuckled and snapped the switch on the coffee maker. As the machine began to gurgle, she came over and joined me at the table. The clawdad scurried around to her far shoulder and chattered at me some more.

"But let me back up," she said. "I was a veterinarian for more than thirty years. Had a practice over on Amsterdam Avenue. I've always adored animals, and they always seemed to take to me. I was the woman you'd see walking half a dozen dogs down to the park. Had twice that many cats back in the apartment. But after losing everything in the Crash, my husband and I ended up in this rent control. Maybe you saw the sign in the lobby? No dogs or cats? Broke my heart to give them away. Then my husband passed." Her eyes went misty behind her glasses.

"I'm really sorry," I said.

"To be honest, there didn't seem much point in going on. A horrible thing to say, but it's the truth. Then I saw you on the news." Her face broke into another of her warm smiles.

"The things you could do. It all just seemed so ... so miraculous. I cut out the articles they ran about you in the papers. They're around here somewhere." She peered over a shoulder as if she might spot one. "I can't explain quite how, but your magic spoke to me. I wanted so much to talk to you, to ask you how you learned to do that stuff. Then I said to myself, 'Mae, if you want something bad enough, you've got to get out of this funk and do it yourself.' So I went out that very day and bought every book on magic I could afford and started practicing. Nothing much happened, until I found this one old book at a store in Queens."

"The *Khafji Scrolls*," I said.

She stopped and blinked at me. "How'd you know?" But she immediately broke into laughter. "Well, of course you know. You're a wizard!"

I gave a modest shrug.

"Anyway, one of the spells in there was supposed to call up a god. Sort of a hunk from the way the book described him." She laughed and shook her head. "I know how that probably sounds, but I'm old, not dead. And I was doing it more for the powers than anything."

"Nothing wrong with that," I said, to keep her talking. But I was thinking of everything that *should have* gone wrong.

"Well, the critter that popped out of that circle was no god, and it sure as sin wasn't handsome. Had about twenty legs and a face so ugly you wanted to forget you ever saw it. But I'd brought it into the world, and that was that. I looked after it like it was my own."

"And it never tried to hurt you?"

"Hurt me?" She looked at me in honest surprise. "It crawled right up under my bosom that first night and snuggled there like I was its mother."

I considered what she was telling me while trying my hardest not to visualize it. I opened my wizard's senses again. An ink-like energy surrounded the clawdad, but I still wasn't picking up anything on Mae. The maternal aura she gave off was natural. I was beginning to wonder if the nether creatures sensed it too, interpreting her, not as sustenance, but protection.

Regardless, the important thing was figuring out why the wards hadn't alerted me.

"Do you remember the date the first one came into the world?" I asked.

"I never forget my babies' birth dates. March the twenty-second of this year."

I pulled out my small notepad and pencil and jotted down the information. "And the others?"

She recited each of their birthdates proudly. "And finally little Buster, who came into the world two weeks back. He'll probably be the last. Apartment is crowded enough as it is. He's a cutie, though, isn't he?" The clawdad's tendrils undulated as she scratched its head.

"Sure..." I said.

We were definitely looking at a malfunction in the ward grid. It had failed to detect the first four manifestations and was two weeks late on the fifth. I'd have to let the Order know. In the meantime...

I put the pencil and pad away and took a deep breath. The clawdad shrank back, as if sensing what was coming.

"Mae, I'm going to be frank."

"Hold that thought," she said. "Coffee's ready."

She stood and shuffled back to the machine. As she poured out two mugs, the smell of the fresh brew filled the kitchen in a warm wave. She manipulated the walker with her thighs on the return trip in order to carry the mugs, making me wonder why she used the device in the first place.

"Here you go," she said, handing me mine. "There's a container of sugar on the table, if you can find it."

As sweet as Mae seemed, and as much as I liked coffee, I couldn't entirely trust someone who kept nether creatures as pets and garnished their meals with blood. I blew politely on the mug and then set it on the table's edge. Mae took a sip from her own cup and sighed contentedly.

"Yep," she said, "it's just me and my babies now. And I'm happier than I've ever been since my husband passed." She leaned forward and lowered her voice. "Happier than some of the years we were together, but that's just between you and me. All those thoughts of giving up?" She waved a hand. "Long gone. And I have you to thank. I never would've gone looking for that spell book if you hadn't shown up on my TV. I keep at it, and I believe I *will* be like you someday. Hey, maybe we can even work together!"

Oh boy.

She took another sip. "So, what was it you wanted to tell me?"

"Well..." I shifted uncomfortably. How would my father have handled something like this? "When I came in earlier, your babies..."

Mae's forehead collapsed in concern. "They didn't get out, did they?"

Before I knew what I was doing, my head began to nod. "Yes," I said. "Yes, they did. Bolted in every direction." I made a running motion with my fingers.

"*All* of them?" she demanded. Buster's tendrils wriggled in excitement and he ran back and forth across her shoulders. In my mind's eye, I saw his four siblings exploding.

"Unfortunately, yes."

"Well, you have to find them!" Mae was standing now. "They don't know how to survive out there on their own!"

I glanced down at my mechanical watch. Crap, class in thirty minutes. I stood in front of Mae and started to reach for her shoulder to reassure her (of what? my lie?) when the clawdad hissed and snapped his claws. I jerked my hand back and searched for something to say.

"I'll, ah, I'll do my best."

"No, I need better than that, Everson. Those are my babies."

"Mae, listen. They really shouldn't be in our world in the first place."

She narrowed her eyes at me. "What are you trying to say?"

"That, um, maybe they're better off..." I watched her eyes narrow further until they looked sharp enough to cut me. "Maybe they're better off staying inside from now on."

She gave an exasperated sigh that Buster attempted to imitate. "What do you think I was *trying* to do? You burst in here, not even bothering to knock. Then you let my babies run right past you, and don't even tell me?" She snatched up my mug from the table. My biggest fan was telling me it was time to go.

"So I guess I'll start looking for them?"

"You do that." She turned and made for the sink.

"Oh, just one thing."

She rounded on me, her look telling me not to press it.

"That spell book, the *Khafji Scrolls*? I'm going to need it to find them."

She grunted and gestured for me to take it. I thanked her and told her I'd be in touch. With a Word, I broke apart the locking spells I'd placed on her doors and entered the bedroom. Peanut shells slid off the cover as I lifted the book and flipped through the pages. At least I could prevent her from calling up any more nether pets. I'd worry about Buster later.

Shaken, I tucked the book under an arm and headed back down the corridor. This was my first call in more than a year where I hadn't succeeded in putting down the creature that had triggered the alarm. And all because I had a weakness for bossy old women on walkers, apparently.

"Close the door behind you," Mae shouted. "Tight!"

Buster punctuated the order with a tiny shriek.

I complied.

4

I arrived at Midtown College with ten minutes to spare and headed straight to the faculty restroom. My pre-class routine included a shirt change, a face scrubbing, a hair combing, and an application of cologne, all done inside five minutes. I also spoke an affirmation into the mirror:

"I will strive to be my best professor today."

I felt stupid, but better. Routines—and yeah, affirmations —did that for me. I'd learned the value of both in a book I'd picked up almost a year back called *Magical Me*. Contrary to what the title suggested, this wasn't an esoteric tome. It was a self-help book.

Smirk all you want, but by the time I arrived at my class-room, the morning's fiasco at Mae's had evaporated from my thoughts. I even had a slight pep in my step. Of course, knowing that a classroom of adoring students awaited me didn't hurt.

Though my reputation as a wizard had faded for the average man and woman on the street, at the college, a mystical aura still enveloped me. I had played down my role in the mayor's eradication program, of course, suggesting that the reporting had been grossly exaggerated, but the rumor mill at Midtown College had other ideas. More than a year later, my ancient mythology and lore courses boasted wait lists ten and twenty deep. Most of the students weren't even history majors, just curiosity seekers. More than a few had become ardent fans.

I smiled at the thirty-odd attentive faces, most of them female, as I passed through the door and fake-limped to my desk. Probably a good thing I was already spoken for. Sort of. Detective Vega and I had started dating shortly after the episode with the Whisperer, but in the last few months our relationship seemed to have stalled. We had plans to meet that evening for dinner, where she wanted to talk. I couldn't imagine that last part was good.

After some friendly banter with the students, I got right to the morning's lecture: the Hero's Journey Across Cultures.

My wizard's voice began working on the students immediately, lulling them into light trances. Not an intentional act on my part, just an effect of speaking to an impressionable audience. I felt good as I spoke, in control. And not just because of the entrancement. After researching and writing on mythology topics for the past fifteen years, I'd attained a kind of mastery in my field that I'd not yet realized in wizardry.

I was getting there. I was making progress. But not fast enough.

Before I knew it, our hour and twenty minutes were up. With a sharp clap, I broke apart the misty currents of energy that bonded us. The students blinked, images of strange beings, mystical assistants, and foreign battles evaporating from their minds' eyes.

"The reading for next week is in your syllabus," I said. "There's a chapter from Gertz and two articles for you to pick up in the library. They all deal with atonement with the father as a theme. Be ready to discuss. Oh, and I want the proposals for your term papers—*with* a sample bibliography of no fewer than five sources." I held up the fingers of my right hand.

Playful groans sounded as students gathered books and backpacks.

"Have a great weekend," I finished. "Try not to strain yourselves."

One of the students lingered. Heather, I think. I needed to do a better job learning my students' names. Anyway, she was this term's bold student. While the others exercised degrees of discretion when probing into my wizard's life, Heather was direct. Too direct. In fact, she was starting to become down-right aggressive. As the rest of the class filed out, she strode up to my desk. She was bigger than me and probably stronger. She scared me a little.

"And how are you spending *your* weekend, Prof?" she demanded.

"Oh, you know, research." I pretended to become occupied with digging through my satchel.

"No magic stuff?"

The thought of having to return to Mae's apartment to finish the job squeezed my gut. I suppressed the feeling and gave Heather one of my practiced answers. "Only if you consider a comparative analysis of early Serbian and Baltic folklore magical. Most outside my field wouldn't."

"So when are you going to give us a demonstration?" she pouted, her hands balling into fists.

"A demonstration?"

"Your *magic.*"

She stepped closer until she was all but towering over me.

"Professor Croft," a prim voice called from the doorway. "Might I have a brief word?"

I never thought I'd be relieved to hear that voice. "Professor Snodgrass," I called back. "Sure, come on in." I turned to the student. "I'm sorry, Heather. We'll have to finish our discussion another time."

Her face furrowed angrily. "It's *Hannah.*"

My department chairman smirked as she stormed past him and out of the classroom.

"Tough start to the term?" he asked me.

The relief I'd felt turned quickly to annoyance. "With all of my classes at full capacity? Hardly."

He snorted. "The glow of adulation will fade. Give it another couple of terms."

"Since you bring it up, how's *The Historiography of the Early British Empire* going? I understand you've had a few drops." He'd had more than a few. There were rumors of the course being cancelled.

"Which is just the way I like it." He clasped the lapels of his tweed jacket as he arrived in front of me and gave me a critical up and down. His gaze settled on my right shoe, where I'd missed a dash of flour from Mae's apartment. "I bring rigor to the discipline," he said, his cold eyes returning to mine. "If a student can't handle it, I would prefer he or she seek instruction elsewhere. I'm an academic, not some magical *story teller.*"

"Well, this magical story teller is tenured now, which

means I'm practically untouchable." I waggled my fingers toward his little oval glasses. "Whatever your latest beef, go ahead and get it off your chest so I can nod in my most unconvincing show of sympathy and be on my way."

Snodgrass only had to breathe to bring out the asshat in me. I was starting to think he knew this. In my defense, he had turned me over to the NYPD the year before, when the vampire Arnaud had tricked the city into believing I was working for the bloodsuckers. Never mind that I'd gone on to slay Arnaud or that my position at the college had been restored and then some. Things had almost ended *very* badly for me. And all because of dick nose here.

"*Practically* being the operative term," he was saying. "There are still offenses for which the board will not hesitate to revoke your tenure and terminate your employment with the college."

I couldn't think of what the man could possibly have on me. Since becoming tenured, I'd been a model professor. Besides filling my classes and getting to every one on time, I'd put together a conference, published several papers, and even begun to earn grants by my own sweat. And all of that despite that I was on wizard duty more than ever. As much as it made me blush to admit, I owed most of my turnaround to the *Magical Me* program.

"All right," I said, circling a hand, "let's hear it."

"That's *not* why I'm here."

"Oh, a friendly visit? I'm flattered."

"That's not why I'm here, either."

"I can keep tossing one-liners if you can."

"Professor Croft," he said abruptly. "This has nothing to do with us."

I was preparing something snarky when I noticed he'd

lowered his tone slightly. He snuck a look toward the closed door, confirming my suspicion that he didn't want to be overheard. I wasn't sure whether to be interested or creeped out.

"Should I sit down for this?" I asked.

"Stand, sit, whatever you like."

I hoisted myself onto my desk, which seemed to prompt Snodgrass to take a seat in the first row of desks. He looked smaller than usual, more petite, and then it struck me that this was our first one-on-one meeting where he wasn't peering down at me from his massive desk.

"I'm here at..." He cleared his throat. "I'm here at the behest of my wife."

"Whoa, let me stop you right there," I said, showing my hands. "I don't do that kind of magic."

"It has nothing to do with that," he snapped. "Let me get right to the point so we can get this over with. My wife has built a very regimented life around herself. She lives and breathes her schedule, and if anything throws it off she ... well, she falls to pieces. She's weak that way."

He narrowed his eyes as though daring me to comment, but I had never met his wife. I only knew Snodgrass had taken advantage of her family connections to secure his position at the college. Hell, if I'd said anything, it would have been to express my sympathy for the woman.

"For the last two weeks, our cable has been on the fritz," he continued. "Miriam has been unable to watch her bedtime show, some sort of regency romance nonsense." He snorted. "She couldn't handle it. To pieces, like I said. When the cable company failed to find the problem, Miriam called in an energy expert."

"You mean someone in utilities?"

"No, someone in your line of work," he said bitterly.

"Oh, someone who can *sense* energy. Gotcha."

"I told Miriam the expert was most likely a fraud..."

"Many of them are."

"...but she wouldn't be dissuaded, so I humored her. Naturally, the so-called *expert* spoke some mumbo-jumbo about an inconsistency in *ley* energy, whatever that is. Nothing he could fix, he said, but that didn't stop him from charging a king's ransom for the reading."

"I still don't see what this has to do with me."

"My wife read about your *feats* during the mayor's reelection campaign. She knows you're a member of my department, and she's asked me to..." He tugged at his plaid bowtie. "To invite you to dinner."

I nearly burst out laughing. "Dinner? With you?"

Snodgrass's face reddened. "It's just a pretext to have you look at the so-called energy problem. And let me make myself clear—I'm only doing this to humor her. You would come, eat quickly, say little, and then investigate the problem. If you can fix it with whatever it is you do, fine. If not, that will be the end of it as far as you're concerned."

"What's in it for me?"

"In addition to dinner, I'll reimburse you for your time." He glanced at the door before lowering his voice further. "How does two hundred dollars sound?"

Now I did laugh. "All the years you've been trying to get me tossed from the college, the last time because of my magic, and now you want to *hire* me for a consultation?"

He pressed his lips together. "Yes or no, Professor Croft?"

"Two hundred, huh?" Between my raise at the college and monthly payments from the Order, I didn't need the money. But I *was* curious. I squinted at him. "Why do I smell a rat?"

"I'm not trying to lure you to my home for some nefarious

purpose," he said indignantly. "You can tell your detective friend where you'll be, if it makes you feel better." He was referring to Vega.

"When?" I asked.

"Tonight at seven. My wife is—"

"No can do, chief," I interrupted. "I have a date with said detective friend."

"Well, surely you can cancel. Surely you can reschedule. I've already told my wife to expect you."

"Not tonight."

"How about now, then? Or—or later this afternoon?"

Something like desperation took hold in his smallish eyes.

"That won't work, either. I need to get in some research before my next class. And right after I'm done here, I'm going to the gym for a session with my personal trainer. That's the rest of my day."

Naturally, I didn't mention that I also planned to check the wards around Mae's apartment. The rest was true, though —even the personal trainer part. I had started scheduling the workouts after someone, I forget who, remarked that I was getting beat up too much.

Snodgrass's lips began to tremble. "W-w-well—"

I winced. As much as I enjoyed the shoe being on my foot for a change, watching him struggle like this was painful. I held up a hand for him to stop. "All right, how about this? *If* I get a break this weekend, I'll set up a time to come over. You don't even need to bother with dinner."

Basically a commitment to do nothing.

Snodgrass's mouth relaxed. He smoothed his thinning hair as though trying to restore some dignity to himself before saying, "That would be fine. You'll find my number in the directory."

As I watched him stand up and make his way stiffly toward the door, I honestly couldn't have said what was stranger: my morning encounter with Mae and Buster, or *that.*

5

Back at my apartment that evening, I dropped my gym bag and cane in the foyer, snapped home the three bolts, and checked to ensure my defensive wards were at full strength. As I turned up the floodlights, Tabitha let out a noisy yawn.

"Shit, darling," she muttered. "I can smell you from here."

"Yeah, there's this thing that happens during exercise called sweating. You should try it sometime."

"I'd love to, but I don't have the glands."

"Not the sweating, the exercising. You know, moving your arms and legs?" I demonstrated on my way to the dining room table.

She made a scoffing sound and repositioned her forty plus pounds of bulk on the divan. "If you mean running in place and lifting metal plates only to put them back down, I'll leave that to you mortals."

"Have you gotten up at all today?"

She narrowed her green eyes at me.

"I'll take that as an 'only to eat and—'"

"What's that concoction you're holding?" she cut in. "My god, it smells worse than you do."

I held up the plastic cup with a straw poking through the lid. "It's a tofu/wheat-germ shake. Supposed to be a good post-workout source of protein and healthy fats." I took another sip as I deposited my mail on the table. I didn't let on to Tabitha how awful it tasted.

"Don't even *think* about trying to sneak that crap into my diet," she warned.

"No, you're getting a lamb shank tonight. But it's going into a stew that you'll need to remember to turn off at 7:30."

"Might as well go out and catch dinner myself," she muttered.

"I'd pay a lot of money to see that."

"Well, why am *I* having to cook?" she pouted. "Where are you going?"

"You're not. And a dinner date with Ricki."

"Oh. Her."

Vega had been over a few times since she and I had started seeing each other. I'd told Tabitha she could remain in the apartment if she promised to be on her best behavior —no evil stares or catty remarks. Of course I also spiked her milk with a sleeping potion as insurance.

"You barely even know her," I pointed out. "And I thought you said you liked her."

"I said she was *tolerable*."

"Given that's where your rating system tops out, I took it as an endorsement."

"Whatever, darling. I'm just surprised it's still going on. How often do you see her? Once a month?"

"We both lead busy lives," I said defensively. "She's a homicide detective and single mother, and I'm a full-time professor and working wizard. Unlike certain cats, we don't enjoy a glut of free time."

"Are you sure your little self-improvement projects don't have anything to do with that?"

I stopped sorting through the backlog of mail. "What are you talking about?"

"Oh, come now, darling. You're up at five in the morning, which you *never* used to do. After chanting some nonsense or other in the bathroom, you spend the next three hours up in your laboratory doing spell craft. You're out all day, and when you do come home, typically late, it's straight to the lab for another hour or two. Hell, darling, *I* barely see you anymore. And to top it off you're drinking wheat germ?"

"Oh, that reminds me. I need to record my day's calories." I set the drink on the table and started searching around my reading chair. In the back of the *Magical Me* book was a great set of charts.

"Would you look at yourself?" Tabitha said.

I turned to her in annoyance and then felt my heart leap into my throat.

"What are you doing? My book!"

"What?" she said.

The book was facedown and open beneath her divan, the front cover and first several pages jammed beneath one of its legs. Tabitha craned her neck as I fell to my hands and knees to rescue it.

"Oh, that," she said, relaxing again. "It felt like my perch had a wobble."

"Well this isn't for leveling!" I worked the book free and inspected the cover. Fortunately, it wasn't torn.

"At least you know I got up today," she said.

I fought to control my voice. "*Ask* next time, all right?"

"That's what I'm trying to tell you, darling. You're hardly around *to* ask. I wouldn't doubt your lady friend feels the same way. And it's all because of that infernal book. Are you sure it's not cursed?"

"It's not," I said thinly.

"I mean, look at that man's hideous face." She shuddered.

I turned the book around to the back cover, where there was a photo of the author, Jocko Wraithe. I'd never really looked at him, but my cat had a point. Beneath a styled shock of white hair, his dark eyes glinted over an almost nonexistent nose and an enormous smile of too-bright teeth.

"Well, this *infernal book* is the reason I was able to banish four nether creatures this morning," I said, "all while maintaining a form-fitting defensive shield and two locking spells." I didn't mention Mae or Buster, of course. "Whatever your problem with my new routine, it's working. I'm a better wizard—hell, a better everything—because of them."

Tabitha smirked. "But are you your *best* wizard?"

She'd no doubt overheard my morning affirmations. With a tight breath, I let the remark go. "The point is that this has nothing to do with Vega and me."

"I know what this is about, darling."

"Oh, this oughta be good."

"I've seen the way you moon over your sword. You want to be like him."

"Like who?"

She lowered her eyelids at my attempt to play dumb.

"Well, what's wrong with that?" I challenged.

"Nothing. I spent time with your father, remember? The most powerful wizard I've seen up close. Handsome too. What son wouldn't want to emulate him? Not as charming as Chicory, granted, but then few are."

I stared at her for a moment. "Chicory's real name was *Lich*, and he tried to destroy the world."

"Since when does that disqualify someone as a charmer?"

But I barely heard her. Mention of Chicory had brought back a flood of images. Largely through luck, I'd managed to kill the Death Mage in his keep, but the thrill of victory had been short lived. I'd watched helplessly as my father leapt into a portal that extended beyond the Deep Down, shouting a Word powerful enough to repel Dhuul. A Word that only someone of his strength and constitution could have channeled ... if only for a few moments.

He'd sacrificed himself to save humanity.

In the moment before Arianna had pulled me from that realm, I had felt something being passed to me: a responsibility to become the wizard and leader my father had been for the Order in Exile. No more irresponsible Everson. No more falling ass backwards into one lucky solution after another. No more solo wizarding. It was time for me to develop my abilities and lead the team Arianna said would find me "one by one."

"Anyways, I understand what you're trying to do," Tabitha said. I blinked her back into focus. "And it's admirable, I suppose. Just don't be surprised if Vega feels the same way I do."

Vega *had* said she wanted to talk tonight, but not about what.

"Whatever. I need to get ready." I spun toward my room, the book clutched to my chest.

"See?"

"This has *nothing* to do with Vega and me," I repeated.

"Hmph. Don't say I didn't warn you."

6

Ricki Vega was still dressed in her work clothes—black suit and blouse—when she arrived at Da Vinci's, an Italian restaurant not far from her place in Brooklyn. Her midnight hair, usually secured in a ponytail, was down over her shoulders in a wavy luster. I stood from the table I'd reserved and waved to her. Spotting me, she smiled tightly and walked over.

"Sorry I'm late." She gave me a light kiss. "Had to finish up some paperwork."

"No worries. Just got here myself." I pulled out her chair and scooted it in as she sat. I returned to my seat across from her and spent a moment taking in her smooth Latin face, dark, intelligent eyes, and the tiny mole beside her lips.

"What?" she demanded.

"Sorry, but you're a dream."

Vega rolled her eyes and took a sip of her water. "Good day?" she asked.

There it was, dammit. The formality I'd started to pick up in the last month.

"Interesting day. I responded to a call this morning up in Harlem." I lowered my voice as I told her about meeting Mae. "The woman's been living with five nether creatures for the last half year. *Five.*"

"And you didn't know?"

"They never tripped the wards for some reason. Not until this morning. After class I checked out the wards that triangulate for her neighborhood, and they all seemed to be working."

Following Chicory's death, the Order had reestablished the network of twenty-one wards to monitor the city. A nether creature's entrance into our world was accompanied by a discharge of energy that the creature continued to emit for a time. The powerful wards were calibrated to sense that energy and pinpoint its origin. After triggering a gem I'd installed in my watch, that information went into a hunting spell that directed me to the source, normally without fail.

"Have you told your Order?" Vega asked.

"I left them a message, but there's no telling when they'll be able to check it out. Could be tonight, could be next week."

"Still stitching up the rips, huh?"

"Yeah," I said, wishing I possessed enough skill to pitch in, or at the very least to reboot the wards over the city myself. The Elder members of the Order had enough on their plate without having to help out the junior varsity.

The waiter came and greeted us with a *"Buona sera."* We ordered and then waited until he was out of earshot again before resuming our discussion.

"About those five creatures," Vega said. "I'm not gonna get called to Harlem, am I?"

"Not because of them, no. At least I don't think so." I described how I'd destroyed four of the creatures before running into Mae, who would have bludgeoned me with an assortment of kitchen implements before allowing me to lay a finger on her precious Buster.

"Great, so there's a homicidal lobster running loose," Vega muttered.

"Only until I can go back and take care of it. Anyway, it's not loose. Mae housetrained it."

She snorted a laugh. "I feel so much better."

"Seriously, it's small time, like a lot of what's been coming up here in the last year. Well, except for the White Dragon. But he was a shifter, not a nether creature. And the Blue Wolf did the heavy lifting on that one."

At mention of the Blue Wolf, Vega arched an eyebrow.

"He's *not* make-believe," I said with a laugh. It had become a running joke between us. Vega hadn't been around the times I'd worked with the Blue Wolf in the past year, and she was having a hard time picturing a seven-foot werewolf with blue hair. She accused me of having a Mr. Snuffleupagus, Big Bird's imaginary friend on *Sesame Street*.

"I'll believe it when I see him."

"I actually invited him to team up. If he'd said yes, you would have seen a lot of him by now."

The Blue Wolf's decision not to join forces had smarted a little. A part of me still held out the hope he'd change his mind. I had taken Arianna's counsel about forming a team to heart.

The waiter returned and set down Vega's red wine, my beer, and a cutting board of steaming bread.

"Do you mind?" Vega asked me, reaching for the bread. "I'm starving."

"Hey, it's not going to eat itself."

"Well, what about Wesson's replacement?" she asked,

tearing off a chunk and dipping it in olive oil. "Have you worked with him yet?"

She was talking about the wizard who had taken over the five boroughs shortly after James Wesson's relocation to Colorado. Someone named Pierce Dalton, from London. He'd actually covered for me the few times I'd gone out West to help James, but that had been mediated through the Order. I knew little about him other than that his magic related to Japanese Himitsu paintings.

I shook my head. "I keep meaning to get in touch, set up a lunch or something, but ... well, other things keep popping up, I guess."

As the city's senior wizard, I really should have contacted him months before, oriented him to the area, even accompanied him on his first few calls to make sure he knew what he was doing. Then again, he had my number too. If he needed help, he would have called, right?

It seemed a little strange now that he hadn't.

Vega snapped her fingers in front of my eyes. "Dispatch to Everson."

I forced a chuckle as she returned to focus. "I'm here, I'm here. So how about you? How was your day?"

"It was fine." She finished the piece of bread she'd been working on, took a swallow of wine, and then leveled her gaze at me. "Everson, we need to talk."

"I thought we were."

"I'm serious."

Oh boy. She *did* sound serious. I set my beer to one side and clasped my hands on the table to show that she had my undivided attention.

"What are we doing?" she asked pointedly.

I glanced around. "What do you mean?"

"I mean this. Us."

"Enjoying each other's company?" I offered.

"That was fine for the first few months—a dinner here, a movie there, a sleepover now and again—but we're going on a year now. Shouldn't we be beyond that? Like *way* beyond that."

"Yes?"

"Well, why aren't we?"

I opened my mouth without knowing what I was going to say. Thanks to my double life as a wizard, none of my romantic relationships in adulthood had lasted beyond a few months. I always assumed relationships just matured from repeated encounters over time. Before I could attempt to bumble that into words, Vega answered the question herself.

"I'll tell you. Because you're not committed. I need to know why."

"Wait, back up a minute. Not committed? How am I not committed?"

"When have we ever spent more than one day or night together?"

"We're busy people. We—"

"When have you ever said, 'Let's sleep in this morning, then take Tony to brunch and hit the park after? Never. It's always, 'I've gotta be up at five so I can do this or that'—even on the days you're not working. Then, boom, it's straight to your lab, and I don't see you again."

"You're starting to sound like my cat."

"Twice last month I left your apartment in the morning without saying anything. I wanted to see if you'd notice. And guess what? No phone call to ask where I'd gone, no visit to my office or apartment later in the day. Nothing. Did you even remember I was there?"

"Of course I did," I said, struggling to recall what two mornings those would have been. "I just—"

"Speaking of my son," she cut in, her eyes softening even as her voice hardened, "he looks up to you, Everson. He wants to spend time with you. Tony got so excited back in June when you mentioned the fair out on Long Island, and then you never brought it up again."

"Didn't I?"

"You can't *do* that to a seven-year-old."

I couldn't quite remember that episode either, but I believed her. I nodded and took Vega's hands, half surprised when she let me. A weariness had fallen over her face, and I wondered how much of that I was responsible for.

"Look, I'm sorry," I said. "You're the best thing in my life right now. I mean that. You know who I am. You get what I'm doing. My mind's just been ... other places, I guess."

I hated it when Tabitha was right.

"Everson, I need to know if this is the way it's going to be from now on. Because if it is..."

I gave her hands a gentle squeeze and released them. "When you were trying to make detective, you put in a lot of late nights, right? Early mornings. Extra hours. Time you wish you could have spent with your son. But you told yourself it was going to be the best thing for him in the long run, right? The best thing for the city?"

When she saw what I was doing, she pressed her lips together.

"I'm just saying that sometimes we have to make sacrifices in the short term in order to be..." I almost said *the best at what we do*, before remembering Tabitha's dig from earlier. "To be in an optimal position to help others. Arianna made it clear that there are going to be more threats to the city. Big threats. On top of the rips, New York has a high concentration of ley energy. And when those threats come, I want to be ready. I *need* to be ready. That's what this is about."

She sighed through her nose, but it sounded conciliatory. "I know that, Everson. I live the part about needing to be ready every day. But in the last year, I've learned something else. If all you do is go, go, go, you're gonna burn out. Then you'll be no good to anyone."

"It's just until I get—"

"Your feet under you?" Vega finished. "I used to tell myself that too."

"Regardless, it's only for a few more months."

"Until those months turn into years."

For a long moment, neither of us said anything. As I searched Vega's eyes, I remembered why we had ended up together. Despite our outward differences, we were fundamentally alike: driven by the memories of our fallen fathers, committed to protecting the innocent. Now she was asking if we were going to do anything with that, or if we—if *I*—was going to sacrifice it in my quest for perfection.

"I need to know," she said at last.

"Look..."

The gem in my watch began to flash. I seized my cane before it could launch itself in the direction of whatever had just popped into our world. I started to explain to Vega what was happening, when her phone rang. Following a terse exchange, she ended the call.

"I've gotta go," she said, already standing. "There's been an attack on East Houston."

I dropped some bills on the table and lined up the strong pull of my cane with a mental map of the city.

"I'll go with you," I said. "Looks like we're being called to the same location."

Suspension cables flashed past my window as Vega sped over the Manhattan Bridge. She was speaking into a Bluetooth, and between her side of the conversation and the bursts of chatter coming over her radio, an ugly picture of the crime scene was taking shape. Someone or something had attacked a group of movie goers at a theater on Houston Street, and it didn't sound like a shallow nether creature.

We bombed down the off ramp and squealed right onto Forsyth.

Vega ended the call. "Two confirmed dead, scores of casualties, and four still trapped inside the theater. Eyewitnesses say the suspect is a man who can summon black fire. Have you heard of anything like that?"

"Could be any number of things," I said, looking down at my kicking cane. This felt big. "Make sure they're keeping everyone back, officers too. I should be the first one in."

While Vega relayed that information, I proceeded through the steps I had been practicing every morning for the last year: centering myself, fortifying my mental prism, tapping into ambient channels of ley energy. They were the basic steps to prepare oneself for casting, but they were also steps I'd gone about haphazardly in the past, not taking full advantage of their potential. It was similar to plumbing in that, sure, you could piece together pipe segments willy-nilly and get a flow, but you were also going to get a lot of leakage.

I was doing it the right way now, tightening each joint to maximize the flow's volume and force. My body vibrated with powerful energy. It wasn't until Vega frowned at me that I noticed her instrument panel flashing.

"You mind?" she said as the radio began to bray static.

"Sorry." I tamped down my thrumming aura enough to restore her electronics. I was anxious to get to the victims—and yeah, also anxious to test myself.

Vega veered right onto Houston. We passed a cluster of ambulances and pulled up to a police cordon. We both got out, and I followed Vega to an official at the scene. I groaned as his portly body rounded toward us. It was Hoffman.

"Detective," I managed.

Instead of returning the greeting, he directed his scrunched-up face at Vega. "What'd you bring Merlin for?"

Thanks to the NYPD's Byzantine politics, the corrupt detective had managed to remain in Homicide as Vega's partner. A situation made more frustrating considering the kinds of cases they worked. Hoffman didn't believe in the existence of magic or the supernatural, despite recent glaring examples to the contrary, and he believed even less in me.

Vega ignored his question. "Are there still people inside?"

"Yeah," Hoffman said. "Four of 'em. Sounds like we've got a real nutjob down there."

"How many ways in?" she asked.

"Just the front door. No windows."

I looked down the street where more police and ambulance lights flashed. Between us and them, about a half block away, I spotted the entrance to the theater. The smoke that curled from the below-ground entrance gave it away. I was preparing to cross the cordon, when I noticed the silhouette of someone with a bald head in the back seat of Hoffman's car.

"Is he a witness?" I asked.

"*She*," he said. "And no, you can't talk to her."

I looked at Vega. "It'll just take a sec. I need to know what I'm dealing with."

"You're dealing with a homicidal freak and a bunch of drugged-out kids seeing things," Hoffman said. "We should've breached the theater ten minutes ago."

"Let him talk to her," Vega ordered.

With a grumble, Hoffman jerked the door open. Inside, a thin girl with a shaved head peered up at me, eyes large and dilated. She was done up in punk chic: dark makeup and black leggings that looked as if someone had attacked them with a razor blade.

"I'm here to help," I said. "Would you mind if I talked to you for a minute?"

The girl nodded and scooted over to make room. "My girlfriend's still inside," she said hollowly.

"What's your name?"

"Star."

I settled onto the seat beside her, and Hoffman closed the door.

"All right, Star. We'll get your girlfriend out. But first I need to know what happened, as briefly as you can tell me."

"Um, the second movie had just begun when the theater started filling with smoke. I think we all thought it was an effect, 'cause it had this funny smell. But when the smoke thinned, there was a man standing in front of the screen." Star stared straight ahead as she spoke. "I think it was because of the projector, but he looked really big. Someone yelled for him to sit down, and that's when the fire came out of his body. A fire so red it looked black. He shot it at the girl who'd yelled, and she screamed, and it was like, it was like the life had been sucked from her body. She just shriveled up and fell over. Me and my girlfriend started running for the exit along with everyone else. I heard more screams behind me. And this horrible laughter. Someone knocked us over, and we got separated. I got out right before the door slammed shut. When I made it to the street, I saw people with horrible burns. Clothes melted to their skin. Another guy was carrying a shriveled body. I looked everywhere, but I couldn't find my girlfriend. She—she's still inside."

"You said the smoke smelled funny. What did it smell like?"

She gave a slight shrug. "Rotten eggs?"

Sulfur, I thought.

"What's your girlfriend's name?"

"Emma."

"I'm going to get Emma right now." I gave Star's shoulder a reassuring squeeze, but it remained stiff and cold. She didn't even glance at me. I knocked on the window for Hoffman to open the door.

"Her earrings are crosses," Star said as I climbed out.

"What'd I tell you?" Hoffman scoffed as he closed the door behind me. "Whacked out of her mind."

"She's in shock, dipshit."

Vega silenced Hoffman's comeback with a stern look. "Anything?" she asked me.

"Said she smelled sulfur, which means we could have a dark mage casting from a demonic realm." Probably what the wards had picked up tonight, though it bothered me they hadn't detected anything earlier. Surely the mage had practiced before unleashing his infernal magic on the theater goers. So either the mage had come from somewhere else, or the wards had malfunctioned again.

"Demonic?" Vega's brow furrowed in concern. "Can you handle something like that?"

I pulled my sword from my staff, then summoned enough energy to bat my coat and frizz out Hoffman's wreath of curls. *The question should be,* I thought, *can he handle something like me?*

Invisible power stormed around me as I marched toward the theater.

"Keep everyone back!" I shouted.

7

A fter last summer's successful campaign to eradicate the ghouls from the subway lines, an edgy nightlife had started to take hold again in the East Village. Recently profiled in *The Village Voice*, the Flicker Theater was one example. It catered to a diverse crowd of rebels, independent artists, and university students. Its two a.m. closing time would have been unheard of a year ago.

As I approached the entrance, evidence of the stampede appeared ahead of me. Stray shoes, bags, and bits of clothing, some bloodied, littered the sidewalk and steps leading down to the closed door. Dark smoke curled around the door's seams, breaking apart in a cone of street light.

Underground, I thought. *Always underground.*

But before my phobia could kick in, I replaced the grim thought with a silent affirmation. *I will focus only on being the most powerful, most capable wizard I can be. My* best *wizard.*

The tightness in my chest released. Hardening my protective shield, I descended the steps and inspected the door. The dark tendrils of a locking spell writhed around the frame.

With an uttered Word, the spell dissolved and joined the leaking smoke.

My nose wrinkled. The eyewitness had been right about the smell, meaning our boy *was* dancing with the devil.

I took a moment to visualize the next steps: open the door, expel the smoke, and hit the mage hard enough to make him think twice about getting back up. While I contained him in a shield, I'd locate Emma and the others trapped inside and get them out. If the mage had any fight left, I'd be happy to oblige. Then I'd find out who he was and where he'd developed his black art.

I was feeling confident, yeah. Maybe even overconfident. But I was also willing to lay odds that my opponent hadn't put a fraction of the practice into his craft as I had in the last year.

"Time to *Magical Me* this assclown," I muttered.

With a shouted Word, I blew the door open. Foul smoke poured out. With another Word, I created a funnel to pull the smoke into the street. With the doorway clear, I entered low.

The indie theater was smaller than I'd expected. Beyond a corner bar were rows of toppled chairs. Except for a low-budget movie still projecting onto a standing screen, the theater was dark. I picked out the kids who'd been trapped inside, their bodies now shriveled and smoking. A cross-shaped earring glinted from the ear of the nearest one. Star's girlfriend.

Dammit.

On the surface, the victims looked like they'd been char-broiled. But my wizard's senses showed me souls being yanked from their bodies with such force that their corpses had succumbed to the resulting vacuum, collapsing in on themselves. The mage had spared no one.

I couldn't let him out. But was he even here?

My gaze swept the theater as I took two more steps forward. I was picking up a vibrating in my inner ear, as if from an energy source. A sudden scream made me start, but it was coming from the movie. On the screen, robed figures surrounded a desperate-looking man in a flannel shirt and glasses. Creepy organ music spiked and fell. *Yeah, that's not helping*, I thought.

I hit the speakers with a pair of low-level invocations.

"What's wrong?" a man's voice asked in the sudden silence. "Not a fan of *avant-garde* cinema?"

The ensuing laughter seemed to drip more than echo from the brick walls, the sound thick with malice. The mage. But where in the hell was he? I pivoted in a circle, careful not to step on any of the victims' remains. Though I couldn't see him, I could feel him watching me.

"Who are you?" I demanded.

The laughter stopped. "Oh, you're going to come to know me quite well in the coming days. *If* you survive tonight."

From nowhere, a wave of fire washed over my shield. I saw what the eyewitness had meant. The red fire was so dark, so intense, that it was nearly black. And I could feel its biting heat, even through my protection.

With a grimace, I shouted, *"Respingere!"*

Light and force detonated from my shield, knocking back the chairs in a wave and toppling the screen. The flames disappeared in what sounded like a sharp intake of breath. I'd surprised him.

"Impressive," he said.

I looked around. The mage remained invisible to me. Meaning I had nowhere to direct my attack.

"Who are you?" I repeated. "What do you want?"

"In good time, my friend," he replied with a chuckle. "In good time."

"Friend?" I peered behind the bar and then into the projection room. "Getting a little ahead of ourselves, aren't we? Anyway, I try not to befriend mages with homicidal tendencies."

For the second time, the mage's laughter ended with unnatural suddenness.

"Very well, wizard."

Another burst of fire exploded over my shield, only this time it was accompanied by something else: a swarm of blazing imps. The screeching creatures threw themselves against my protection, sparks falling where they impacted. Like with the fire, I felt them: tiny gouges all over my body.

Fueled by the souls he'd claimed, the mage was calling up some demonic shit.

I hacked and slashed at the creatures with my sword. I didn't want to divert energy from my shield into another invocation. The blade's runes glowed white as the metal cleaved through the imps' pint-sized bodies, reducing them to smoke. But the cursed things found new life in the mage's flames. They took fiery shape again and resumed their assault.

Using my wizard's voice, I shouted, *"Be gone!"*

The creatures hesitated mid flight and looked at each other with soulless insect eyes.

"Attack," the mage countered softly.

With a collective shriek, the imps complied, this time with even more fury. The mage was trying to wear down my defenses—and succeeding. I kept the creatures at bay with my blade while squinting past them. Beyond their bodies and the licks of red-black fire, I could see the movie projecting onto the wall. Only now a large shadow blocked half of the picture.

There you are.

I blew the creatures and flames back with an invocation. Then, thrusting my sword and staff at the shadow, I shouted, *"Vigore!"*

A torrent of energy stormed through my body, down my implements, and into the mage. The fire and imps disappeared entirely as the mage grunted and staggered backward.

"Entrapolarle!" I called.

Light burst from my staff and surrounded the mage in a crackling orb. Expecting the light to bare his features, I was surprised to see only a figure composed of what looked like smoke.

"Tell me your name," I said, shrinking his confinement.

Grunting again, he motioned with his right hand and drew it into a fist. In the next moment, dark, taloned fingers appeared around my shield. Rank smoke rose from the manifestation, but the force was far from insubstantial. My protection buckled and pressed into me.

I opened my prism further, channeling more energy into both my protection and my opponent's confinement. I bore down on the orb around him, shrinking it further. He responded in kind, the infernal fingers digging my shield into my ribs as they gripped more tightly.

We were locked in the ultimate nut-squeezing contest, but I was game. One of us would give, and it wasn't going to be me. Not after all the hours of practice I'd amassed in the last year. Wincing, I focused through the pain and pressure. I blocked out everything but the twin invocations. I had grown my capacity, yes, but the efficiency remained key. I needed every last ounce of energy.

When I felt his grip around me waver, I managed a trembling grin. The son of a bitch was weakening. "I'm not backing off ... till you talk," I said between pants. "Your choice."

Without warning, the orb confining him burst in an explosion of light. I squinted away, gasping with the release of energy. Expecting a follow-up attack, I drew the energy furiously into my own protection. But the mage was gone, I realized, along with the crushing fingers.

"Are you all right?" a voice asked from behind me.

I spun to find a figure standing at the theater entrance. I tensed my sword arm, an invocation on the tip of my tongue. The man stepped into the soft aura of my blade. Tall and dressed in a tailored blue suit, he looked to be in his mid forties. Gray touched the temples of his neat chestnut hair. My gaze fell to his hands. He was holding what appeared to be a slender wand.

I shuffled back a step and opened my wizard's senses. A subtle energy moved liquid-like around the man, but it felt nothing like the dark mage's aura.

"Everson Croft, I presume?" the man said with a slight smile.

All in a moment, I put the man's aura together with his English accent.

"That's right," I answered, slotting my sword into my staff and dispersing my shield. "And you must be Pierce."

"Yes, Pierce Dalton."

It was James Wesson's replacement, the wizard in charge of the boroughs.

"I'm sorry for not getting in touch with you earlier," I said. "There's no excuse, really. I just..."

I had extended a hand to shake, but he was already

moving past me. His cool blue eyes took in the shriveled bodies, then the rest of the theater. "A rather bold attack," he remarked. "Six souls ripped from their owners. Almost seven. A good job I arrived when I did."

I lowered my hand. "Actually, I had the situation under control."

"Did you?" he asked offhandedly, looking around the theater as if trying to locate something.

I bristled at the insinuation. "Not only that, I was on the verge of getting him to talk."

"Oh, I doubt he would have said anything useful."

"And you know that how?"

"You were grappling with a smoke golem. How do you think it dispersed so easily?" He collapsed the wand so that it was pen-sized and slipped it into the front pocket of his shirt.

"A smoke golem?" I echoed. *And easily?*

"Yes, a flimsy form animated from elsewhere."

I felt my face warm over. He was making it sound like child's play.

"Well, a golem can still be made to talk," I countered. "The key is preventing the spell-caster from breaking the bond. With enough pressure, the caster will say anything to be released." Not that any of that was forefront in my mind while I'd been tussling with the golem.

"Yes, *anything* being the key term," Pierce said. "Not necessarily the truth."

"My point is that I could have used a few more minutes with him."

But Pierce was no longer listening. He had stopped in front of the wall on the left side of the theater and was running his slender fingers over the glazed bricks. "Hm," he said, pausing at one and donning a pair of latex gloves. Who in the hell carried latex gloves? He jiggled a loose brick free, set it on the floor, and reached inside the hole. I watched his lips work as he probed around. A moment later, his hand reappeared holding a small leather pouch.

I walked over. "A hex bag?"

"An infernal bag." He undid the black lock of hair holding it closed, and the gray pouch opened in his hand. Removing his collapsible wand from his pocket, he poked around the bag's contents. "Black powder, magnesium, devil's ear…"

I winced inwardly at suggesting it had been a hex bag. "So the caster planted it here to animate the golem and claim unsuspecting souls," I said, trying to redeem myself.

Pierce raised his wand above the pouch and moved his lips. A transparent light glowed throughout the pouch's contents, then quickly retreated. I felt the bag's lingering energy discharge in a dark rush. The sensation had me tasting bile, but it didn't appear to effect Pierce.

"Shouldn't we have tried to trace the energy back to the source?" I asked.

"Any caster worth his salt would have covered his tracks, and our friend is no exception. I checked."

"You checked already?" I usually needed a casting circle for that.

"It's all right to come down!" he called past me.

Footsteps sounded on the stairs, and Vega and Hoffman entered the room. That Pierce had been the one to give the all-clear bothered me. It felt like an invasion of my turf. That he had given the all-clear to Vega bothered me even more. I walked over to meet her before he could.

Vega's concerned eyes inspected me for injuries. Finding none, she scanned the room. "What are we looking at?"

"Well, someone, a magic-user presumably, stashed what's

known as an infernal bag in the wall." I pointed to the dark gap left by the brick. "He used it to animate a smoke golem, which claimed six souls. To what purpose, I'm not sure yet. Maybe just to empower himself."

"Great," Vega muttered. "Any leads on who he might be?"

"Not yet," I admitted. "I had him—or his golem—entrapped. He was about to talk when—"

"I believe I have enough information that I can have an answer within a day or two," Pierce interjected. He had walked up behind me. When I turned, I realized just how tall he was. And, yeah, good-looking. His face was lined in a way that spoke to experience rather than age. He also had one of those tanned complexions that looked so damned effortless.

"That would be excellent," Vega said.

Hoffman, who was kneeling over one of the victims, snorted.

Pierce turned toward him. "Is there a problem, Detective?" The inquiry sounded innocent on the surface, but it wielded a dangerous edge underneath. Hoffman looked like he was about to say something before thinking better of it and returning his attention to the victim.

"Here's the bag Everson mentioned," Pierce said. "It's quite harmless now."

Vega called a crime technician over, and Pierce handed him the evidence.

"You have my card, right?" Vega asked Pierce.

He smiled as he stripped off his gloves. "I do. You gave it to me outside."

"That's right." Vega's face flushed slightly. "Then we'll take it from here. Thanks for your help."

Pierce nodded politely and stepped past us.

I stared at Vega for another moment—I couldn't

remember ever seeing her blush—and then hurried to catch up to Pierce.

"Hey, uh, mind holding on a sec?"

Pierce had been speeding up, as if he had somewhere to be, but he slowed to a stop and faced me. "Yes?"

"If you think you have a lead, we should meet up," I said. "Discuss strategy. The mage said something about us getting to know him 'quite well' in the coming days, which suggests that whoever we're dealing with isn't done. He could have more bags stashed around the city."

Pierce watched me with compressed lips as I spoke, eyes squinting slightly. It took me a moment to understand he was considering something, but not what I was saying. His eyes returned to focus.

"Yes, yes, of course," he said absently. He reached into the inside pocket of his jacket and snapped out a white business card. "Call this number and my assistant will set something up."

Assistant?

I looked down at the sleek card. The embossed print read:

Pierce Dalton
Art Appraisals

"Art, huh? Does that have anything to do with Himitsu paintings?"

But when I looked up from the card, he was gone.

8

I looked at where Pierce had been standing, feeling like I'd been slapped in the face. He'd done nothing overtly dickish. Nothing I could really point to, anyway. But then why did my face smart?

There had been something about him—several things, actually. His confidence and competence, his total understanding and mastery of a situation he had all but happened upon. A situation that, until that point, I thought I'd been mastering. His intrusion left me feeling like a tool.

"So that's the new wizard, huh?" Vega said, coming up beside me.

"Yeah," I said, giving my head a shake. Then I remembered the way her face had flushed a moment ago. Embarrassment for forgetting he had already given her his card, or something more? "Why did you let him past the cordon?"

"What do you mean?"

"I was already down here."

"Yeah, which is why I let him in. He introduced himself, explained who he was—"

"And you trusted him?" I interrupted.

Anger flashed hot in Vega's eyes. "I was the police contact you gave to the Order, and he knew that. Plus not an hour ago, you told me a Pierce from London was Wesson's replacement, and this guy's name just happened to be Pierce from, wait for it, London. I'm not stupid, Everson," she said in a lowered voice. "I wouldn't have let just anyone in. I was trying to *help* you."

I released my breath and nodded. "I know. I'm sorry. I just..." I gestured around the theater. More police officials had come down, and one was snapping photos of the victims. "I had the smoke golem in the equivalent of a chokehold. I could feel the mage powering him. We're dealing with a really bad dude."

Vega searched my face before relaxing hers. "Why don't you go home and get some sleep. You're exhausted." For the first time, I felt the burning strain in my eyes. That no doubt explained my irritability.

"What about you?"

"We're going to be a while processing the scene."

It still bothered me that Pierce had picked up enough to feel confident he could name a suspect in a day or two. "Do you mind if I do a final tour?" I asked. "See if I can sense anything?"

"Go for it. Just watch where you step."

I moved gingerly around the crime scene. The last remnants of the smoke golem had dissipated, the scent of sulfur fading. I attuned my wizard's senses to the infernal bag that had spawned the being. Pierce had neutralized the bag's magic—and it felt inert now—but I wondered whether he'd also pulled some of the magic into his wand for later study, explaining his confidence.

But why would he have kept that to himself?

I looked around the rest of the movie house before determining there was nothing more to glean. Basically, a bad guy stuck an infernal bag in the wall, focused enough energy into it to produce a smoke golem, and then used it to attack the theater and suck down a few souls.

I found Vega. "Sure you don't want me to wait for you?"

She shook her head. "There's no point. And yes, I'm wearing the amulet."

She had picked up my glance at the front of her shirt. Shortly after we had started seeing each other, I'd taken an enchanted amulet from my collection, imbued it with protective power, and made her promise to wear it, especially while working. I threatened her with random pat-downs until the amulet-wearing became a habit, right along with her badge and sidearm.

She tapped her sternum where the slender amulet was nested.

"Okay, good." Then remembering our dinner conversation, I said, "Hey, do you want me to check in on Tony?"

"He's fine. Camilla's spending the night."

"It's no problem."

"Go. Get some sleep."

Though she said it sternly, I could tell by her eyes she was pleased I'd asked. That was a start. I was about to lean down to kiss her before remembering our professionalism agreement: no PDA while working. Instead, I clapped her shoulder, which felt lame as hell.

Despite everything, that made her smirk. "Night, Croft," she said.

"Night, Detective."

IT WASN'T EVEN NINE BY THE TIME I RETURNED TO MY apartment building. But so much had happened tonight, between my dinner talk with Vega, to the theater attack, to Pierce's surprise appearance, that it felt much later.

As I climbed the stairs, I replayed the smoke-golem encounter in my mind. Golems were only as powerful as the magic-user powering them, and this one had been up there. The fire, the imps, the clenching hand—not to mention the violence with which the golem had ripped the souls from the victims' bodies.

If there was a recent pattern of similar killings, Vega would be on it. But I couldn't remember anything like that during my time in New York. Maybe we needed to go further back. I would consult my books.

You were grappling with a smoke golem, I heard Pierce saying. *How do you think it dispersed so easily?*

"Because I loosened the lid, you opportunistic ass," I shot back. The comeback might have arrived thirty minutes late, but it was true. Looking back, I was proud of the way I'd combated the golem: strongly, capably, never losing focus or resorting to my luck quotient. The mage had tried desperately to hold onto his creation, but I weakened him, nearly overpowered him. And that's when Mr. Fancy Pants sauntered in and gave the final twist.

"How do you think it dispersed so easily?" I mimicked in a kid's voice.

My growing anger suggested Vega had been right. I was shot. My keys seemed to blur as I inserted them into the locks.

I usually spent an hour or two in my lab before turning in

—Tabitha's observation hadn't been a stretch—but not tonight. I was more likely to blow the roof off the building than make any breakthroughs on the case. After contacting the Order about the killings, I planned to bury myself under my covers until five a.m. A morning dose of *Magical Me*, and I'd be good and focused again. Inside my apartment, I cycled through my door-locking routine so automatically I almost missed something.

My wards had been breached.

I spun at the same moment the toilet in my bathroom flushed.

"Tabitha," I hissed at the orange mound on the divan. *"Are you awake?"*

She slept on, my voice not loud enough to stir her.

Pulling my cane into sword and staff, I stole forward and eyed the slender bar of light between the bottom of the bathroom door and the floor. Shadows appeared along it. A moment later, the light turned off and the door opened. I recoiled at the sight of the emerging figure. She was large with a wild shock of hair, a mottled face, and a witch's hooked nose.

A night hag!

"Vigore!" I shouted, thrusting my sword forward.

The force invocation warped the air as it blasted across the open space. The hag, who was hacking into her fist, never saw it coming. Or so I'd thought. She waved her hand irritably, and the invocation veered off course, blowing apart my potted Ficus tree. Soil and leaves rained everywhere.

I switched to my staff. *"Entrapolarle!"*

An orb of light encased the hag, but only for a moment. She looked it over, then poked it with a finger. The orb shuddered before cascading to the floor like a waterfall, where it glimmered out.

I fumbled to pull my coin pendant from inside my shirt. Night hags were fae creatures and thus susceptible to iron. Grasping the pendant, I spoke quickly. Blue light shone through my fingers.

"Bah," the hag said, flicking her own fingers.

A force hit the coin hard enough to knock it from my hand and snap the chain. Both went skittering off behind me. She squinted at me now, her irises cycling through several colors. I felt the mesmerizing effect immediately. My body stiffened into a kind of rigor mortis. Straining, I tried to raise my sword and staff, but I couldn't lift my arms from my sides. When I attempted to invoke, thin murmurs leaked from my locked jaw.

Desperately, I went back in my mind to my last encounter with a night hag a couple of years earlier. What had I done then? With a sinking feeling I realized I'd cast through my coin pendant.

Crap.

And here I'd been congratulating myself for how I'd handled the smoke golem.

The hag arrived in front of me, fists on her wide hips. I braced for her rancid odor, but she smelled like sandalwood. And I saw that though her hair was wild, it was stylishly wild, held in place with product. She had even attempted to soften her several warts with makeup.

What kind of night hag was this?

I strained my eyes in search of the skin bag for storing her souls, but I couldn't spot one.

"Everson Croft, hm?" she grunted, looking me up and down and not appearing at all impressed.

I tried to ask who she was, but my mouth still wouldn't move. Searching for another way to communicate the question, I widened my eyes a few times. She widened her eyes back.

"Oh, darling," Tabitha murmured from the divan, half asleep, "someone's here to see you. She says she's your new teacher."

My new teacher?

I let out a straining moan.

"Oh," the woman said. The colors receded from her eyes. Her force released me so suddenly that I collapsed to my hands and knees. I pressed myself up and stood on shaky legs.

"The Order sent you?" I asked.

"Well this wasn't just a pee stop."

"I-I had no idea you were coming," I stammered.

"So you weren't welcoming me just now?" she asked dryly.

"Yeah, sorry about that. I thought you were an intruder. But you're ... my teacher?" I scratched the back of my neck and laughed. "I guess I was expecting a call or something. Some kind of heads-up."

"Have you read your mail lately?"

I followed her gaze to the dining room table, where the mail for the past week plus remained in a pile at one end. With an exasperated huff, she waved a hand. The pile shifted, leaving one letter behind. I walked over and picked it up. The plain letter was addressed to me, but without a return address. I vaguely remembered pulling it from my box on Monday.

I tore open the letter and unfolded the neat hand-written note inside.

Dear Everson,

A teacher has become available. Her name is Gretchen Wagonhurst. She is a highly capable magic-user who has spent considerable time in the faerie realm. She escaped Lich's notice this way, though unwittingly. As such, she is more skilled than most who were not in exile.

The faerie realm, I thought. That probably explained her resistance to my magic.

Her teaching style is likely to be unorthodox. However, we believe she is the best fit for your current level of experience. She is scheduled to arrive this Friday. Please allow her the use of your apartment until we can arrange more permanent accommodations for her.

Congratulations on the next phase of your development.

Love,
Arianna

I reread her name, this time aloud. "Gretchen Wagonhurst."

"*Vah*-gonhurst," she corrected me.

"And you're staying here?"

"Would you rather I slept on the street?"

"No, it's just that if I'd known—I mean, if I'd read the letter in time—I would have prepared for your arrival."

"Your room is adequate. I've already unpacked my bags and arranged the bed to my liking."

I waited for the indication she was joking, but it never came.

"Yeah, sure, sure," I said quickly. "That'll work until I can set something up. Let me grab a few things out of there, and the room's all yours."

"I'd rather you didn't."

"Huh?"

"I just rinsed my hose and draped them around the room. I'm modest, all right?"

"Oh." I swallowed. "Okay."

"As much as I'd like to stay up and yap, I'm also beat. Traveling all day does that to a broad. Think I'm going to file a few stubborn corns on my big toe and turn in. Might even sleep late."

"Sleep as late as you need to," I said, recovering from the thought that she'd be filing her feet in my bed. That's what antiseptic spells were for. "And listen, I'm really glad you're here. I've been anxious to take the next step, and the Order is confident you're the one to get me there. I think you'll be pleased to hear I haven't been idle. I've been waking up early for the last several months and—"

"Wonderful," she interrupted, "superb, excellent, great. Good night."

She disappeared into my room and shut the door behind her. I looked after her for a moment, then snorted. By *unorthodox* Arianna must have meant lacking entirely in social skills.

I called the Order and left a message, telling them about the night's attack and that Pierce and I would be working together. I finished by saying that Gretchen had arrived and was settling in.

After getting ready for bed myself, which involved

cleaning Gretchen's hair out of my sink, I pulled some sheets from the linen closet and arranged them on the sofa. I climbed in and tried to get comfortable, but the sofa was lumpy in all the wrong places. I sighed. Just twenty minutes before, I'd been walking through the door thinking about how wonderful my bed was going to feel.

"How does she seem?" Tabitha murmured.

A tractor started in my bedroom. I realized it was Gretchen snoring.

"I'm suspending judgment," I answered.

9

I opened my eyes the next morning to the ringing telephone and morning light streaming through the bay windows.

Wait, light?

In a panic, I pawed around for my alarm clock before realizing it was still in my bedroom. I checked my watch. Nine o'clock! I had expended more power last night than I'd thought. Kicking the sheets off my legs, I stumble-ran to answer the telephone. It was probably the Order, returning my message from last night. And here I should have been up four hours ago, at peak focus and power, primed for the day.

"Hello?" I gasped into the phone.

"That Everson?" A familiar voice asked.

"Budge?"

"That's right," he said with boyish cheer. "Your friendly city leader."

I was never quite sure how to feel about Mayor Lowder. We had a checkered history. Almost two years before, his half-werewolf wife, Penny, had tried to kill me. I put her in a coma that eventually killed *her*. But I also spear-headed the mayor's monster eradication program the following summer, a program that had been a huge success for all intents and purposes, propelling the mayor to an improbable reelection victory. I hadn't heard much from him since. I wasn't under the illusion that our relationship had been anything other than convenient, but an invite to his second inaugural ball would have been nice.

"Something I can help you with?" I asked.

"Well, I'm looking at the report from last night's attack. Some guy whipping black fire around? Shriveling up kids like they're made of cellophane? Sounds like your kind of case."

"Yeah, I'm, um..." I turned from the phone to hack the sleep from my throat. "I'm working on it."

"That's what Vega told me, but I wanted to hear it from my favorite wizard. What the hell are we dealing with, Everson?"

"By all appearances, someone with access to the demonic realm."

"Christ, that doesn't sound good."

"No, it doesn't," I admitted.

"Well, listen. We've managed to keep the details from the press. Good thing it was dark in that theater and half the eyewitnesses were on something funny. Right now the public thinks the killer was a guy with a flamethrower, and I'd like to keep it that way. Because the second the word gets out it was a supernatural, people will get cold feet about the neighborhood again."

"What people?"

When Budge replied it was with a lowered voice. "All right, you didn't hear this from me, but I've got a major developer interested in the East Village. The plan is to raze the

ruined blocks and burned-out shells and put in brand new
buildings. You should see the proposal, Everson. I'm talking
condos, commercial, mixed use. Quality stuff. But if they
think we've got supernatural problems again"—he paused to
give a sharp whistle—"see ya."

"Developers need renters," I said in understanding.

"And shoppers, and buyers. And no one's gonna do any of
that if they think they'll end up like those theater kids. This
thing needs to be wrapped up, Everson. Homicidal maniacs
the city can stomach. The minute you throw in smoke and
magic, forget about it. The killer pops up again—there, or
anywhere in my city—and the story's gonna grow legs and
stomp all over my deal."

"Let's not forget the tragedy of more senseless deaths," I
pointed out.

"Yeah, yeah, of course. That too."

I shook my head. As sincere as Budge could appear, it
took examples like that to see him for the political animal
he was.

"All right," I said. "I should probably get started."

"Oh, hey. Vega mentioned another wizard getting
involved?"

The straps of muscle in my neck tightened as I remembered Pierce. I'd thought a good night's sleep would dissolve
the resentment, but oversleeping actually seemed to have
hardened it.

"That's right," I said. "His name's Pierce. We work for the
same organization. He sort of happened on the scene while I
was there, and ... well, I guess that means we're partners
now."

"Good, keep me up to date," Budge said. "In fact, why
don't we meet in my office this afternoon."

I had no interest in adding a pointless meeting to what was already going to be a busy day, especially given my late start. But making the mayor happy would grease the wheels of whatever city resources I might need for this case or future ones. Maybe I had a little political animal in me too.

"What time?" I asked.

"Let's see..." Budge made a puttering sound with his lips. "Aw hell, my calendar's on the computer, and I never learned how to work that thing."

"The calendar app?"

"No, the computer. And I've got two of 'em in my office for some reason. Tell you what. Soon as my secretary gets back, I'll have her clear a time and then give you a call."

"Sounds good."

"Hey, I'm looking forward to teaming up again, Everson," he said in that buddy-buddy way of his. "We've got a solid record, you and me. Haven't let our city down yet."

Though the mayor hadn't stressed the word "yet," it lingered as I hung up the phone. Probably because there was too much negativity swimming around my head. I hadn't gone through my morning practices, and between the lumpy sofa and Gretchen's snoring, I hadn't even rested that well.

The one time I managed to fall into a decent sleep, I was awakened by Gretchen rooting around the fridge. She did that for twenty minutes before fixing what smelled like a left-over lamb-and-onion sandwich. I hope she enjoyed it. She had devoured it noisily enough.

I checked my watch, then eyed the door to my bedroom. Still closed, and I had things to get out of there.

I was heading for the bathroom when the bedroom door swung open and banged against the wall. Sporting the most violent bed head I'd ever seen, Gretchen staggered out and peered at me with crinkled eyes. She cleared her nostrils and then disappeared into the bathroom without a word.

Assuming she was going to be in there for a while, I rifled the pockets of my hanging coat until I found Pierce's card. I went to my phone and dialed. Pierce claimed to have information from last night, which I had apparently missed. I still didn't see how that was possible, but just in case, I wanted to talk to him before sitting down with the mayor. The line rang twice before a young woman answered.

"Pierce Dalton's office."

"Yes, is he in?"

"I'm afraid he can't come to the phone right now. Can I ask who's calling?"

"This is Everson Croft. I'm an ... associate of Pierce's." I had no idea if his assistant knew anything about his wizarding life. "He told me to call to schedule a time to meet with him."

"Hmm," the woman said. "He didn't mention anything about that. Hold one moment, please."

"The earlier the better," I said quickly, but canned violin music was already piping through the line.

The woman returned a minute later. "He has an opening in forty minutes?"

Crap. I'd been hoping to go through at least an expedited version of the *Magical Me* program and then swing by Mae's apartment. I'd already incinerated the old woman's spell book, but I still needed to take care of Buster. I hadn't worked out exactly *how* yet, but with the mage case looming, I wanted to tie up all of my dangling threads. Guess that would have to wait.

"Sure," I told Pierce's assistant. "I just need his address."

"Oh, that won't be necessary. We'll send a car."

"A car?"

I could hear her tapping on a handheld device. "You're on West Tenth, correct?"

"That's right," I said uncertainly.

"Great, we'll have a car there in twenty."

"Great," I echoed, and hung up.

Who in the hell *was* this guy? On top of being a wizard, he appraised art and had a personal assistant and a chauffeur? I couldn't wait to see what he drove. Feeling my jealousy gathering again, I spoke a quick affirmation, then headed to the bathroom. Twenty minutes didn't give me much time. I knocked tentatively on the closed door.

"Hey, ah, how much longer—"

"Do you mind?" Gretchen barked. "I've been stopped up for three days, and I'm finally getting some movement."

I backed away from the door. I'd skip the bathroom. Instead, I scrubbed my face in the kitchen sink, finger-combed my hair, and rinsed my mouth with baking soda and water. I was heading to my room to grab a clean set of clothes, when Gretchen emerged from the bathroom with a loud, satisfied sigh and strode into my room ahead of me, closing the door.

Wonderful.

I pulled last night's clothes from the back of my reading chair, put them on along with my shoes, and grabbed my cane. Tabitha slept while I dressed, which was just as well. My black pants and shirt looked more appropriate for another date, and I didn't need any commentary. Then again, I wasn't aware of there being standard attire for meeting a fellow wizard.

"Where you going?" Gretchen called from my bedroom.

"I have to meet someone. Another wizard. I shouldn't be too long."

"Well, come straight back when you're done. Your training starts today."

She was testing my patience as a roommate, but for the first time that morning, I actually smiled.

Training! Finally!

10

———

The car that arrived to pick me up was a Rolls Royce. Its silver body glistened as it pulled up to the curb. I took two steps forward, then stopped. Was I supposed to wait for the driver to do the whole chauffeur thing? I squinted, but couldn't see anything past the tinting.

The rear door on my side opened.

I hunkered down and peered into the empty back seat. "Neat trick."

I slid onto the supple leather seat, and the door closed. Cool air moved around me. It wasn't until the car pulled from the curb that my eyes began to adjust to the dimness. I was opening my mouth to make conversation with the driver before realizing there was no one behind the wheel either. I rose from my seat to make sure the driver wasn't just really short before settling back down.

Great, the car was operating itself.

I opened my wizard's senses until I felt the magic moving throughout the vehicle. I'd had modest success animating golems, but a frigging car? Jealousy curdled my gut again and I had to talk it back down.

The truth was, a part of me was excited to be meeting another wizard. Until discovering the Order in Exile and then James Wesson, the only wizards I'd known had been my first trainer, Lazlo, and then Chicory, who turned out to be Lich. Which meant the majority of my wizarding life in the city had been pretty lonely.

I was also starting to see how Pierce's skill—demonstrated by the car's smooth turn and acceleration onto Sixth Avenue —could be to my benefit. His appearance last night had bothered me, sure. After the hundreds of extra hours I'd put into wizarding in the past year, after all the early mornings and late nights, I'd started to believe in my own affirmations. Last night's one-two punch of Pierce and Gretchen had taken care of that. I *was* a better wizard now than I'd been a year before, but I was nowhere close to where I thought I was—or should be.

Gretchen would help. But so too could Pierce. By collaborating on the case, I'd be able to observe him, ask questions, learn how he did what he did. It was just a matter of keeping my ego in check.

And you can do it, I told myself. *Think of it as a necessary step in your journey to becoming your best wizard.*

By the time the Rolls Royce pulled in front of a townhouse just south of Midtown, I was feeling good about where this could lead. And damn, he had a nice place. I climbed the stone steps to the front door, where I was greeted by Pierce's assistant, a young Asian woman dressed in smart business attire. I suddenly felt self-conscious in my date-night get up.

"Mr. Croft?" she said, giving me a firm handshake. "I'm Sora. This way, please."

I stepped into a giant foyer, where a staircase wound up and natural sunlight fell through large windows high overhead. The panes of light glowed over a series of beautiful landscape paintings that circled the room. Sora led me down a wainscoted corridor hung with more paintings before stopping at an open door. "Your ten o'clock is here," she announced.

His ten o'clock?

Ego, I warned sternly.

"Ah, yes," Pierce said. "Show him in."

I thanked Sora as I stepped past her and into an office. Ahead of me, Pierce stood over a large desk, shirt sleeves rolled to his elbows. His brow was creased, and it took me a moment to realize he was studying a painting on his desktop, a rendering of seemingly random lines and shapes.

I looked around. No paintings hung from the walls, though large numbers of them were stacked here and there, protected by thin paper. Subtle magic moved throughout the ample space.

Pierce remained staring at the painting for another few seconds before looking up.

"Everson," he said, recognition seeming to take hold in his blue eyes. "Have a seat."

"Thanks." I sat in one of the leather chairs facing his desk. Sora returned a moment later with a cup of tea and a saucer, which she placed efficiently on a small table beside my chair.

"Oh, Sora," Pierce said before she could leave. "Go ahead and package this one and prepare the certificate of authenticity." He handed her the painting he'd been studying.

"I'll have it ready to sign following your meeting," she said.

"Very good."

Sora left with the painting and closed the door behind her.

"When your assistant said you were sending a car, I didn't think she meant by itself."

Pierce gave a modest chuckle. "I found it saves on staff."

I took another look around. Like the rest of the house, the office demonstrated expensive tastes without being flashy. Wooden fixtures glowed handsomely in the light through the window.

"Nice place," I remarked.

"Yes, well, property values have been depressed for some time, so when I received the request to relocate, I decided to take a chance on buying. Perhaps the housing market will come back fully, and perhaps it won't." He smiled in a way that suggested it didn't really matter to him either way.

"So how did you get into appraising?"

"By accident, really. I grew up outside of Tokyo. My father was an officer in Her Majesty's Armed Forces, you see. They had a presence in Japan well into the '70s. In the region where we lived, a kind of painting called Himitsu is widespread. The style dates back to an early religion called Jiko."

"I've heard of Jiko," I said.

"Yes, well, then you probably know that the religion was forbidden during the Muromachi period, its practice punishable by death. As such, devotees developed subtle ways to communicate with one another. One was through Himitsu paintings. On the surface they appealed to the common tastes of the era, but their true purpose was to transmit messages and teachings."

I gave my best scholarly nod, even though I'd known little of that.

"We studied the local culture as part of the curriculum

at my school," Pierce went on. He had never sat down, and now he began to stroll the space behind his desk. "One day, a Himitsu painter spoke to our class. He showed us an original Himitsu painting and asked if anyone knew what it depicted. Various classmates of mine described the tree and the woman sitting beneath it. I couldn't for the life of me understand why no one had pointed out the painting's most obvious feature: directions to a meeting place. After class, I asked the painter about this. He looked at me intently for a long moment before decreeing, 'You will study with me.' Then he left. Two weeks later, my mother announced she wanted to add art to my extracurricular activities. In fact, she had already found someone to instruct me—a painter. Naturally, it was the man who had come to our school, Gaku."

Whether it was Pierce's ability as a storyteller or his wizard's voice, I felt myself being pulled into the account.

"For the next eight years, I studied under Gaku. He taught me the language of the Himitsu paintings, which were even more layered than I'd first intuited. The painting he showed to our classroom? It also contained the history of an important period in the past as well as information on a *mirror period*, an epoch in the near future that would reflect the referenced history."

"So the Himitsu paintings were also used for divining."

"By the masters, yes. Eventually I could not only read and reproduce the paintings, but compose my own. The practice unlocked other abilities."

"Your magic," I said, unable to hide my interest.

"Some of the old Himitsu masters were practitioners themselves. Their teachings were found in the paintings. My teacher was a devotee rather than a master, but he had collected images of all the old works. We experimented in secret, developing my abilities."

"So you learned your magic through paintings?" Though I'd heard of such things, the concept still seemed incredibly foreign. In my defense, the Far East wasn't my specialty. "What about books?"

Pierce's laugh carried the slightest hint of condescension. "I consulted books to round out my studies, but I found them too linear. With a Himitsu painting, you can take in everything at a glance. This one for example." He walked over to a bookshelf that I'd assumed held reading material. But when he selected a leather folio and opened it for me to see, I was looking at an old painting on parchment.

"What do you see?" he asked.

"A lily pond with mountains in the distance?"

"What if I were to tell you that this contains a complex spell on translocating objects?"

I squinted and tilted my head, unable to see anything other than the image. Could Pierce really perform translocations? I'd taken a few stabs at it that year but without anything approaching success.

Pierce's eyes gleamed as he closed the folio and returned it to its place on the shelf. "In any case, all of that was a long way of telling you that in the process of studying the Himitsu paintings, I developed an uncanny eye for authenticity. I become an appraiser, and here we are."

Judging by *here*, his services were expensive and highly sought after.

I took a sip of tea. "How did the Order find you?"

"Oh, I found them."

"You found *them*?"

"Yes, through a painting I was working on. You asked

about divination, and it is quite true that some paintings begin to speak to you." He cocked an eyebrow. "Has that ever happened with one of your books?"

"Yeah, but it was cursed," I muttered.

"This was about a year ago," he went on. "I had been living back in England and was working on a large piece. By the time I finished, I knew the recent history of the Order and understood they were looking for magic-users. I had been taking nightly strolls though London, protecting its citizens from unnatural threats, if you follow, so it seemed a natural fit."

"Lich never came after you before that, never tried to recruit you?"

"He didn't. The ethos of the Himitsu masters was to be 'soft in their practices,' as they put it. Subtle. A history of persecution, remember. And this was the manner in which I myself practiced. I must never have made enough of a light show to be noticed." For the second time, I picked up a hint of judgment in his tone. "Not only that, I managed to remain ... unattached."

At first I thought he meant being a swinging bachelor; his fourth finger was ring-less. But when he gave me a thin smile, I realized he was referring to Thelonious, the incubus spirit that remained affixed to my soul. The anger I'd felt last night climbed my neck, and I set my tea down.

"You mentioned the recent history of the Order," I said. "You must have learned about the being Dhuul."

"Ah, yes. The Whisperer. Chaos. The effects were beginning to spread through London."

"Well, did you know I killed Lich?" My heartbeats pounded through the words. "Did you know my father sacrificed his life to repel Dhuul and collapse the portal to his realm?"

Pierce became preoccupied with a document on his desk. "I did pick up something about that, yes," he replied. "Quite a lucky break."

"It wasn't *luck*."

He blinked up at me, startled by my show of anger. "Just a turn of phrase, Everson. No harm meant. Would you like Sora to bring you some more tea? How about something to snack on?"

I glared at him another moment. What was the deal with his off-handed comments? His show of disinterest? Were they deliberate tactics meant to demonstrate his mastery over me? Or was he just one of those types who became bored by someone's company the instant the focus shifted from himself? Choosing to believe the second, I exhaled through my nose.

"Let's talk about the case," I said.

"Certainly. What exactly would you like to discuss?"

"Last night you said you had enough information to name the suspect in a day or two."

"That's correct."

"Well, I don't see how that's possible. I didn't see a damn thing at the crime scene." I stopped short of accusing him of taking evidence without telling me.

Pierce smiled.

"Is something funny?"

"My being on Houston Street last night was no accident."

I stiffened, ready to grab my cane. Had he been involved in the attack?

He seemed to take in my reaction, his eyes touching on my ring and coin pendant, before turning his back. "I mentioned mirror periods to you earlier? Well, they don't have to involve major historical epochs. They can reflect smaller events too. Mirror events. While working on a recent painting to hone my intuiting, I picked up on a reflection. One that foretold the attack that occurred last night. Unfortunately, I arrived too late."

"How did it foretell the attack?" I demanded.

When he turned to face me again, he gave another one of his thin smiles. "It's impossible for someone unfamiliar with Himitsu paintings to fully understand. It would be like..." He rested his chin on his thumb. "Well, it would be like a sphere trying to explain its three-dimensional existence to a circle. There are almost no common points of reference."

He gave no sign that he'd just landed another one of his stinging jabs. Regardless, I believed that divination had led him to the crime scene. My body relaxed slightly. "Fine, let's go back to last night. So when you told Vega you'd have an answer in a day or two, you're going to *divine* that info?"

"With the help of the painting, yes."

"Then what are you doing"—I threw a hand out—"appraising art?"

The smile again, as though he was enjoying a private joke. "A Himitsu painting cannot be rushed, Everson. It takes time to fully express itself. Hurry the job, and you'll end up with nothing."

"Well, can I be doing anything in the meantime?" I asked in frustration.

"No, honestly. Like I said, the attacker did a good job covering his tracks. But he's locked into a mirror pattern now, most likely unknowingly. And those are extremely hard to escape."

"The infernal bag," I said. "The ingredients are common,

except for devil's ear. The crushed leaf is sold in a handful of specialty shops around the city. I can talk to the shop owners, see if they remember anyone buying some."

"If you wish," Pierce said, consulting something else on his desk.

"It beats waiting around for a painting to talk," I muttered. But if he heard me, he gave no sign. I took a few calming breaths. He wasn't trying to be a dick, I reminded myself. Or was he?

I stood with my cane. "I have a meeting with the mayor later today," I said, for no other reason than to sound important. "He's worried about another attack. More than anything, he needs to be reassured we're making progress."

"Oh?"

"So if you learn anything more before this afternoon, could you let me know?"

He raised his eyes. "If you want to hang around, I'll be checking in with the painting shortly."

Did he seriously expect me to operate on his timetable?

"Can't." I headed for the door. "I need to get a head start on the shops."

"You're more than welcome to the car," Pierce offered. "Cheaper than a cab."

"Thanks, but I'm feeling extravagant."

11

I caught a cab and gave the driver the address of a medicinal shop on the Upper West Side. I hadn't forgotten Gretchen's request to come straight home following the meeting, but I felt a burning need to find a lead before Pierce did.

It wasn't just the way he'd talked down to me. It was the subtle critique of my magic and then my incubus. It was the insinuation that I couldn't possibly understand the complexity of the Himitsu paintings. But most of all, it was the way he'd dismissed my father's and my efforts to repel the Whisperer.

He'd called it luck. And while, yes, luck had played a part, it didn't change the fact we had spared the world—including *him*—from Chaos. A little gratitude would have been nice.

To top it off, none of Pierce's sleights had seemed deliberate—which only made them more humiliating. It was as if he didn't even have to try. And then he'd had the gall to offer me his car.

"*Pfft*," I said as I looked out the cab's dirty window.

I knew I needed to get a handle on my ego, to be the bigger wizard...

Screw that, I thought. *I'll let him in on this one case, and then he can go back to covering the boroughs.*

I didn't ever want to hear about Himitsu art again.

By early afternoon, none of the shop owners I spoke to recalled any recent purchases of devil's ear. Several didn't even keep it in stock. My next-to-last stop was Mr. Han's Apothecary in Chinatown. Because I was in the domain of Bashi, the local crime lord, I had the taxi idle while I hustled inside.

I found Mr. Han at the register, ringing up a woman customer. Her small daughter tapped on the side of a fish tank full of live scorpions. I browsed the narrow aisles as I waited, looking for devil's ear. As I went, I picked out a few items I was getting low on. Though I shopped at Midge's Medicinals for convenience, Mr. Han still had the best prices in the city.

"That Mr. Croft?" he called in his sharp accent.

I turned to find the shop owner standing ramrod straight behind his register, a collared shirt buttoned to his chin. The door made a *tring* sound as the customer and her daughter left.

"Hey, Mr. Han." I walked up and deposited the items on the counter. "How are things going?"

The last time I'd been here was almost a year before when I helped the Blue Wolf. I braced now for Mr. Han to ask why the upstairs room he'd rented to Jason had been trashed and bloodied, but he fell back to his old refrain.

"Oh, you know, just *chilling out*." His fingers punched the register as he inspected each item and dropped it into a bag. "You see special on dried bull wang today? Buy one get one two-third price."

"That's an interesting deal. I'm actually looking for devil's ear, but I couldn't find any."

"Because someone buy it all," he said. "Devil's ear on backorder. Be here two week."

A charge went through me. "Do you know who the buyer was?"

"I never see him before."

"Can you describe him?" When Mr. Han looked up, I caught a glint of suspicion in his eyes. "I might know him," I added quickly. "I was thinking I could maybe, you know, talk him into sharing some until you restock."

"Must want devil's ear very bad."

"I do."

Mr. Han placed the final item in my bag. "Forty-two dollar, thirty-five cent," he announced.

I paid him in cash, then waited as he produced my change.

"So," I said, taking the bag, "about the person who bought the devil's ear..."

Mr. Han looked at me blank-faced. I'd known him long enough to recognize that as his thinking expression. But after another moment, he looked past me. "I no can say, Mr. Croft."

"No can or no will?" I pressed.

Mr. Han's response was to fold my bag and push it toward me.

"All right," I said, "how much did he pay you to remain silent?"

Mr. Han didn't hesitate. "One hundred dollar."

"Here." I reopened my wallet and placed a scatter of bills on the counter. "That's another hundred."

Mr. Han swept the bills into a pile, tapped them into a neat stack, and deposited them in his register. "White man, a little shorter than you. Wear long black coat."

"Well, that narrows it down to a million or so," I muttered.

"Oh, and he wear funny hat."

"Funny how?"

"No, *furry* hat, with parts that go over ear. But look funny too, especially with big sunglasses and scarf around mouth."

I sagged as I pictured the ridiculous disguise. Knowing someone might come asking, the mage had not only concealed his distinguishing features, but paid Mr. Han to remain silent. I started to ask if the man had bribed him with a credit card, before remembering Mr. Han's cash-only policy.

"How much devil's ear did he buy?"

Mr. Han's eyes canted to one side as he searched his memory. "Ten pound, I think."

I whistled inwardly. That would make a lot of infernal bags.

"Do you remember what his voice was like?"

"He talk in whisper. And he have ... How you say? Lip?"

"Lip?" I repeated.

"Like when someone pronounce special *spethal*?"

"A lisp!" I said.

"Yes, yes, *lisp*." He repeated the word a few times to lock it into his still-growing vocabulary.

I hadn't heard a lisp last night, but the magic-user had been speaking through a smoke golem. He could have manifested any voice he'd wanted. *So, a lisp,* I thought. That didn't necessarily give me a lead, but it gave me an identifying feature rare in grown men. That was something.

"Is there anything else about him you can tell me?" I asked. "The way he walked, maybe?"

But Mr. Han had stooped down. When he stood again, he was aiming a fire extinguisher past me. I had begun to feel a vibrating in my inner ear, like in the theater last night—an unpleasant sensation of building energy. I turned to find sulfurous black smoke growing from the back of the store. And not just growing, but writhing toward us.

Well, crap.

My watch began to flash as my cane jerked toward the smoke.

"Yeah, yeah, I'm right here," I told my alarm, dispelling it quickly.

I caught Mr. Han as he tried to rush past me with the fire extinguisher. "Get down!" I shouted. I shoved him back behind the counter, pulled my sword from the cane, and called forth a shield invocation. Light burst from my staff into a dome that covered both of us.

"Have to put out fire," Mr. Han insisted.

"It's not a fire! We're under attack!"

No sooner than I'd said that, red-black flames began snapping from the smoke. At the center, the smoke was coiling into the same figure I'd encountered last night— another smoke golem.

"Careful, wizard," the golem said. "You're putting your nose where it doesn't belong."

"Vigore!" I shouted, thrusting my sword forward. A shield hardened from the golem's right arm, blocking and scattering the force invocation. The shelves to either side of him toppled in a Domino effect. The large fish tank fell and shattered, sending scorpions scrambling in every direction.

I followed up with an attempt to trap the golem. But the

mage animating him had prepared for that as well. A spiky suit of armor appeared over the golem's form, breaking apart the light energy.

"As for you..." The smoke golem trained his glaring red eyes on Mr. Han. "I thought we had an agreement."

The golem threw his left arm forward. Flames shot from his hand and blasted around our shield. Before I could stop Mr. Han, he shouted something in Mandarin and shot back at the golem with the fire extinguisher. A layer of thick foam coated the inside of the shield, rendering me blind.

For the love of...

I shoved Mr. Han past the curtained entrance to his living quarters with a force invocation and shielded the doorway. I then inverted my own shield so the foam was on the outside. With another invocation, I blew the foam away and shrunk the shield until it conformed to my body.

The smoke golem rose up in front of me.

"What's wrong?" he asked. "Your wizard friend isn't here to help you?"

My face burned at the suggestion. "I can handle you just fine on my own, thanks."

I drove my sword forward, but even though the runes glowed with power, it only passed through his body. With a laugh, the golem seized my wrist and twisted. Pain shot up my arm, until I could feel the ball of my shoulder straining in the socket. Grunting, I rotated with the pressure and ended up on my knees.

"Respingere!" I managed.

Light and force detonated from my shield, but the smoke golem didn't budge.

"I'm far too adaptable for you, wizard," he said. "With

each encounter, I develop more immunity to your magic. It was a deadly mistake for you to come looking for me."

He gave a hard twist. I shouted as the shoulder dislocated. The ball bulged beneath the front of my shirt like a baseball. Gritting my teeth, I drove my sword into his smoky form again. He reached for my face, flames licking from his fingers. Sweat leapt from my brow.

Adaptable, huh? I thought. *Then let's try something you haven't seen.*

I gathered all of my power, even the portion shielding Mr. Han's doorway, and channeled it into a single word: *"Disfare!"*

The invocation I used to banish nether creatures erupted from my blade and into the golem. With a pained cry, the golem's smoky form blasted out in all directions as if it had been hit by an industrial-strength fan. The smoke didn't coalesce again. My invocation had worked.

I pushed myself to my feet and peered around the trashed store. Other than a few small fires, smoking scorpion husks, and the golem's lingering fog, there was no sign of him.

Mr. Han's head appeared from behind the curtain. Seeing the coast was clear, the rest of him followed. He was still carrying the extinguisher. He ran around, putting out small fires.

"I'm really sorry about your store," I said.

"Rented room, now this?" he asked sharply. "Disaster follow you everywhere?"

I started to shrug, then winced as the pain of dislocation discharged down my arm. Mr. Han set the extinguisher down and walked quickly over to me. Clasping my shoulder in his small but surprisingly strong hands, he said, "Relax. On count of three, I fix. One..."

With a sharp thrust, he jerked the shoulder. I gasped in

surprise as the ball popped back into the socket. I rotated the shoulder a few times. Everything stayed put. I would apply some healing magic when I left.

"Thanks," I said. "Here, let me help you get the shelves back up."

We worked together righting them. His wife appeared shortly with a fan to blow out the remaining smoke. She then began sweeping up the detritus with a small broom and dustpan. Every so often, Mr. Han would snatch up a live scorpion and drop it into a plastic bag he'd tucked into his belt.

As we righted the final sets of shelves, I spotted what I'd been looking for: a small leather pouch like the one Pierce had discovered last night. While Mr. Han chased another scorpion, I picked up the infernal bag from amid a pile of books on channeling. A small amount of dark magic stirred inside the pouch. I slipped the bag into my coat pocket.

When we got the last of the shelves up, I checked my watch. It was after two o'clock. Gretchen was expecting me back at the apartment. It had also been awhile since I'd checked my voice mail. The Order and the mayor's office had probably called. I picked up my purchased spell items, which by some miracle had remained on the counter, and turned to Mr. Han.

"If that man who bought the devil's ear comes back, could you give me a call?"

"Give you call?" he said. "Only person I going to call is insurance company."

I glanced around his ruined store. "Good point." I held up my shopping bag. "Well ... thanks."

"Wait," he said when I turned to leave. "Twenty dollar. For shoulder."

"Huh?" I said before realizing what he was asking. "Oh, right. The medical bill."

I reached for my wallet, figuring it was the least I could do, but he waved his hands.

"Mr. Han make joke," he said, turning to his wife, who started laughing too.

That got me chuckling as well, even though the joke was only mildly funny, especially in light of the destruction around us. But I realized I had some things to feel good about. I had just defeated a smoke golem more powerful than last night's, I had obtained a description of the mage behind it, and I had recovered an infernal bag with some magic still kicking inside.

Add them up, I thought, *and I just might be looking at an advantage over Pierce.*

12

When I returned to my apartment in the mid afternoon, it looked like a bomb had gone off in my kitchen. The counter was scattered with mixing bowls, milk cartons, and heaps of flour; burnt pans and batter covered the stove top; and the sink was crammed with dirty pots and plates. I picked my way across a kitchen floor mined with egg shells to shut off the running faucet.

"Where's Gretchen?" I asked.

Tabitha stirred on her divan. "She made breakfast and then went back to bed."

"Back to bed?"

At that moment, I heard her choke on a snore in my bedroom.

"I'm not surprised," Tabitha said. "I've never seen someone eat that many pancakes in one sitting. You should have seen the stack. It was like something out of a cartoon. I'm surprised she didn't fall into a diabetic coma. Or maybe she did." Tabitha lowered her head back down, unconcerned either way.

"Did she seem upset when I didn't come back?"

"She seemed more upset when she ran out of maple syrup."

"Have *you* eaten?" I asked.

"Yes, darling. But not because she offered to share. In fact, she behaved as if I were hardly here."

"Join the club," I muttered, thinking of my meeting with Pierce.

"Thankfully, she fried up a pile of bacon and then forgot about it. A little greasy for my tastes, but sometimes a girl needs to indulge."

The girl in question *always* indulged, but I didn't say so.

"Well, here, let me warm up some milk for your lunch."

"That would be marvelous, darling."

I opened the fridge—also trashed—and rooted around until I found a bottle of goat's milk. I pulled out an apple for myself.

"Any calls?" I asked.

"At least one. I thought Gretchen was going to answer, but she was too involved in her breakfast."

I crunched into the apple while filling a pot with Tabitha's milk and cleaning a burner to set it on. When I finished, I checked my voice mail. The service indicated one message, probably from the mayor's office.

But when the recording started, I recognized the voice as belonging to a functionary of the Order, an older man I'd met in the Refuge named Claudius. His messages always sounded harried, as if he was in perpetual catch-up mode, but that was the current state of the Order. In addition to stitching the tears in reality, the senior members were trying to track down magic-users. Still, even their delayed response time was a huge improvement over the artifice Lich had been running.

"*Yes, hello, Everson,*" Claudius said. "*We received your two messages. On the matter of the wards ... let's see ... yes, we checked the wards in that sector and they're operating as they should. It seems your colleague in the boroughs anticipated the situation some months before and investigated for himself.*"

Pierce? I thought.

"*He found the situation stable, so instructed the wards not to call you to that particular address.*"

My hand tightened around the receiver. *He messed with my alarm system?*

"*The signal must have leaked out,*" Claudius continued. "*In any case, I trust you found everything in order. Now, to the matter of last night's attack ... Yes, a mage casting infernal magic does sound serious. We'll see if there have been similar patterns elsewhere. In the meantime, continue to work with ... let's see ... oh, yes, Pierce. A fine magic-user. Extremely capable.*"

Sure, I thought. *Everyone loves Pierce.*

"*Also, you mentioned that Gretchen arrived. She can assist you as well.*"

I actually hadn't thought of that, but of course she could. Hell, I'd welcome some of that fae-style magic in my corner.

"*That should do it,*" Claudius said. "*If anything else comes up, let us know right away. Keep up the good work.*"

Harried or not, the last words placated me as I hung up. But still, who in the hell was Pierce to screw with my alarm system? And without telling me? It made me wonder how many other calls he'd intervened in over the past year. There had been a few stretches of little to no action, which I'd thought unusual.

"Well, two can play at that game," I muttered, patting my coat pocket that held the infernal bag.

Though I was anxious to begin testing the bag, I had shot

my payload back at Mr. Han's to disperse the smoke golem. My power needed time to recharge. When Tabitha's milk began to steam, I poured it into a bowl and swapped it for the empty one beside her divan. The smell roused her.

"Thanks, darling," she said in a languid voice.

She willed herself to stand and stretch before thudding to the floor. As I returned to the kitchen with the empty bowl, I thought about calling the Order with an update on the afternoon's attack. But I was bothered by the fact the mayor's office had never called back.

I picked up the phone, intending to dial Budge's office, but decided to call Vega first. I wanted to see how the rest of last night had gone. I was also curious whether there were any new developments in the case.

"Hey," she answered in a tired voice.

"Sounds like someone needs a cuddle."

Vega was a lot of things, but a cuddler was not among them. She snorted. "Is that why you called?"

"I actually called to see how you're doing."

"Well, it took till after midnight to wrap up the scene, then I was back at it early this morning, interviewing friends and families of the victims. Also the theater owner and employees."

"For a random attack?"

"Even if it looks random we still have to rule out the perp targeting the location or someone inside. I mean, they knew about the loose brick in the wall as a place to hide that bag."

"Good point. Speaking of bags, I found another one."

"You did? Where?"

I told her about my visit to Mr. Han's, how a man had bought a large quantity of devil's ear, paid Mr. Han to remain silent, and then mined his store with an infernal bag to be sure. I played down the encounter with the smoke golem just enough so she wouldn't worry, but that battle had *not* been easy. And I hadn't liked what the golem said about adapting to my powers.

Vega blew out her breath. "So there are more bags out there."

"Yeah. Any hits with the interviewees?"

"None of the vics seem to have had any of the usual enemies. The theater did fire someone several months back for stealing from the register, but she doesn't look like a hot lead. To be safe, we're getting a warrant for her place. Should have the judge's sig by this afternoon."

In cases of suspected magic use, I'd instructed Vega on what kinds of books and items to look for during a search. "I'd be happy to tag along," I offered, even though it sounded like a dead end. But it would give my magic time to recharge. I could also start addressing the absentee issue Vega had raised last night. "I just have this meeting with Budge I'll need to work around. He wants to talk about the case. In fact, I was just about to call over there to see if he'd scheduled a time yet."

Silence on the other end.

"Hello?" I said.

"Everson, the meeting just ended."

"What meeting? With the mayor?"

"I thought you knew."

"How was I supposed to know if no one told me?"

"Pierce was there. I figured you'd sent him so you could—"

"Pierce was there?" I interrupted. *"Pierce?"*

"Why are you raising your voice at me," she demanded.

I forced a steadying breath through my nose as I worked

out what had happened. During my visit with Pierce, I had mentioned the meeting with the mayor. As soon as I left, he must have called his office and scheduled himself in my place. That fucking rat.

"What did he say?"

"Everson, what's going on?"

"What did Pierce say?" I repeated.

"I want you to talk to me."

"And I want you to tell me what he said."

She sighed. "He mostly listened, but he told the mayor he'd be working closely with the NYPD and that we'd have a suspect shortly."

"Did he say *he* would be working with the police department, or *we*?"

"*He*, but I'm sure he meant both of you."

I shook my head and swore through clenched teeth. "That son of a bitch."

"Okay, Everson, what's this all—" She stopped as an explanation dawned on her. "Are you jealous of Pierce?"

"No, I'm not jealous of Pierce," I said. "But this is the second time he's..." I almost said *invaded my turf* before realizing that would sound exactly like jealousy. "...encroached on my responsibilities. I'm getting a little sick of it. The next time he shows up somewhere like that, I want you to tell me. You know what? Forget it. I'm going to call him right now."

"Don't you think you're overreacting?"

"I think I'm showing incredible restraint. I'll call you later."

My heart was slamming my sternum when I thumbed the phone's switch hook and dug Pierce's pretty little card out of my pocket. I dialed the number with hard strokes and waited.

"Pierce Dalton's office," Sora answered.

"I need to talk to him. Is he in?"

"May I ask who—"

"Everson Croft."

"Hello, Mr. Croft. No, I'm sorry, he's out right now."

"Does he have a cell number?"

"He prefers all communications to go through me."

"Even in emergencies?"

"Is that what this is?"

Instead of answering, I said, "Tell him to call me right away. I mean that. I don't care what he's doing."

"Sure ... I'll pass on the message."

I hung up and paced the room. My temples were pounding and my stomach felt sick. Tabitha, who had already lapped up her milk, watched me from her perch with sullen eyes.

"Not a word," I warned.

"Don't worry. I'm content observing your unraveling from afar."

I was about to shoot back, but she was right. I was unraveling.

"Where's my book? It better not be back under the divan."

"Relax. It's over there."

I followed her lifted paw to the sofa, where half of *Magical Me* was sticking out between the cushion and armrest. I snatched it out, flipped it open at my chest, and resumed pacing.

You need to relax, Everson, I told myself. *Reestablish your center.*

I took a breath and began whispering the first fill-in-the blank aspiration. "I will do something every day toward becoming a better *wizard*. That's the only way I will develop into my best *wizard*."

Tabitha scoffed softly.

I glared at her, then tried again, but the affirmation wasn't helping. I couldn't stop myself from replaying Pierce's little digs in my mind. And then there was the going behind my back, boxing me out of my own city. I pictured him at the mayor's meeting with his cool blue eyes and know-it-all smile.

With a cry, I flung *Magical Me* across the room. I then grabbed my cane and hit the book with a force invocation for good measure. In an explosion of pages, *Magical Me* leapt fifteen feet into the air and landed in a mangled pile. I panted as I watched the torn pages flutter down around it.

"Have you gone mad, darling?" Tabitha asked with wide eyes and the hint of a grin.

I ignored her and stalked to my bedroom. The only thing that was going to make me my best anything was finding and defeating the mage before Pierce could. I pounded on the closed door.

"Gretchen!" I called.

I heard her snort and then stir on my bed.

"I'm ready to begin training!"

13

"All right, all right," Gretchen called back. "Hold your horses."

I heard the bed shift some more followed by the sounds of slippered feet shuffling around the room. For the next couple of minutes, Gretchen alternately hacked and grumbled. By the time she opened the door, she'd put on a floral housedress and touched up her face. I glimpsed an array of open suitcases behind her, their former contents draped and slung everywhere. Clothes of mine that had been in my dresser stood in piles on the floor, while the top of the dresser had been converted into a messy makeup counter.

"So you're raring to go, huh?" Gretchen said, closing the door behind her. "Where were you earlier?"

"Yeah, sorry about that. After the meeting, I wanted to get a jump on a case I'm working. It took longer than I thought."

She leaned toward me and sniffed twice. "Black magic?"

"Someone's casting through infernal bags and creating smoke golems. I managed to get ahold of one of the bags, actually." I started to dig into my pocket for it. "Maybe you could—"

"Let me stop you right there," she interrupted. "I'm here to train you, not play mentor to your current project. You know, the wise hag who gives you cryptic clues that sound like nonsense until the final act when you're staring death in the face, and then—whammo!—a flashbulb goes off, all those clues make perfect sense, and you save the day?"

"Not quite what I had in mind."

"Anyway, I shouldn't have to tell you not to noodle with an infernal bag. That's just stupid."

I felt my face grow warm. "Fine, forget the bag. I was just thinking that the best way to go about the training might be to align it with something I'm already working on. You know, applied learning." Plus, I could really use her power and expertise to outmaneuver Pierce.

But she folded her thick arms across her body. "Who's doing the teaching here, me or you?"

"You," I said meekly.

She nodded. "Maybe you're not as hopeless as you look."

"Hopeless?"

"Let's have another gander at you."

She began circling me, lips pursed, one eyebrow cocked in critical assessment. When she'd made one revolution, she started muttering about me in third person. "His wards are rubbish ... Didn't give me much of a fight last night. And what about his aura?" She shook her head. "All over the map. Small wonder he can't handle electronics. Oh, look—there's his debauched companion." She poked my belly button. A small charge detonated through me and hit Thelonious. I felt him rumble, then sink his hooks into my soul more deeply, stealing my breath for a moment.

"Is there a point to this?" I demanded when I'd recovered.

Gretchen seemed to be echoing Pierce's criticisms, only more pointedly. And she wasn't done.

"Behold his famous luck quotient," she muttered, circling behind me again. "Wow, that *is* a big one ... He should have been maimed or killed at least a dozen times by now."

At last she stopped in front of me and extended her right hand. I took it uncertainly.

"Congratulations on still being alive." She gave my hand a pair of hard pumps. "That's about the best I can say."

"Gee, thanks."

"You're going to be a real project. Hurts my head even thinking about it. I guess the first thing I should ask is what *you* want."

I didn't hesitate. "To solve this case."

But she was shaking her head. "No, Everson. Big picture. What do you want as a magic-user? I don't want to hear about your case again."

"But Claudius said you could help."

"That's because Claudius is a senile idiot. Why do you think he's stuck answering phones?"

I considered that.

"I want you to listen to me because I'm only going to say this once," she continued. "I've been in the faerie realm for the last twenty of your years, which is like a jillion years over there. The fae don't care for humans, and frankly, neither do I."

I thought about the pact Caroline had made to help me out the year before, a pact that had meant sacrificing her feelings for me. A distant sadness brushed my heart. I wondered how her princess life with Angelus was going.

"I'm mostly human myself, but what can I say?" Gretchen

went on. "Their realm has a way of rubbing off on you. I'm not going to apologize for that. The fae have their shit together a lot better than we do. But back to my point. I don't care about your case. Not how important it is, not who it affects, not how I can help. I have a finite amount of energy, and I'm going to apportion it in equal amounts to keeping myself comfortable and to your training. That was my agreement with the Order. So I'll ask you again. What do you want?"

I cleared my throat. "To become a great mage, like my father."

"What in the hell am I supposed to do with that?"

"You asked me what I wanted," I said defensively.

"Yeah, and you gave me the worst answer imaginable. You're not auditioning for a role in a television movie. Seriously, what am I supposed to do with an answer like that? Tap my feet, throw my arms out, and cry, 'Hallelujah, I declare you great!' Steps, Everson. What can we accomplish today, this week, this month? Not in a thousand years."

"You really think it's going to take that long?"

She leveled her gaze at me. "What do you want?"

"To, um, become more capable?"

"Still too general."

"Double my current casting capacity?"

"Give me one goal, Everson. One, *specific* goal."

"Well, since everyone and their mother keeps bringing it up," I said irritably, "how about my luck quotient?"

"What about it?"

"I don't want to depend on it anymore."

I braced for another round of goal-jousting, but Gretchen stood back and grunted. "I can work with that."

"Yeah?" I said, recovering my enthusiasm. "Okay, what do you want me to do?"

"Close your eyes."

I squinted at her. "Can I ask why?"

"I'm not gonna sneak a kiss. Though I won't lie, I'm tempted."

I did as she said, wondering if this was meant to be some sort of trust-building exercise. I could hear her breathing in front of me. Then the door to my bedroom opened, followed by the sound of Gretchen walking away and rooting around. A minute passed, then another.

"All right, you can open them."

When I did, I saw that she'd put on a coat and a red bucket hat with plastic flowers. She was carrying a wire shopping cart.

"What's going on?" I asked. "Are we going somewhere?"

"*I'm* going somewhere. Your kitchen's not going to stock itself. A person would starve inside a day living here." She walked past me.

"Um ... okay. So we'll finish up when you get back?"

She stopped and blinked at me. "Finish up what?"

"The day's lesson."

She waved a hand. "Oh, the lesson is done."

"Done? But ... we haven't accomplished anything."

"Patience, Everson. Ha! Now there's some mentorly advice."

I watched dumbfounded as Gretchen opened the front door, adjusted her hat, and then walked out, slamming the door behind her. Prolonged exposure to the faerie realm could drive a person mad. Figured. After almost twelve years, I finally get a real instructor, and she's fae touched.

Tabitha stirred on the divan. "What's the Order's return policy on teachers?" she asked.

"Exactly what I was wondering."

14

W ith my plan to enlist Gretchen's help a complete bust, I taped together my *Magical Me* book and climbed to my library/lab to find out what I could about the infernal bag. Fae touched or not, Gretchen had actually been right. Infernal bags shouldn't be messed with. But the magic in my specimen had all but expired, making it less dangerous. And, yeah, I was desperate.

That didn't mean I had to be stupid, though.

I removed the stuffed leather pouch from my pocket, placed it on the iron table, and sprinkled a small circle of copper filings around it. Aiming my cane, I incanted until the circle glowed with protective power. I did the same to a second circle inset in the floor, the circle I would be casting from. Those were the standard precautions, but I didn't stop there.

From beneath the table, I pulled out a bin full of potions. One of my projects this past year had been to pre-mix an assortment of them, right up to the brink of the potions becoming active. Now when I needed one, I only had to perform the final steps. Hours of prep reduced to minutes.

I chose a bottle labeled "Slick Wizzy"—short for slick wizard—poured the thick gray liquid into a pot, and placed it on the portable burner. Chanting, I stirred the potion with my engraved wooden spoon. I watched the potion turn thin and green and begin to steam. Another minute and...

Done.

I snapped off the burner and, taking the pot by the handle, tipped it to my lips. Most potions tasted awful, and this one was no exception—especially since it had spent a few months in storage. I forced the entire concoction down, then leaned my arms against the table to allow it to settle in my stomach.

Within moments, my palms slid forward as if the table had been greased. The potion was taking effect. I stepped back into my casting circle and examined my hands. An oily film was beading from my pores. I could feel the same thing happening over the rest of my body, toes squishing inside my shoes. But the physical manifestations were only byproducts of the potion's intent: to keep one's soul from being grabbed.

"Okay," I said, taking a deep breath and reorienting myself to the bag.

I had to use both hands to lift the cane without it slipping in my grip, but I finally managed to aim the cane at my target.

"Rivelare," I said.

The reveal spell sprang from my cane in ribbons of white light and encircled the infernal bag. Almost immediately, the pouch began to jerk. It scooted from one side of the casting circle to the other. Then it started to pooch out, as if tiny fists were beating the bag's inside. Like most objects imbued with black magic, it didn't want to be probed.

But after another minute of resisting, the bag finally sagged, exhausted, at the circle's center. Black smoke leaked from its cinched mouth.

"Now to find out who made you," I whispered.

Carefully, I drew the smoke along the ribbons of the reveal spell and into my cane. This was the dangerous part. By connecting to the bag, I was exposing myself to an attack.

As I pulled a little harder, I began to see an image above the leaking bag. It was the residual stamp of the mage who had given the infernal bag life. With no safe way to cast against him, I could only attempt to will his dark, dull image clearer. But after several attempts, I realized Pierce had been right. The mage had taken pains to cover his tracks. Where there should have been a face or aura, I still saw only the vaguest silhouette of a head.

I had my mage, but he was hidden, dammit.

I pulled some more, but it was no use. I was preparing to break the spell when the smoky silhouette shifted into another one. I stopped.

Two mages?

The silhouette shifted again. And again. And again. It then cycled back to the first shape I'd seen. I watched the merry-go-round of images for a few more cycles, counting the silhouettes.

Five individuals had a hand in creating the infernal bag?

I was considering the implications when the next silhouette grew into a hideous head with narrow, blood-red eyes. Something shot through the connection. Powerful taloned fingers raked my throat, trying to grab hold, but they slipped over the potion and lost their grip.

"Disfare!" I shouted.

The ribbons of the reveal spell dispersed in a flash, and

smoke belched from the infernal bag. My heart thundered as I held up my cane defensively. The bag gave a final hiccup before the last of its magic expired. I felt around my throat, but the potion had done its job. I was unharmed.

"Holy hell," I said, releasing my breath.

I stepped from my casting circle and paced the office on slick feet and trembling legs. Not one mage, but five. And powerful enough to attack me through a dying infernal bag. And I mean *attack* me. If it hadn't been for the potion, that thing would have torn out my lungs.

Time to hit the books.

I turned toward my shelves. With a Word, the veil of encyclopedias and classical titles dissolved away, revealing my library of magical tomes and grimoires. I wiped my slick hands on my pants—the potion was starting to wear off— selected several titles, and set them in a stack on my desk. Flipping my notepad to a blank page, I started with the topmost book, intent on learning everything I could about infernal bags, innocent souls, and the dark mages who loved them.

———

TWO HOURS LATER I SET THE FINAL BOOK ASIDE AND, TAPPING my pencil between my teeth, looked over my pages of notes.

I had jotted down some items about the history of infernal bags, but I was more interested in their use. The bulk of the information confirmed what I already knew. Infernal bags contained ingredients that reacted to magic channeled from the infernal realms. Hence the name.

The more powerful the mage, the more powerful the infernal bag's manifestations, and the more control the mage had over them. Judging from the strength and intelligence of the smoke golems I'd encountered, the magic-user in question was pretty damned powerful.

But what if the reveal spell had been right? What if I was dealing with the collective power of *five* mages? My research had uncovered several examples of multiple magic-users sharing infernal bags. Besides sounding gross, it worried me. Especially since the mages appeared to be going after souls.

I thought about the shriveled bodies in the movie house.

Souls could be used in powerful spells. One only had to go back to Lich for an example. He'd stolen and harvested the souls of countless magic-users to sustain his nightmare portal to the Whisperer. I feared the five mages had something similarly awful planned.

Then again, the mages could be feeding the souls to a demon.

My final page of notes was devoted to this second theory. It wasn't any more reassuring, though. I had come across a case of a demon taking control of a cult devoted to his worship in Medieval Europe. Through them, the demon directed assaults on several settlements, emerging to claim the souls of the victims and grow his power. A member of the Order had ultimately broken up the cult and banished the demon, but it had been close.

Chewing on my pencil, I thought about the final silhouette that had taken shape through the reveal spell. The way it had attempted to seize my throat, my soul. At first I'd assumed it was a manifestation of the infernal bag. But I'd been in the clutches of a demon before—a greater demon—and this had felt too damned familiar.

With enough power, a greater demon could enter our world. How many souls that would require depended on the demon in question. A lower-level demon might only need a handful. But for a greater demon, it could mean hundreds or thousands. And cults tended not to worship the weak ones. That would mean lots of infernal bags—and lots more attacks.

I hovered the tip of my pencil over my last line of notes, which dealt with the Medieval cult that had called forth the demon. "All the cultists were mortal," I read aloud. "No magic-users."

I underlined the last sentence twice. *No magic-users.* If that was the case now, my job had just become infinitely more difficult. There couldn't have been more than a few true magic-users in New York City, but there were millions of mortals. And I still only had Mr. Han's description of a man with a lisp to go on.

No names of the five people I'd seen in the reveal spell, no faces...

The thought trailed off as I remembered what Vega had said about the woman who'd been fired from the theater. I'd dismissed her as a candidate because she didn't sound like a magic-user. But she didn't need to be. Though the woman remained a long shot, she was the best lead I had.

I just hoped Vega hadn't executed the search warrant yet.

I stood and tested my footing. The oil had dissipated with the potion, and my skin was no longer slick.

Halfway down the ladder, I slipped anyway and landed awkwardly. Pain speared through my right knee. I grimaced and gripped the leg as I limped toward the kitchen. Too minor to waste healing magic on. I considered grabbing an ice pack from the freezer, but the kitchen floor remained littered with the detritus from Gretchen's breakfast, and I didn't want to risk another fall. Instead, I propped myself against the counter and called Ricki.

"Vega," she answered formally.

I hesitated. Hadn't she seen it was me on her phone's display? Then I remembered the way our last call had ended, with me raising my voice and then practically hanging up on her.

"Hey," I said carefully. "Sorry about losing my temper earlier."

"I don't have a lot of time right now. Is there something you want?"

I could tell by her tone I was in a hole, one that was going to take time to dig out of. Because of our closeness, it felt worse than the old days when she just thought I murdered people. But just like the old days, my first job was to make sure I didn't make my hole any deeper.

"There is actually," I said. "That search warrant on the former theater employee? Has it been executed yet?"

"No, but we're about to head over."

"Can I come with?"

Vega gave a tired sigh. "If this is about wanting to make up, I'd rather you didn't."

"I do want to make up, but this isn't about that. I took a look at the infernal bag this afternoon, the one from Mr. Han's? I might have hit on some new information. It's pretty vague, I admit, but if the woman's place turns up anything, this case could be blown wide open."

I was pretty sure it would get me out of my hole with Vega too.

"Can I say something about Pierce without you hanging up?" she asked.

My stomach tightened into an acid fist, but I managed a neutral-sounding "Sure."

"He called not too long ago. Apparently he's seeing some things too. Thinks he might have a lead."

I felt my pulse quicken. "Oh? Did he say what it was?"

"Just that we might be looking at multiple perps. Does that jibe with your findings?"

I couldn't frigging believe this. "It might," I hedged. "Why? Does he want to come too?"

"No. He said he needs to tease out more info."

I relaxed a little. Pierce was chasing something else.

"So, do you have an address for me?" I asked.

Vega hesitated before answering. "It's in that apartment tower on Madison and Sixty-Eighth. The Sophia." She gave me the street and apartment numbers. "Her name's Becky McKay."

"A former ticket-ripper on Madison Ave?" I whistled in amazement.

"Yeah, I thought the same thing. We'll be pulling up in about fifteen minutes." Even though Vega's voice had thawed, she usually offered to pick me up in these situations, or at the very least to send a car. Right now, though, I'd take what I could get. And that meant a cab.

"I'll meet you there," I said.

15

I had more trouble than usual catching a cab, and once I did, we seemed to hit every red light going north. When we finally pulled up to the address, the skies opened in a late-afternoon thunderstorm. Making an umbrella of my coat collar, I hobbled from the cab toward the armed doormen. Like most of the apartment towers on the Upper East Side, the Sofia was palatial.

I showed the doormen my NYPD identification card, and they opened the doors. Safely inside the lobby, I stepped in a puddle and went straight down. My cane clattered from my outflung arm.

Oh, for chrissake.

One of the doormen rushed in to help me up.

"That's funny," he said, handing me back my cane. "These floors are supposed to be slip proof."

"Yeah, well, tell that to the floor." I rubbed my tailbone, but my ego was bruised more than anything. Two falls in the last half hour, and I couldn't blame them on the slick wizard potion. It had expired more than an hour ago.

The young man straightened my coat. "Can I help you to where you're going?"

"I'll manage, thanks. Why don't you clean up that puddle before someone else steps in it and breaks their neck?"

While the doorman radioed a janitor, I staggered my way to the elevators and pressed the up button. In the polished reflection of the brass doors, I watched a pair of elderly women enter the lobby. Before I could spin and warn them, they walked right through the same puddle in high heels— and kept right on walking.

I exhaled and lowered my arm.

Becky's apartment turned out to be on the top floor. Ahead of me, about halfway down the corridor, several police officers were clustered. I saw Vega talking to a young woman —Becky, I assumed. She was short with a Mohawk that went from dark purple at the base to neon pink at the tips. And she did not look happy about having her penthouse tossed.

I walked toward them, relying heavily on my cane. I'd been worried I was too late, but from the bits I was picking up, it didn't sound like the search had started yet.

"If you don't calm down," Vega was saying, "we're taking you to the precinct."

"Am I under arrest?" Becky demanded. "Huh? Am I?"

Hoffman, who was beside Vega, muttered, "Not yet."

"We've already explained everything to you," Vega replied. "No, we're not arresting you. We're executing a search warrant. That's the copy in your hands. I'm giving you the choice of remaining out here with the officers, or they can give you a lift to a precinct. Your call."

"This is because of my neighbors, isn't it?" Becky said. "Can't stand someone like me invading their sheltered sanctum."

"While we're on the subject," Hoffman said. "How is it that you can afford a place like this?"

"I inherited some money," she said defiantly. "Is that against the law now too?"

Vega stepped up beside Hoffman and spoke into the ear Becky couldn't see. "Check it out," I saw her mouth.

But Becky's attention had been diverted by my arrival. As Hoffman separated from the group and pulled out his phone, the suspect gave me a critical up and down. "Oh, look," she said. "Another member of the goon squad."

I gave her my most charming smile, which only deepened the scowl across her pierced lips. I opened my wizard's senses and assessed her in return. She wasn't a magic-user or super-natural—I could see that right off. I focused on her aura, where I caught ashy bits of gray orbiting. But that could have been her anger. Nothing screamed black magic or demon.

"Stay or go," Vega said to her. "This is the last time I'll ask."

Becky sighed and waved a hand. "Do whatever you want."

"All right, but no more problems. Understood?"

Becky looked away with a scowl.

Vega nodded at me and a pair of officers, and we followed her into the apartment. The other two officers remained in the hallway with the suspect.

"Whoa," I said as the door closed behind us. The main room was an enormous open plan, stocked with brand-new furniture and one of the largest entertainment centers I'd ever seen. The speakers alone were taller than me. Posters of obscure movies and indie punk bands covered the walls. Little in the room really went together, but I doubted Becky cared.

Across the room, a massive window overlooked south

Central Park. Budge was still promising the city a new, improved park, but following last summer's slash and napalm campaign, it remained a mostly brown lot. His priority right now was rebuilding Lower Manhattan. That's where the money was.

"Look for any computers or devices," Vega was telling the officers. Then to me, "What do you see?"

"Someone who has more money than she knows what to do with."

Vega frowned. "You know what I mean."

Her look and tone reminded me I was still in her doghouse. I nodded and paced around the room for the next several minutes. There was no evidence of casting circles or spell items. No esoteric books or ingredients for an infernal bag. And no matter how wide I threw my wizard senses, I wasn't feeling anything.

I grew anxious as I remembered what Vega had said about Pierce pursuing another lead. I needed *this* to be the lead, dammit.

"Let me check the bedrooms," I said.

Three of them were completely empty, while the one Becky had claimed for herself held an obscenely large bed with black satin sheets. Her belongings were slung everywhere: mostly ratty clothes that reeked of cigarette smoke. I started to poke through them before deciding I was wasting my time. If I was in close proximity to something magical or demonic, I would have felt it. And the only thing I felt was a young woman's rebellion.

Poof. There went my lead.

I checked the kitchen to make sure, but it was mostly bare. Empty take-out cartons and soy sauce packets littered the massive central island.

I reentered the main room to tell Vega I had nada and ran into a standing lamp. When I lunged forward to catch it, my cane became entangled in my legs somehow, and *I* went over. Hollering, I grabbed for a speaker. The end result was that the lamp, speaker, and I ended up on the floor together.

"Oh, for..." Vega muttered.

Embarrassed, I scrambled to my feet. Something clunked inside the speaker as I righted it. The lamp's decorative shade was shattered. Shards of stained glass glinted over the hardwood floor.

"That's coming out of our department budget," Vega said. "You know that, right?"

"Crap, sorry about that. The lamp sort of ambushed me."

I wasn't always the smoothest number, but I honestly couldn't remember a streak of clumsiness like the one I was having this afternoon. Had the months of marinating caused the slick wizard potion to stay in my system longer than usual? I rubbed my hands to double check, but they felt dry.

"Well?" Vega said, raising her eyebrows.

I looked around a final time. "Nothing," I admitted. "Becky doesn't seem to have been involved in the attack."

Vega turned to the two officers. One was holding a laptop and the other a computer tablet and smartphone. Vega shook her head, and the men returned the items to where they'd found them.

"Then let's tell her we're done here," she said.

"What?" Becky said when we emerged. "Didn't find my secret plans for world domination?"

"Thanks for your cooperation," Vega told her in what I recognized as her official voice. "In the process of the search, one of your lamps was damaged. Our department will reimburse you the full cost of the item." She reached into her pocket and produced a card. "If you call this number—"

"Keep your number," Becky interrupted, drawing her hand from the offered card. "I'll gladly pay for a new lamp if it means never seeing you again. Can I go back inside *my own apartment* now?"

Vega pressed her lips together as she returned the card to her pocket. She jerked her head for the officers to back off. "Yeah, we're all done here."

"The Nazi fucking Gestapo," Becky muttered as she returned to her penthouse. She slammed and locked the door behind her.

"Wow, touchy," I said before hustling to catch up to Vega.

I reached her as Hoffman was walking up to meet us. He'd been hanging around the elevators, making calls. Now he pocketed his phone.

"Story checks out," he said to Vega. "She had a couple wealthy grandparents out West. Had the foresight to invest in precious metals, apparently. When gold jumped, so did their net worth. They died a few months ago. Within a few days of each other, in fact. Heart attack and stroke. One of those freak things. Anyway, it all went to Miss Charming over there."

"Thanks, Hoffman," she said. "I'll join you downstairs in a minute."

As Hoffman and the officers boarded the elevator, Vega turned to me.

"Hey, about the lamp—" I started to say.

"Forget the lamp. When we talked earlier, you said you had some new information?"

With the search over and the other officers gone, Vega's stance seemed to soften. She sounded more like the Vega I'd come to know over the past year. But she was counting on me now for information I didn't have.

"I'm pretty sure we're looking at more than one perp," I said. Realizing I was repeating the same info she'd gotten from Pierce, I quickly added, "Possibly five. And there's a chance they're not magic-users, but mortals under the influence of a demonic entity."

The skin between Vega's eyebrows furrowed in thought. "Pierce said the same thing."

"He did?" My stomach churned. "Even about the demonic stuff?"

"Do you have anything else?"

"That's ... Well, that's it for right now," I confessed. If there was demon energy out there, the wards should have detected it. I would call the Order anyway and ask them to double check. Pierce's tampering with the wards could have screwed them up. The thought made my stomach churn even more.

Vega pulled out her phone.

"Who are you calling?" I asked.

"I promised Pierce an update on the search."

"Well, wait, hold on a sec."

She paused. "What?"

"I thought you said he wasn't interested in the search."

"I said he wasn't planning on coming."

"Well, does he have to know every little thing we're doing?"

Vega cocked her head in impatience.

"He has a tendency to go overboard," I said. "He's been messing with the wards I depend on for closing breaches. Those creatures I told you about in Harlem? I almost missed them because of him. Hell, there are probably things about *this* case I'm missing because of him."

"Do you know that for a fact?" Vega asked.

"Well, no, but ... My point is that it's starting to feel like too many chefs in the kitchen."

"He found the infernal bag last night, right?"

"I would've found it eventually," I grumbled.

"And everything he's uncovered since—multiple perps, possible demonic involvement—jibes with what you're telling me, right? It sounds like he's on track. And if you think you've hit a dead end—"

"I never said 'dead end.'"

"Everson, I'm calling him."

I throttled my cane in frustration. "Fine, but don't let him be vague. Make him tell you *exactly* what he's working on."

If I *was* at a dead end, maybe I could piggy-back off his leads. Shameful as sin, yeah, but there was no way I was going to let him crack the case before I did.

"I'm not your gofer," Vega said.

"What are you talking about?"

"If you want Pierce's help, ask him yourself."

Crap, she'd seen right through me. Something she was getting better at.

"All right, one? I don't need Pierce's help. And two, I already approached him about collaborating and he blew me off. Not only that, he went behind my back."

"I asked him about that."

I blinked at her. "You did?"

She allowed a smirk. "Maybe I was just being the protective girlfriend. He said he offered to show you what he was working on, but that you were anxious to begin interviewing the shop owners. He took your place at the mayor's meeting as a courtesy, knowing you'd be a few hours. He said he even tried calling you before the meeting, but no one answered."

"Oh, bullshit."

I hadn't meant to voice the thought, but there it was.

Vega glared at me, then turned with her phone to make the call.

I clenched my jaw. *Way to dig yourself out of that hole,* I thought.

Without warning, Vega's phone began to sparkle and smoke. She shouted in surprise and dropped it. By the time the phone hit the floor, flames were licking around the edges of the shattered screen.

She looked from the device to me. "Did you just blow up my phone?"

Her voice was cold and dangerous. "O-Of course not," I stammered. But had I? I looked around. My wizarding aura sometimes jagged a little when I got angry, but it couldn't have jagged *that* much. I remembered Pierce's and Gretchen's critiques of my control.

Vega left her smoking phone on the floor and jabbed the button for the elevator.

"Wait, where are you going?"

She faced the closed doors, arms crossed, body tense.

"Ricki, listen, I did not blow up your phone. At least not … intentionally."

The elevator doors opened. Vega cut past the man stepping off and hammered the button to take her down. When I tried to join her, she showed me her hand in a sharp, martial arts-like gesture.

"Ricki," I said.

She wouldn't meet my eyes. The doors closed in my face. I hit the button, but her elevator was already descending.

"Damn," I muttered.

Vega and I had had our spats since we'd started seeing

each other, sure, but this one felt different. Worse. Maybe because it had come on the heels of last night's talk about moving the relationship forward. Something told me I'd just managed to slam it into reverse. It was also the first time we'd fought publicly. We'd only had an audience of one, but still.

I snuck a look around at the man who had just gotten off the elevator. He was peering back at me, probably wondering what I'd done to piss off the woman who'd almost knocked him over.

But then I noticed something strange. He'd been slowing toward Becky's door, but now he sped up again. At the far end of the hallway, he opened a door and disappeared. Before the heavy door clattered closed, I picked up the descending patter of footfalls.

He just went down the exit stairwell.

I started down the hallway at a fast walk.

I'd been so fixated on Vega that I hadn't gotten a good look at the man, just a glimpse. The thirty-something man had been wearing a gray flat cap over a bald head. His face had seemed normal enough, maybe a little surly. It was in his mouth, the way the upper lip bent and curled around the faint track of ... a scar.

Not surliness, I realized. *A harelip.*

Which meant the man was a lisper.

Heart pounding, I broke into a run.

16

I was still gimpy enough from my spill in the apartment as well as the falls in the lobby and at Becky's place to make running awkward. I wished now I'd applied some healing magic, but I hadn't wanted to deplete my power stock. The pain wasn't bad, just annoying—especially since my gym trainer and I had spent the last month on speed drills.

At the far end of the hallway, I spoke a Word, and a shield crackled to life around me. I opened the exit door and stepped onto the landing. I could hear Harelip's footsteps echoing off the walls. He had a good three-story head start. I started down, wracking my brain for ways to close the gap.

"Stop!" I shouted. "NYPD!" Because it was still a crime to impersonate a police officer, I added, "Consultant."

None of it mattered, though. Harelip's footsteps never slowed.

Could I chance a force invocation? I'd gotten pretty good at controlling them. I could probably manage to bend one down the stairwell and send the man sprawling. But was it the same man Mr. Han had described? If not, I could be maiming someone who had nothing to do with the attacks.

I imagined Pierce studying his Himitsu painting, teasing out more info.

No guts, no glory, I decided.

"Vigore!"

I aligned myself with the charge that pulsed from my cane and whipped it down the stairwell. But after two floors, I got my turns mixed up. The next thing I knew, the invocation was back and slamming into my shield. The impact lifted me from my feet and drove me into the wall. I rebounded and landed on hands and knees. Had it not been for the shield, I would've been KO'd. In my fog, it took me a moment to recognize the sound of a door opening.

He's getting off on one of the floors.

I all but threw myself down the next three flights until I arrived on a landing for the fifteenth floor just as the door clicked closed. Opening the door, I flung myself out into the hallway. I expected to find Harelip racing toward the elevators. But the hallway was empty.

Meaning he's in one of these rooms.

I stole down the hallway and listened. But all I could hear was the steady whoosh of air-conditioning. I'd progressed a quarter of the way along the hallway when the door to the stairwell closed behind me. The sound was followed by a second click. And then soft footsteps.

Son of a bitch never left the stairwell.

I spun and ran back, but the exit door was now locked.

I aimed my cane at the door, shouted a force invocation, and jerked the cane violently back. The bolt broke through the door frame, and the entire door swung out, narrowly missing my face.

The descending footsteps sped up.

I started to lunge into the stairwell after them, but stopped. It was clear the man wanted out of the building. Which meant he was headed for the lobby.

I can get there first, I thought.

I stamped my feet on the landing a few times to make it sound like I was in pursuit, then slipped back onto the floor and made for the elevators. By a minor miracle, one of the doors slid open just as I arrived. I stepped past an elderly couple getting off and pressed the button for the lobby. The doors closed, and the elevator dropped with stomach-dipping speed.

My pulse pounded as I planned my next steps.

I'll catch him at the bottom of the stairwell before he comes out. Trap him in a shield invocation.

I took that as a cue to disperse my own shield. The last thing I needed was to short the elevator. As the energy broke apart, the lights dimmed for a moment and the car shuddered, but our descent didn't slow.

At the ninth floor, I estimated that I'd passed Harelip.

At the eighth floor, the car came to a sudden stop. *No, dammit.* The elevator door opened, and a mother boarded with her preschool-aged son. I smiled stiffly at them as I punched the button for the door to close again. A few seconds of lost time, but I still had my lead.

The boy glared up at me. "*I* wanted to press the button!"

"Be nice, Dylan," his mother admonished, but with a smile that said, *Aren't you just the cutest little thing?* "Anyway, this man was already on the elevator. He pushed the button before we came on."

The logic escaped the child. "I wanted to press the *button!*"

"Dylan," she warned, but while reading a text on her phone.

The boy advanced on me with hands that were red and sticky. I backed away, not wanting whatever he'd been handling on my coat. Snarling, the boy trained his anger on the elevator buttons themselves.

My heart leapt into my throat. "No!" I shouted.

Before I could stop him, he slapped his sticky hands against the buttons for the lower floors, lighting them all up.

"Oh, you little shit," I muttered.

"Dylan!" his mother cried, pulling him to her side. "And you!" she said to me, eyes engorged with anger. "You have no right to talk to my little boy that way."

When the doors opened on the sixth floor—thanks to junior—I stepped off. If I could catch another elevator, I still had a chance. I waited for the doors to close so I could hit the down button again, but the mother wasn't done. She stepped into the path of the sensor so the doors *wouldn't* close.

"What's your name?" she demanded. "Do you even live here? I've never seen you here before."

"Get back on the elevator," I ordered as I dug around for my NYPD card. "I'm here on official business."

"Oh, and that gives you the right to cuss out my son?"

He peered at me from behind her legs with a sharp grin.

"I'm pursuing a suspect and he ... interfered."

"He's *four!*"

She had a point. Regardless, I didn't have time for this.

I angled my cane up. *"Vigore,"* I whispered. The soft force invocation sent the woman and her devil child stumbling into the back of the elevator. The doors closed and *finally* I was able to punch the down button.

Not my proudest moment, and probably not something

my father would have done, but I was thinking about Harelip —and yes, Pierce. I needed a jump on this case in the worst way.

I shifted my weight as I watched the digital displays above the doors. One elevator was on the upper floors and climbing, the other was in the lobby, just sitting there. The one I'd abandoned was plodding its way down.

"C'mon, c'mon, c'mon," I muttered.

Ten seconds passed, then twenty. In my anxiousness, it felt like my bladder was going to burst. Finally, the elevator that had been heading up reversed and started back down.

Thank God.

Several long seconds later, the door opened, and I joined a middle-aged man. No kid this time. I estimated that Harelip was almost to the lobby by now. It was going to be close. Damn close.

The elevator began its descent.

5 ... 4 ... 3 ... 2 ...

The car jerked to a halt and went dark. Red emergency lights came on.

"Oh, you've gotta fucking be kidding me," the man said before I could. "I called maintenance about the problem just this morning. I got stuck on the same elevator around seven a.m. Twenty minutes I was sitting here before it started up again. Something must be screwy with the wires."

"Twenty minutes?" I said, punching the lobby button.

When nothing happened, I hopped up and down a few times, then wedged my fingers between the doors. With a whispered force invocation, I managed to open the doors a few inches. But we had stopped between floors. Short of trying to blow a hole through the roof or floor of the elevator, which was sure to cause more problems than it solved, I was stuck.

The man, who had been speaking to someone on the emergency phone in the control panel, hung up. "Lucky for us, it's just a fuse," he said. "They should have it running again in ten."

"Yeah," I said, sliding to the floor. "Lucky."

BY THE TIME THE ELEVATOR CAME BACK TO LIFE AND DEPOSITED us in the lobby, I knew Harelip was long gone. I approached the building's doormen.

"Did a bald man in a gray cap just leave here?" I asked.

The doorman who had helped me up earlier smiled in recognition. "Was that you got stuck on the elevator just now? Man, some day you're having."

"He's about my height," I pressed on. "And he has a scar here, above his lip."

"Oh yeah, I know him. Talks with a lisp."

Hope surged inside me. "What's his name?"

The doorman shrugged.

"I thought guests had to show ID."

"Only if we've never seen 'em before," the other doorman said. "He's been in and out a few times with Becky."

So he *had* been going up to see her.

I looked back into the lobby. Panoramic security cameras studded the ceiling. I checked my watch and estimated that Harelip had come in around 5:15 and left around 5:25. Good to know if we needed to pull the security footage. Right now, though, I needed to head back up and talk to Becky.

Rather than risk another elevator ride, I took the stairs.

Ten minutes later, I arrived on the top floor, panting, but without any mishaps. At Becky's door, I knocked loudly. Moments later, a shadow moved over the peephole.

"What do you want?"

"I need to ask you about something." When she didn't respond, I added, "It's about someone you know. A bald man with a scar on his upper lip."

"I just got off the phone with my lawyer, and she said I don't have to tell you shit."

"It'll only take a minute," I said lamely.

"If you're not *gone* in a minute, I'm suing for harassment. She said I could do that too."

Great. As desperate as I was, I had to weigh my need for a lead against the knowledge that Becky and the guy who'd just fled might have nothing to do with the infernal bags. For all I knew, Harelip could have been her drug supplier, and he'd thought I was a narco agent. In any case, rich, pissed off, and lawyering-up was not a combo you wanted to mess with.

"Fine," I said.

I walked far enough away that I was out of view of the peephole, then reached into my coat pocket for my small overnight bag. In my effort to become my best wizard, I'd put the bag together to hold small everyday items that I might need in a pinch. It was surprising how often I'd used it over the last few months. I pulled out a set of tweezers now and winced as I plucked a slender hair from inside my ear. Holding up the hair, I uttered, *"Attivare."*

The hair trembled with energy, then stood straight up like an antenna. If I couldn't get Becky to talk to me, I could damn sure listen. I pulled out a thin tube of adhesive and one of my business cards—just my name and number—and glued the hair to the card's backside.

When I returned to the door, Becky was still at the peephole. Probably waiting to ensure I'd left.

"You're down to ten seconds," she said.

"Yeah, I'm just going to leave you my card, in case you change your mind."

"Wanna know what you can do with your card?"

"Not really." I wedged the card between the door and frame and quickly made my way back to the stairwell.

My little bugging spell would absorb noise for the next hour or so, noise I could access back at my apartment. And I was laying odds that Becky would call Harelip as soon as I left.

I was just stepping out into the lobby when my cane began to wriggle and tug. My watch flashed urgently. Damn, I was being called to another breach.

"Careful, buddy!" the doorman shouted as I blew past him. "Sidewalks are still wet!"

No sooner than he'd said it, I skidded on a manhole cover and splashed down.

Swearing, I got back up and hailed a cab.

17

The scene this time was a Midtown delicatessen. We'd hit several traffic snarls en route—which gave me time to heal my knee—but by the time I paid the cabbie and stepped out, I could see from the black smoke rising from the stairwell that I'd arrived too late.

A crowd was gathered out front. A wiry woman with frizzy hair was telling everyone in frenetic gestures what had happened.

"...paid for my lox bagel and I was coming out when this blast of heat hit me from behind. The doors slammed and I heard screams and smelled smoke and I just clutched my bagel and ran!"

"How many people were in there?" I asked.

"A couple dozen, at least. Oh God, it was horrible!"

The crowd murmured excitedly as I stepped past them.

"We already tried," a man called. "Door's melted shut. The fire department's on its way."

I ignored him and the distant wail of sirens and went down. I summoned a protective shield and hit the door with a force invocation. Cries rose from the street as a burst of sulfurous smoke blew past me. Through the haze, I could already make out the victims. They were everywhere, some sitting at tables, others piled on the floor in front of the counter as well as behind it, their bodies violently shriveled, just like the victims of the theater attack.

It *was* horrible. They hadn't stood a chance.

I waded into the smoke, my sword and staff drawn, but the golem was gone. The cane-tugging had petered out by the time we'd pulled up, and my watch was no longer flashing. No vibrating in my ears either.

I swallowed hard and did the math. The six from last night plus the couple dozen here meant we were up to thirty souls. That put us past the realm of lower demon. We were looking at something middling to large.

I peered around the deli for the infernal bag. A shelf along a back wall held gift items such as wrapped salamis and cheese wheels. On the bottom shelf, behind jars of pickles, I found the leather pouch. I doubted there was anything more to glean, but I cast a protective orb around the bag and pocketed it anyway. At the very least I could neutralize its residual magic.

As I surfaced, I considered looking for a payphone to call Vega before remembering I'd killed her device. I still had no idea how that had happened, but it had *not* been intentional. Just as well. My priority right now was to get home and check my eavesdropping spell.

I ARRIVED BACK TO AN EVEN MESSIER APARTMENT THAN THE ONE I'd left a couple of hours earlier. The disorder in the kitchen had spread to the living room, where my chairs and couch had been shoved around. I noticed my bedroom door open a crack, but I couldn't hear anyone inside.

"Where's Gretchen?" I asked.

Tabitha moaned and rolled onto her back so that her head hung off the divan, mouth open. She looked half dead.

"You all right?"

"No, darling ... I'm terrible."

"What happened?"

"Your teacher ran off to some play. She left the rest of her dinner out for me. At first it was delectable. But when it landed in my stomach, it turned sour and crappy."

"It *was* sour and crappy," I said, picking up the nauseating scent of fermented fish. I looked over at the kitchen, where empty jars and strange packaging littered the counter. "She probably disguised it with a glamour."

"Why would she *do* that?" Tabitha demanded.

"Vanity? Malice? There's no telling with the fae touched."

As Tabitha held her swollen belly, her next moan turned into a loud caterwaul.

I sighed. I was never going to get any work done with her carrying on like that. "Here," I said. "Let's see what I can do."

I swirled the end of my cane over her stomach and started into a healing chant. Soon, white light wrapped her in a misty halo. Her caterwaul softened and became a noise of satisfaction.

"Oh, that feels so much better, dar—"

A jet of vomit shot from her mouth and soaked the front of my pants.

Twenty minutes later, following a shower and a change of clothes, I was up in my library/lab.

I had placed another one of my ear hairs into a casting circle, and I concentrated toward it now, fingers pinching the corners of my closed eyes. The equivalent of white static filled my head. Pairing with an eavesdropping object was like tuning a radio. The key was finding the right...

"...I want to stay..."

There!

I dialed back a little until I recovered the frequency. Then I accessed the listening spell from the moment I had activated the hair. I would hear everything that had gone on in her apartment in the last hour.

"Hey, it's me," Becky said.

"What were the cops doing at your playth?"

A lisp. Just as I'd hoped, she'd phoned Harelip right after I left. Even better, she was using her phone's speaker feature. I hunkered my head down to hear better.

"It was just a search," she replied.

"Just a search, my assth. One of them chased me."

"They didn't catch you, right? So what?"

"Shut up and listhen! Everything was supposed to be random. Random! Random! Random! And you went and fucked it up. Now we've got polith searching your place and chasing me."

"Yeah, random. So how do you know it was me? How do you know one of the others didn't stick it there?"

I stiffened. Were they talking about the infernal bags?

"Because you're a vindictive little bitch," Harelip replied. *"And I asked them."*

Becky fell quiet for a moment. *"Well, the cops didn't find anything. There's nothing here to even find."*

"Doesn't matter. You broke the pact."

"So what do you want me to do?" she asked.

"Not over the phone. Hardman's."

"When?" Her voice broke slightly.

"Now."

A double beep signified the end of the call. I listened to hear if Becky would dial anyone else, but for the next few minutes, I could only pick up pacing and indistinct whispers. She was talking to herself, debating something. Her footfalls faded into the back of her apartment, then returned several minutes later, only now in heels. Having come to some decision, she picked up a set of keys and opened the door. When it closed again, I heard her lock it.

"Oh," she muttered. *"That dumbass's card."*

She'd just spotted the card with my contact info, fallen to the floor when she'd opened the door.

Please, take the dumbass's card, I pled, tapping my foot.

I winced at the harsh sound of my ear hair brushing something. I heard more footsteps, then the ding of the elevator. She'd put the card in her pocket. Which meant I'd not only be able to hear her, but hunt her down—along with Harelip and whomever else she was going to meet.

I pulsed the spell forward until I heard her getting into a taxi.

"Ninth and West Twelfth," she told the driver.

A charge went off in my chest. That was only a few blocks away, in the old Meatpacking District. I considered casting a hunting spell and heading there myself, but I needed to find out what I'd be walking into. I pulsed the eavesdropping spell forward some more until I heard the slamming of a car door and the clopping of heels over pavement. I was getting close to real time. Moments later, Becky used her phone again.

"I'm here," she said.

For an answer, a metal door rolled up and then back down again. Two sets of footsteps, one sharp, the other heavy and dull, echoed together. When Becky spoke again, the acoustics warped her voice.

"*I want to stay in the Ark,*" she said with what sounded like equal parts fear and resolve. "*I'll take the penalty.*"

"*Fine. Then do as I say. Shtand there.*"

"*Here? I can barely see anything.*"

"*Shh,*" Harelip said.

"*Hey! What the fuck are you—*"

My gut knotted up as Becky's words became lost to gargles and the muffled sounds of struggle. I stood and grabbed my cane. For a split second, I considered casting a hunting spell, but there was no time. I was still on a slight delay, meaning what I was hearing had happened minutes before. And what I was hearing was clear enough: Harelip meant to kill her.

"*Help!*" she gasped right before I broke the connection.

A minute later, I was breaking out of my building and bolting northwest on Bleeker Street.

18

I arrived, heaving for air, at Ninth and West Twelfth. It was a historic intersection of brick row houses as well as large slaughterhouses and packing plants that had been converted into stores and restaurants, though many had closed following the Crash and never reopened.

All right, I thought, looking around. *She got out of the cab and walked for about a half minute to a roll-down metal door.*

I didn't see any metal doors. I peered down several streets until a narrow lane caught my eye. I hustled toward it, wary of the uneven cobblestone street. I'd already fallen enough for one day, not to mention blown up a phone, gotten stuck on an elevator, and been hurled on by my cat—though whatever had been responsible for the accidents seemed to have left my system.

It probably *had* been some lingering effect of the slick wizard potion.

I ducked into the lane. Halfway down the block, I spotted a roll-down metal door, the first of three. The faded words above the doors read HARDMAN'S MEATS—where Harelip had told her to meet him.

I summoned a shield and seized the handle of the first door, but it wouldn't budge. I blew out the lock with a force invocation and tried again. This time, the door rattled up and slammed into the space above, the sound crashing through the building's dark interior.

"Illuminare," I whispered.

The light from my staff lit up what looked like a large storage space, but the junked conveyances and rows of hanging hooks identified it as an old packing plant. Rusting support beams broke up the open space.

I peered around, but didn't see any sign of Harelip or Becky. Wispy currents of dim black energy eddied inside the space, the remnants of something no longer active.

"Becky?" I called.

A choked rasp sounded from the back of the plant. A support beam blocked my view of its source. I hurried across the plant, sword drawn. In the middle of the floor my light glowed over a large demonic symbol, recently drawn and surrounded by thick melted candle stubs.

It was looking more and more like I'd found my "mages."

I skirted the symbol, stepped around the beam, and came face to face with Becky. She was suspended, impaled on a large hook. The cruel metal had entered beneath her right shoulder blade and punched out through the front of her tank top, just below her breast. Harelip had also done a number on her face. Her jaw was lumpy, one eye nearly swollen shut.

But she was still alive, her bloodied lips moving, her good eye imploring me to help her.

"I'm getting you down," I told her.

I touched my staff to her head and uttered an incantation. It was the precursor to a healing spell, meant to dump endorphins into her system. I didn't want her tissue to start repairing while she was still impaled, but I didn't want her in agony either. When her eye rolled up, I slid my sword and staff through my belt and gripped her above the waist.

Three ... two ... one.

With the aid of a gentle force invocation, I lifted her up along the curve of the hook until she was free and falling into my arms. I expanded the light shield to protect both of us. She gurgled against my ear as I stooped and set her against the support beam, her right lung no doubt collapsed. Her arms flopped out to her sides as blood began to pool on the floor.

Have to work fast.

Touching the staff to her torso wound, I began my healing incantation. Soft white light grew from the opal and moved around her, thickening over her injuries like pads of gauze. I caught myself standing to one side of her while I worked. Once hurled on, twice shy.

After several moments, the blood pool stopped growing. Her good eye rolled back into view, and I could see her other eye now between the healing lids. Both of them found me, pupils glowing from the soft light.

"Who are you?" she rasped.

"Everson Croft. I was at your apartment earlier."

"No..." She paused to cough. "I mean, how are you doing that thing with your stick?"

"I'm a wizard," I said.

She snorted weakly. "Of course."

I guessed she didn't read the papers.

"Listen, the man who tried to kill you—"

"Quinton," she said. "Quinton Weeks."

I waited. Though her breathing was improving, it still required work, and there was more she wanted to say.

"I didn't know the bags would kill..."

"The infernal bags," I said.

She nodded. "We were told they created fear. That's why I put mine in the theater. The guy managing it, Brad ... he was skimming from the register. Stealing from the owner. When I confronted him, he said I..." She drew a wheezing breath. "Said I was the one stealing. Owner sided with him. If the bag was gonna scare anyone, I wanted it to be those assholes."

"Were the bags Quinton's idea?"

"No, Damien's."

"Who's Damien?"

"The one who talks to us." Her eyes moved past me to the pentagram on the floor, her body giving a small shudder.

"How many of you does he talk to?"

"Five of us. Calls us *the Ark*."

"The Ark," I repeated. The name was probably the demon's idea of a joke. More important was the number five, a member for each point on the pentagram. "What does Damien want?"

"At first he said he wanted to help us. We were the 'Chosen Ones.'" She air-quoted the word with the fingers of one hand. "Told us we were being held down by those who feared our awesome power." Her Mohawk glistened as she shook her head. "He was going to open us to our true potential, turn us into supernatural warriors. I feel so stupid now."

"Most likely you were under a form of possession," I said, remembering the gray I'd picked up in her aura earlier. "How did Damien first contact you?"

"Quinton was working on a cleanup crew downtown. He

found a necklace. Said it called to him. When he put it on, Damien spoke in his head. Told Quinton to gather his four most trusted friends."

A cursed object, I thought bitterly. But from where?

"Quinton and the rest of us go back a while. We used to crash together at different pads in the East Village, before it got really dangerous. Quinton was the depressed one, moping around all the time. But after finding the necklace, he had all this energy. There was a light in his eyes I'd never seen. A manic light. It was because of what Damien was telling him. He couldn't wait to share it." She teared up. "I can't believe he just tried to..."

"He wasn't himself," I said.

Becky sniffled. "Damien told Quinton to perform an induction ceremony. Symbol, candles, strange chants. Right over there." Her eyes cut past me again. "The rest of us went along, mainly for kicks. But then we heard another voice—Damien's. That's when he told us about being the Chosen Ones."

I nodded for her to continue. Time was short, but I needed to learn as much as I could.

"I wanted to believe him," Becky said, her voice gaining strength. "I think we all did. None of us had been doing so hot. Hell, I'd just lost my third job in eight months. To prove what he was saying, Damien told us to wish for something and he would grant it. I was sick of not having enough money, of having to put up with other people's shit. I wished to never need money again. A few weeks later, a lawyer called. My grandparents had kicked it and, for some reason, willed everything to me. I hadn't talked to them in years. Similar things happened to the others. Jodi won a share of the state lottery. Jake found a guitar that made him sound like the second coming of Jimi Hendrix."

"And Quinton?" I asked.

"Being the direct line to Damien was enough for him."

"But Damien asked for something in return," I said. The name Damien sounded a lot like *demon*—probably another one of the creature's jokes—and I knew demons all too well.

Becky nodded. "He told us how to make the bags and then had us place them around the city."

"How many bags?"

"Three each."

"Fifteen bags?" I asked to be sure.

"Well, Quinton had five, so I guess seventeen."

Three had been activated, which left fourteen.

"I need to know where they are."

"I know where I put mine, but I have no idea about the others. Damien told us to stash them in secret. If we told anyone, even someone in the Ark, we'd suffer the *Penalty*, capital P. That's what Damien called the punishment for disobedience. I didn't know the Penalty was d-death."

I watched Becky sympathetically. When Damien gave Quinton the order to execute her, he must have released her from his possession, which explained her recovering senses and morality.

"Where did you put your bags?" I asked.

"I put one in the Flicker Theater, but I swear, I didn't know it would kill people. I didn't. You have to tell the police—"

"I believe you. What about the other two?"

Horror took hold in her eyes as the implications dawned on her. "Oh my God. More people are going to die, aren't they?" When she struggled to stand, I placed a hand on her shoulder.

"We'll take care of them. Just tell me where they are."

"I put one in Café Agora, in the ladies' room. Do you know where that is?" I nodded. "I stuck it behind a foam tile in the ceiling over the toilet. I put the other one in the Cerulean Store on Fourteenth Street. There's a fuse box in the very back with a deep well. It's down there."

I pulled out my notepad and wrote down the locations.

"I need the names of the other members and where I can find them."

Becky drew in a trembling breath and released it. "Quinton Weeks, Jodi Rice, Jake Hornsby, and Arlen Hart." She gave me their addresses. Some had recently relocated because of their newfound wealth or status, but they were all in or close to the city. "I'd give you their numbers, but Quinton took my phone."

"That's all right. This should be enough."

Now it was a matter of tracking them down, breaking the demonic hold over them, and finding out where they'd stashed their infernal bags. Three had already detonated, and Becky had told me the location of her remaining two, which left twelve bags unaccounted for.

But who knew how much longer they'd remain inert?

I would contact Pierce, I decided. I could use his help neutralizing that many bags, not to mention the cursed necklace that had kicked off the whole show. There were too many cursed items for me to handle alone. I could admit that to myself—and even Pierce—because I was doing so from a position of strength. I'd been the one to break the case, after all.

"You're not going to leave me here?" Becky asked worriedly when I peered toward the door.

"No, I'm taking you to my apartment. You'll be safe there. Do you think you can stand now?"

She nodded. I stooped low to help her up.

She wrapped an arm around my neck. "I'm sorry about the way I talked to you back at my apartment."

"You were possessed."

"No, that was pretty much me."

"Either way, it's water under the bridge."

I rose with her slowly, but Becky's legs supported her better than I thought they would, stiletto heels and all. Together, we started toward the door. As we made our way around the casting circle, Becky looked down at it, then suddenly over at me.

"Oh, shit," she said.

"What?"

"How in the hell did I forget about him?"

"Who?"

"There was another member of the Ark, before Jake. His name was Trevor. A couple weeks after the ceremony, he started getting up on Quinton over the necklace. Why was he the only one who could wear it, stuff like that. It got more and more serious. One night Quinton called out of the blue. He said Damien wanted to do another ceremony. He didn't say for what, but this time Jake was there instead of Trevor. I didn't even think to ask why. And then we all just seemed to forget about Trevor, like he'd never existed. How the fuck does that happen? He and I used to date." She stopped. "Do you think he's...?"

I nodded, but more in understanding. By ordering Trevor's death, Damien had created a hole in the Ark, a hole he needed to plug in order to sustain his power. Hence the hasty ceremony to induct Jake.

Now, with Becky's excommunication, the demon had the same problem. He would need to restore the Ark to five, fast, which meant another induction ceremony. Probably tonight.

"Where was the ceremony held?" I asked. "Here?"

"No, up in—"

Something in my coat pocket had been mashing into her side as we walked, and now foul smoke exploded between us. I recoiled from the searing heat, dropping Becky. She screamed and tumbled to the floor. Vibrations rang in my ears as a leather pouch plopped between us.

Shit. The infernal bag from the deli.

I swung my cane toward it, shouting an invocation to enclose the bag again, but the golem had already swirled into shape above it. Black fire and smoke washed around the golem's writhing form. I switched my efforts into placing separate shields around Becky and me.

"Oh, Becky," the golem said, looming over her. "I had such high hopes for you."

"Go to hell," she grunted. She was trying to shove herself away while pressing a hand to her ribs where the bag had burned her.

"Hell?" The golem released a malevolent laugh. "A little late for that."

So we *were* dealing with a demon. With his attention on Becky, I managed to draw my sword and struggle to my feet. Driving the sword into his back, I shouted, *"Disfare!"*

I braced for the golem's dissolution, but the invocation only sent a ripple through his smoke.

"Have you forgotten our little talk about adaptability?" he teased.

He hit me with a vicious backhand. My shield dissolved into sparks, and I crashed into one of the old conveyances. When I flopped to the floor, the right side of my face was warm with blood.

"Now to clean up Quinton's mess," the golem said. Angry flames whisked around him like a sandstorm, growing until they enveloped Becky. She released a withering scream.

I cycled madly through my spells and invocations. In our last two encounters, I'd hit the golems with force, shield, and dissolution invocations. I'd yet to use my coin pendant, though.

Inside the growing maelstrom, Becky's Mohawk burst into black flames, and her skin began to crease. I took the coin pendant in my hand and held it out. Stumbling forward, I shouted, *"Liberare!"*

A shaft of blue light shot from the coin. The golem, who had been delighting in Becky's torture, received the full brunt of the blast. He arced his back to the burst of blue flames and screamed.

I'd hurt the bastard.

He whipped around to face me.

"I'll remember that," he seethed. "And you remember this, wizard. I'm everywhere. *Everywhere.*"

He lunged toward me. I instinctively threw up a shield invocation, but the words had been meant as a parting shot. The golem broke apart, the magic that had remained in the infernal bag fully spent.

Slowly, I lowered my sword and staff.

Beyond the dead infernal bag, Becky was on her back, the stubs of her Mohawk smoking.

"Becky," I called. "Can you hear me?"

She didn't respond, but her chest was rising and falling in

shallow gasps. Burns and bloody scoring covered her body. I wrapped her in another healing spell. That would repair her physical injuries, but she'd just suffered a soul attack—and *that* was beyond my abilities to heal quickly.

I needed her to recover, and not just for her own sake. I had the names and addresses of the four other members of the Ark, but there was a good chance they wouldn't be home. They would be en route to the ceremony to restore the Ark so that Damien could get his program back on track.

Only Becky could tell me where that ceremony was.

Kneeling, I covered her with my coat and lifted her sagging body into my arms.

19

I burst into the apartment and slammed the door behind me with a foot.

"Is Gretchen back?"

Tabitha stirred at the commotion, then looked up at me in puzzlement. I'd gotten a few of those looks on the way here. I moved Becky from my right shoulder to a two-armed under-handed grip. The young woman sagged against my stomach, smoke still drifting from what remained of her Mohawk. Tabitha sighed and lowered her head back to her paws.

"Desperate even for you," she muttered.

I ignored the dig. "Gretchen!"

I carried Becky into my bedroom. Using my foot again, I shoved as much of Gretchen's crap off the bed as I could before lowering Becky. She looked slightly better than when we'd left the packing plant, but she was still in bad shape. I arranged the sheets and comforter to keep her warm while my magic worked on her body. I would need to figure out a way to convince Gretchen to mend her soul. Problem was, I didn't have a way to contact my "mentor."

I emerged from my room. "Did Gretchen say which play she was going to see?" I was already moving toward the phone and the massive city directory. If I knew which theater, I could call and have her paged.

But Tabitha shook her head. "She doesn't talk to me."

"I thought she shared her dinner with you."

"God, don't remind me. Yes, she said she couldn't finish, so here, would the kitty like the rest? But, no, it didn't amount to a conversation. And she didn't say what play she was going to."

"Not even what it was about?"

When Tabitha shook her head, I picked up the phone and dialed Vega's cell from habit before hanging up and calling her office instead.

"Homicide," Hoffman's gruff voice answered.

"It's Everson. Is she in?"

He snorted. "Listen, buddy. There's the doghouse, and then there's the doghouse. I don't know what happened between you two, but I'm pretty sure you're in the second. If I was you—"

"Well, you're not," I interrupted. "Anyway, this has nothing to do with us. It's about the case."

"She ain't in."

"Where is she?"

"Went to meet that other wizard."

"Who? Pierce?"

"Don't care for the guy myself, but did you catch the way the ladies were checking him out last night?" I didn't, but I remembered Vega's flushing cheeks. "Looks like you've got some competition, buddy."

Hoffman was trying to get under my skin, and he'd succeeded. My jealousy returned in a burning rush, incinerating the earlier confidence I'd felt at being able to ask Pierce for help from a position of strength.

"Where?" I demanded. "His place?"

"I think so." He chuckled. "I'm almost tempted to follow you over there. I've never seen a wizard fight. All I can picture are long robes, pointed hats, and a lot of slapping."

"There's not going to *be* a wizard fight," I said, struggling to control my voice. "Is there a number I can reach her at."

"You tried her cell?"

"It's..." I saw it in flames on the floor. "It's not working."

"Then she probably grabbed one from the pool. Couldn't tell you which one, though."

"Then I need to give you a message, in case I can't reach her."

"I'm a little busy over here," he said. "'Cause of you frigging *wizards*, we've got a citywide dragnet going for more of those bags. Every venue you can name, public and private."

"I might be able to save you some time, then. I have the names and addresses of four suspects."

"Suspects based on what?"

"Based on Becky, the woman whose apartment we searched. She just confessed."

"Thought you guys didn't find anything," he said suspiciously. But I could hear an edge of hunger in his voice. Homicide's priority was clearing cases. That's where the promotions happened. Some, like Vega, cleared them ethically. And then there was Hoffman, who would clear cases however he could. Even if it meant working with someone he despised.

"Do you want their info or not?" I pressed.

"Yeah, yeah, all right. If nothing else, it'll prove how useless you are."

I gave him the names and addresses. When I finished, I said, "But I don't want anyone moving on them yet."

"The hell are you talking about? You just said they were suspects."

"They're also possessed, and their places could be booby trapped." You couldn't rule out anything with a demon. Hoffman started to grumble, but I talked over him. "Right now it's about locating the suspects and keeping tabs on them. I need to head out, but I'll have my pager. Fill Vega in as soon as you hear from her, then have her call my pager."

"What about Becky?" he asked.

I thought about the unconscious woman in my bedroom. I didn't want the police getting involved until Gretchen had restored her soul and I'd found out where the ceremony to restore the Ark was being held. Or maybe I just wanted to keep that information from Pierce.

"Let me worry about her."

"I know you get off acting like a detective," Hoffman growled, "but you're not."

"Then I'm in good company."

Before he could fire back, I thumbed the switch hook and dialed Pierce's number. His assistant, Sora, answered.

"Is Pierce or Detective Vega there?"

"They just left."

"Together?" The jealous burn again. "Do you know where?"

"To a crime scene in Midtown. A delicatessen."

A part of me relaxed. Pierce really was behind the eight ball on this.

"I have some important info I need to give Vega," I said. "Could you contact Pierce and tell him to tell her to call my pager?" This was getting complicated, but I didn't want to deal with him directly. Not yet. I'd wait until the suspects I'd identified were apprehended and had given up the locations of the remaining infernal bags. *Then* we'd see how superior he felt.

I gave Sora my number. She hung up before I could thank her.

I climbed to my library/lab and loaded my coat pockets with spell items. With Becky still soul-torn, I needed to move on the two infernal bags she'd told me about and cancel them out.

I activated one of my pre-mades, a neutralizing potion, and funneled it into a tall water bottle. My heart beat anxiously as I worked. I knew the bags could go off at any moment. I kept one eye on my hologram of the city, but except for the lingering glows where the smoke golems had appeared, and a pinpoint of light in Harlem, Mae's pet, the hologram was clean. Nothing was breaching.

Back downstairs, I poked my head into the bedroom. Becky was how I'd left her, the covers to her chin. As my magic shifted around her, I saw that the burns on her face were healing.

I walked over and gave her a gentle shake. "Becky," I whispered.

She opened her eyes and spoke a sentence of gibberish before closing them again. Her soul was in as bad shape as I'd thought. Damn. And no Gretchen. I considered fishing my teacher's hair from the sink drain and casting a hunting spell, but there was no telling what kind of defensive magic she used. If it was fae-based, I could lose my own magic—or worse. Plus, there wasn't time.

I scrawled a quick message in my pocket-sized notepad, tore out the sheet, and set it on Becky's chest where Gretchen would be sure to see it. I repeated the message to Tabitha, who gave a weary paw wave.

My loaded trench coat clinked as I hurried from the apartment.

AT CAFÉ AGORA, I TRIED TO APPEAR INCONSPICUOUS AS I waited outside the women's bathroom. The Greek restaurant was more crowded than I would have expected for a Sunday night, but it wasn't terrible. I heard the toilet flush, and now I waited for the patron to wash and dry her hands. When the middle-aged woman emerged, she startled back at seeing a man in flasher attire hovering nearby.

"Sorry," I said. "Just looking for my wife."

"Well, there's no one else in there," she snapped.

"That so?"

I waited for the woman to leave before slipping inside. The door lacked a locking mechanism, so I sealed it with magic, then surveyed the smallish restroom: a sink and two stalls. I entered the far stall and climbed onto the toilet to reach the foam ceiling tile Becky had described. It lifted easily. I pawed around until my fingers closed over a small leather sack.

Yes!

In my anxiousness to get back down, my foot slipped and landed in the toilet bowl. I yanked it out with a splash, my shoe, sock, and pant leg from the shin down soaked through. I swore silently before returning my attention to the bag. It was heavy with black magic.

I couldn't waste any time.

I set it gingerly in the still-sloshing toilet water and then pulled out my neutralizing potion. I was in the process of centering myself when voices sounded outside the bathroom door.

"Are you sure?" a man was asking.

"Yes, I watched him walk right in," a woman insisted.

Oh, for chrissake...

"Sir?" A tentative knock. "Do you know this is the ladies' room?"

I tilted the bottle over the toilet. As the purplish potion streamed into the water and around the bobbing infernal bag, I began to incant.

The door shook. "Sir?"

I jerked slightly, splashing potion around before righting my aim.

"Did you hear that?" the woman whispered. "He's urinating all over the seat!"

"Blocked the door too," the man muttered.

The voices retreated, allowing me to concentrate on what was happening in my makeshift laboratory. As the potion activated, it turned the water an intense indigo. Capillaries glimmered into being and explored toward the infernal bag. As though sensing what was happening, the bag clenched into a tight fist to protect its murderous contents.

It was frightening how much magic Damien had managed to channel through Quinton and the others.

When the bottle was half empty, I stopped pouring. I would need the rest for the other bag. The infernal bag splashed as it tried to escape, but the thickening capillaries were penetrating the leather now. A cloudy blackness seeped through the vessels and into the water: the evil being drained.

I pushed more power into the incantation.

The potion pumped out more and more of the infernal

magic, blackening the water. The bag continued to thrash, kicking water up over the edges of the bowl. And then the commotion stopped. I waited several moments before leaning forward. Too late, I saw the bobbing bag draw in for one last gasp.

"Protezione!" I called, willing a shield into being and shape.

But the bag had already exploded in a spectacular burst. Black toilet water erupted in founts, one of them hitting me in the face. My shield took form an instant later, sparing me a full soaking.

As I spat and dried my dripping face, I heard something spattering over my shield. I lowered the front of my shirt. The bag had been mined with spiny imps. Their dead and dying bodies littered the tile floor like a strange breed of fish. I'd read some grisly stories about that class of imp, and as I watched them deflate into flaccid bags, I shuddered that they'd nearly been set loose in a crowded restaurant—along with another smoke golem powered by Damien.

I leaned over the toilet and checked to make sure the infernal magic had been neutralized before flushing. The spent bag swirled down with the black water until it all disappeared with a throaty *glug*.

I dispersed my shield, yanked several paper towels from the dispenser to finish drying my hands and face, and then killed the locking spell. I opened the bathroom door to a small crowd of managers.

"What the hell were you doing in there?" the biggest one demanded.

I combed a cowlick of wet hair from my brow and peered over a shoulder. A half inch of black water and a few dozen imps covered the bathroom floor. The imps would soon break down into phlegmy puddles, but for now they looked like a bizarre deep-sea haul.

One of the dying imps let out a croak.

"I, ah, think you've got something breeding in your pipes."

The managers rushed past me, exclaiming over the spectacle. Knowing the imps were harmless, I used the excitement to squish my way through the restaurant and out the front door.

One down, one to go, I thought as I hailed a cab.

Actually, thirteen to go, but until Becky could talk...

20

Thirty minutes later, I was running out of the Cerulean Store. More accurately, I was being chased by four associates in khakis and blue polo shirts, lanyard IDs swinging from their necks. Electric buzzes sounded as they activated the tasers on their high-tech phones.

My night was starting to look like my afternoon—a series of mishaps. Though I'd taken pains to be inconspicuous, one of the Cerulean associates had wandered into the utility room at exactly the wrong moment. My hand wrist-deep in the fuse box, he'd concluded I was a competitor trying to sabotage the store. The biggest provider of smartphones in the city, the Cerulean Store was a popular spot for people to play around with the newest devices, even if they couldn't afford them. Becky had chosen her target well. There had been a good thirty people in the store this evening.

I managed to snag her infernal bag, though, and was holding onto it for dear life. I just needed to ditch these guys so I could deactivate the damn thing. But after two blocks, they weren't giving up.

"Who do you work for?" one of them shouted.

"Apple?" shouted another. "Samsung?"

Wait, a minute, I thought, slowing down. *You're running from a nerd herd.*

When I turned to face them, they spread into a semicircle around me. The crackling nodes on their devices glinted from glasses and bared braces. I decided to level with them.

"Look, guys, I consult for the NYPD. I received a tip that someone had planted this in your store." I held up the infernal bag. "It contains combustible material that I need to deactivate. So if you would let me do my job."

"He works for Huawei!" one of them decided.

Oh, screw this.

As they rushed in, I jagged out my aura. Once again, probably not how my father would have handled things, but it had the desired effect. Their phones erupted in smoke, and two or three exploded.

"My Gamlon!" an associate screamed.

The rest of them stopped, the destruction of their devices seeming to emasculate them. Because I'd never been able to operate a smartphone myself, I couldn't quite grasp people's attachments to them. One of the associates began to weep. But something was happening to the infernal bag. It began to squirm and bulge in my grip. A faint pressure grew in my ears.

Crap, need to get this away from them.

No one gave chase when I ran this time. I cut into an alleyway a block and a half away. Behind a Dumpster, I found a large puddle left over from the afternoon's downpour. Wasting no time, I dropped the infernal bag into the water and poured the neutralizing potion around it.

I incanted quickly, one word slamming into the next. But though the brown puddle turned a shade of purple, no capillaries were forming. The potion wasn't draining the black magic from the bag. The pressure in my ears turned to vibrating.

C'mon, already!

Then I remembered what Damien had said about adapting. After the last bag, he must have already developed a defense against the neutralizing potion. As smoke began to stream from the bag, I tossed the potion bottle aside, reached into a pocket, and withdrew a vial of dragon sand.

Let's see how you handle a two-thousand-degree inferno, you smoking prick.

With my shield in place, I dumped the contents around the bag and shouted, *"Fuoco!"*

The dragon sand detonated in a pluming fireball, enveloping the infernal bag and knocking me back several feet. The heat was so intense it made instant steam of the puddle.

From the cover of the Dumpster, I squinted toward the bag. A smoke golem was taking shape above it. But the animation was off. It swelled to impossibly large proportions before breaking apart in a fiery roar. The wind swirled up the golem's remains and swept them away.

I waited until the dragon sand was spent and the bag had burned down to a crispy husk before lowering my arm and stealing forward. I prodded the infernal bag with my cane. When it broke apart, I was satisfied the magic had too.

That's the last of Becky's stash, I thought.

But there was a problem. If the bags could adapt—and not just the smoke golems Damien controlled—I was going to run out of ways to destroy them. And twelve still remained.

First I have to find them.

I dug around for my pager—maybe Vega or Gretchen had called—but I couldn't find the damned thing. Must have fallen out when I was running. I retraced my steps. When the pager didn't turn up, I went in search of a payphone. I found one a few blocks away, shoved a pair of quarters in, and called Homicide.

Hoffman answered again.

"It's Everson," I said. "Any word from your partner?"

"We sent officers to those addresses," he said, not answering my question. "No one's home. Any idea where they ran off to?" Though he was speaking in his typical surly voice, I could hear how badly he wanted these guys. I wondered if it had anything to do with wanting to get out from under his partner's shadow. Given my situation with Pierce, I could understand the urge. Maybe he and I had more in common than I'd thought.

But what Hoffman was telling me seemed to confirm my worst fears. If the members weren't home, there was a good chance they were en route to the ceremony, along with their newest inductee.

"I'm, ah, working on something," I said. "Still no word from Vega?"

"No. And I heard what you said before you hung up the last time, smartass."

"Hoffman, I've gotta go."

"Keep me in the loop," he warned.

I hung up, fed two more quarters into the slot, and called home. Tabitha answered.

"Is Gretchen back?"

"Yes, and she's *not* happy that someone's in her bed."

"Did she read the note?"

"Yes, and promptly ripped it apart."

"She ripped it apart?"

"The play was a big disappointment, apparently. Oh, it was a modern interpretation of *Hello, Dolly!* She left at the intermission and returned in a foul mood. When she found someone in her bed—"

"*My* bed," I interjected.

"Well, when she found someone there, she threw a fit. I've never seen anything like it. That's when she ripped apart your note. She said she wasn't here to babysit, and I'm quoting this part: 'Why can't he get that through his shit for brains?' Her eyes are turning all sorts of colors, darling. She's starting to frighten me."

"Where is she now?"

"The bathroom." Her voice dropped to a low whisper. "Oh, wait, she just came out." I pictured Tabitha hunkered with the phone behind one of the girder-like columns that ran along the kitchen counter.

"Put her on," I said.

"I don't think that's a good idea."

"Do it," I growled.

Tabitha cleared her throat. "Um, Gretchen? Everson's on the phone."

Gretchen muttered as she stomped over. I heard the loud thud and skitter of Tabitha clearing out.

"What's the big idea?" she demanded.

"You mean asking you to help someone whose soul was attacked?" I shot back. "Who holds key information that—"

"We had a deal," she said over me. "I train you, and you keep your business out of my business. I come home, and not only is your business in my business, it's in my *bed*."

I clenched my jaw. "One, we never made a deal. Two, when have you ever trained me? And three, it's *my* bed."

"One, yes we did. Two, what do you think we did this afternoon? And three—"

"Wait a minute. What do you mean, 'What do you think we did this afternoon?' You had me close my eyes for like two minutes while you got ready to go shopping. You call that training?"

"Well, I wasn't going to make you watch me change."

"The point is," I said through gritted teeth, "there's a demon trying to break into our world, and that woman has info on how I can stop it."

"And my point is that the woman in question is in my bed."

"Fine. Heal her soul, and you can have your bed back."

"Why would I do that? I can just boot her out the door and get the same result."

"You're a member of the Order, goddammit! Don't you know our history? Our creed? Our whole purpose is to protect the innocent against evil, especially demons. That's what we do! But all *you* do is eat, sleep, and—and go to plays. Never mind that there's a major breach in progress or that the city's about to be demon-fucked. You just care that someone's in your bed!"

"Don't you mean *your* bed?"

"What do you want?" I cried in exasperation.

"Now you're speaking my language."

I stopped as her words sunk in. In fae style, she wanted to make a bargain.

"You want something in exchange for healing her?"

"If it's juicy enough."

"Fine. What?"

"You tell me."

I sighed. "I don't have time for games. I have no idea what you could want from me. My blood?"

"That's disgusting."

"Then *what?*"

"That's what I'm waiting to hear," she said with exaggerated patience.

As frustrated as I was, I was also desperate. I calmed my breathing and tried to think like a fae. The thing was, they were so damned strange. Their bargains tended to tilt steeply in their favor, but they also liked to make the other party suffer, depriving them of something they valued. In fact, that alone could be enough.

I resolved not to bring Vega into this. No matter how uncertain our relationship felt, I wasn't going to allow a fae bargain to even breathe on what we had. I'd learned my lesson with Caroline.

So what else did I value?

I thought about the associates crying over their destroyed phones. While I couldn't understand the obsession with their devices, I'd been accused recently of being similarly obsessed.

"My *Magical Me* book?" I said.

"You mean that taped-up mess under the divan?"

"It's back under the divan?" I shouted.

Gretchen laughed until she began to snort. "Relax, it's right here. Is that what you're offering? And I don't mean just the book. The daily exercises, the affirmations..." I could hear her flipping through it.

I surprised myself by hesitating.

"Everson?"

"Yeah, yes, of course," I said. "The book and ... the practices."

"Then you've got yourself a deal. Let me go rouse Sleeping Beauty."

As Gretchen set the phone down, I shook my head. With everything at stake, had I really just balked at giving up my *Magical Me* program? But I'd made progress with that program in the last year. Not as much as I'd hoped, but still ... It had gotten me to levels I wouldn't have reached without it. If the training with Gretchen didn't pan out, I might need it again. Plus, as sappy as it sounded, giving up the book felt like losing a close friend.

"Okey-dokey," Gretchen said after several minutes. "It's done."

"You healed her already? She's coherent?"

"Do you want to talk to her? She's right here."

Before I could answer, I heard a murmured exchange. The next voice was Becky's. "Everson?"

"Hey!" I said in honest surprise. Given the speed with which Gretchen had come back on the line, I thought she was pulling my leg again. "How are you feeling?"

"Like crap, but I understand it could've been worse. Are you all right?"

"Yeah. I found the bags you told me about. They've been defused."

"Thank God," she breathed.

"Listen, when we were trying to leave the packing plant, you started to tell me about the location of an induction ceremony? The one where Damien had you all meet to replace Trevor?"

"Oh, right. It was at the southeast corner of Central Park. You know where that big pond is? Well, at the end near the old skating rink, there's a huge pile of boulders. Damien had us go down a hole around there. We followed an underground passageway to a big room."

The old goblin tunnels, I thought anxiously. "All right, I want you to stay at my place until I tell you it's safe to leave." If Damien's Ark was restored, the demon would send the members to silence her.

"Okay," she said, then lowered her voice. "But I don't think this woman wants me here."

"Gretchen's bark is worse than her bite—though you might want to relocate to the couch. Oh, and don't eat anything she cooks. Remember, stay put until you hear back from me."

"Gotcha," she said. "And ... thanks for everything."

I could hear by the awkwardness that *thank you*s didn't come easy for her.

"Don't mention it."

I hung up and called Homicide again. Hoffman answered.

"Anything from Vega?"

"Still nothing."

I wasn't sure whether or not to believe him, but time was too precious.

"Okay, listen," I said. "If you want in on this, here's what I need you to do. Set up a perimeter around the southeast corner of Central Park, from Sixty-Fifth down. Have it in place in thirty minutes. Grab anyone who tries to go in or come out. I'll be in touch. Deal?"

"Sure. But where are you gonna be?"

I swallowed. "Underground."

21

I t was drizzling again by the time the cab dropped me off on Central Park South. I raised my collar and stepped into an amber cone of streetlight, thin droplets splintering around me. Something else I'd improved on in the past year was channeling energy in the presence of water.

I invoked a shield and scanned the dark expanse ahead of me. The fires from the year before had incinerated the growth and overgrowth, making the roads that wound through the park mostly navigable again. I made my way toward East Drive, which curved in the direction of the old skating rink. A set of tire tracks appeared in the wet cinders.

Someone had come this way recently.

I broke into a jog, my coat bouncing with spell items, until I could see the skating pavilion. Parked behind it was the vehicle that had left the tracks: a large SUV.

South of the rink, I spotted the boulders Becky had mentioned. As I picked my way over to them, it occurred to me that I was at the other end of the pond where Vega and I had fought the bugbear the summer before, narrowly escaping the overgrown park ahead of the napalm drops. The current charred landscape with tree trunks rising like spires couldn't have looked more alien.

When I arrived at the boulders, I circled them, searching for the hole. I risked a bit of light from my staff until I spotted several sets of footprints coming from the direction of the skating pavilion.

I followed them, and I was soon edging sideways between two large boulders.

I spotted the hole that thick growth had once concealed. Budge was supposed to have had the goblin tunnels filled, but a backlog of projects, including the park's restoration, were on hold until the downtown was finished. His eradication program had helped get him reelected, but it had also caused billions in damage. While new businesses and residences had begun to take hold in some of the formerly afflicted areas, the city's coffers weren't exactly overflowing.

As I approached the hole, my light shone over a crude staircase descending steeply. I listened but couldn't hear anything beyond the blackness.

Oh boy, I thought as my chest began to tighten.

I started into one of the *Magical Me* affirmations before catching myself. Bad things tended to happen to those who went back on their fae bargains. I wasn't sure how enforceable our bargain was, given Gretchen wasn't actually fae, but I couldn't afford any badness right now. Especially after seeming to have gotten over my second bout of bad luck.

Old goblin odors, putrid and reptilian, moved around me as I reinforced my shield and started down the staircase. After a twenty-foot descent, I arrived in a low passageway supported by rough-hewn scaffolding. The remains of several goblins that had tried to flee the napalm attack lay off to one side, bones and rags now. The fingers of a hand still clutched the grip of a burnt bow.

I turned from the remains and listened. Within moments, I picked up what sounded like distant moaning, but I couldn't tell whether it was voices or some flue-like effect of the tunnels.

I followed the passageway forward, rehearsing my plan in my mind. I stopped when, a few yards ahead, I could see the tunnel splitting in two. The moaning was coming from the right one—and, yes, it was made up of voices.

I followed the sound past small rooms and through two more intersections. Eventually, light flickered at a bend in the tunnel ahead. I killed my own light and stole forward.

The tunnel opened into a high-ceilinged room large enough to have served as a goblin mess hall. An assortment of small tables and chairs had been shoved to the room's sides. In the cleared center was a pentagram, similar to the one at the old packing plant. I took in the three men and two women, each standing at a different point on the pentagram. Heads bowed, they clasped hands to form a circle. Dozens of thick candles flickered around them.

Their moans were a collective chant, low and drawn out. Dark demonic energy stirred at the pentagram's center. The sharp pressure in my ears told me it was Damien. I looked from member to member, stopping at Quinton's bald head. He was standing across from me, his voice the loudest. My gaze dropped to the necklace glinting on the front of his chest.

Step one, I thought, *grab the cursed item.*

I pulled my cane apart and aimed my sword. *"Vigore!"*

Quinton lurched forward as the invocation snagged the necklace and snapped it from his neck. The necklace whipped through the air and into my hand. Expecting something ancient and evil, I was surprised to find myself holding a thin silver chain. I shoved it into a bag of salt in one of my pockets.

The chanting broke apart, and the members of the Ark looked around in sleepy confusion. Quinton pawed frantically around his naked neck.

Step two: seal the exits.

"Serrare," I called, stepping into the room. The air crackled at my back, barring the tunnel I'd entered from. Shields went up over the remaining two tunnels.

"Over there!" Quinton shouted, pointing at me while reaching his right hand behind his back. When he drew a pistol, I was more concerned for the others. An errant shot could kill someone, and that would mean infernal bags whose locations remained unknown.

I disarmed Quinton with a force blast. The pistol flew from his grip. A second blast to the gut dropped him to his knees. The rest of the Ark began lumbering toward me, as if awakening from a confusing dream.

Step three: confine the members.

"Protezione!" I shouted.

Light swelled from my staff, and crackling domes grew around each member of the Ark, including Quinton, who was still down. I had them, but I was already feeling the strain of maintaining so many invocations at once. The very edges of my vision began to waver.

Step four: exorcise the cursed item.

I sprinkled out a circle of copper filings and dropped the

chain in the center. As I willed energy into the circle, hardening the air around it, the wavering in my vision turned creamy.

Not Thelonious, I pled. *Not now.*

Though I'd increased my casting capacity, I had expended more energy today than I had in a long time. My eyes shifted to the exits. I had sealed them to keep anyone from escaping, but also to prevent any surprises from popping in. They were a luxury I could no longer afford.

I dispersed the barriers. Fresh energy surged into my casting prism. Pulling out a small scroll, I unrolled the vellum paper that contained Latin instructions on performing an exorcism.

"*Exorcizo te, omnis spiritus immunde,*" I read, directing my voice at the casting circle, "*in nomine Dei Patris omnipotentis...*"

The necklace began to flick around, trying to escape the barrier.

"*...sanctum suum vocare dignatus est, ut fiat templum Dei vivi...*"

Once exorcized, the necklace—and the demon that had cursed it—would have no more hold over the Ark. I could release them and then get down to the business of finding and defusing the remaining infernal bags.

As the necklace writhed and kicked, I stole glances at the dark mist that hovered over the pentagram. It was the remnants of the demonic energy, trying desperately to hold itself together.

I read louder, faster.

"*...et Spiritus Sanctus habitet in eo...*"

When I finished, the necklace fell still. The mist above the pentagram broke apart. I watched as air currents carried

the failing energy from the pentagram into the tunnels opposite me.

Good riddance.

I sighed and pocketed the scroll.

"Is everyone all right?" I asked, turning to the Ark.

I expected to find them looking around in confusion as
they recovered their senses. Instead, they were pounding the
crackling domes that confined them, trying to get at me.
Quinton snarled with bloody lips as he threw his entire body
into his shield, murder rimming his eyes.

I looked down at my casting circle. The necklace was
exorcized, the energy that had bonded the Ark to it broken.
That should have freed them, dammit. I opened my wizard's
senses toward the necklace.

Crap—a faint pulse remained.

Swearing, I pulled out my overnight bag, removed a small
flask of holy water, and gave it a shake. A little left.
Unscrewing the cap with my teeth, I dumped what remained
of the water over the necklace. The thin chain came to life in
a fit, leaping around and hissing steam.

I snorted. "Playing possum, huh?"

I unrolled the scroll to exorcize what presence remained,
then froze as the voice I'd come to associate with the smoke
golems sounded through the space.

"Not playing possum, wizard," Damien said. "I'm simply
biding my time. Oh, look. You have company."

I raised my head and almost screamed. The two tunnels
the smoke had departed through were now crowded with
nightmare creatures—imps, mostly, but lesser demon spawn
filled the ranks. They had advanced slowly, quietly, and were
now spreading into the room.

My gaze ranged over the mass of fangs, glowing eyes,

spindly limbs, ragged wings—all of them awash in dark, sulfuric fire. Those must have been the two extra infernal bags Becky had mentioned, stashed farther back in the tunnels for security. Bags Damien had activated as his energy was swept from the main room. And this is what the bags had given birth to.

"Attack!" Damien's voice ordered.

I responded with two shield invocations intended to shove the creatures back into the far tunnels, but the moment the creatures contacted them, the shields failed in brilliant cascades of sparks.

Adaptability, remember? I told myself.

A large creature sprang from the mass on grasshopper legs, its pointed ears almost as long as its horns. Spiny teeth shone bone-white from the creature's gaping jaw. I swung my sword at the same time the creature shot out an arm. Fortunately metal still worked where magic didn't. My blade caught the imp at the elbow, severing it neatly. I whipped the sword back around and removed its screeching head. The body collapsed to the floor, its thin, tendinous legs twitching and kicking.

But as more creatures flapped and raced toward me, I knew that wasn't a winning strategy. They were too many. I cut my eyes to the Ark, realizing the members were vulnerable. Damien could decide to silence them. I shouted a force invocation that shoved their shielded bodies into an alcove. With a second invocation, I shrouded them in deep shadow.

The creatures arrived in a gibbering mass. I hacked and slashed at them while digging my free hand into my coat pockets. I removed three golf ball-sized objects and chucked them into the throng. They ricocheted off creatures and bounced over the floor in separate trajectories.

"Attivare!" I shouted, activating the lightning grenades.

A harsh scent of ozone filled the room an instant before blue-white jags of energy streaked from the three tunnels and detonated inside the chamber to deafening and ground-shaking effect. Creatures shrieked as they blew apart, their appendages raining everywhere.

Though my shield protected me, I could feel the lightning's energy buzzing in my teeth. I looked around. The attack had destroyed half the creatures, but the rest were reorienting themselves, starting to come at me again. I slashed through an imp, but missed the one zipping in behind it. My shield shook and spilled sparks as the imp grazed it.

What else did I pack?

I dug into my pockets, past vials and bottles that contained potions I'd yet to activate and wouldn't have time to. At last I encountered a smooth glass orb the size of a tennis ball.

Yes.

The orb pulsed in my grasp and sent a warm current up my arm. As I drew out the orb, its misty interior glowed through my fingers.

The several dozen creatures stopped and stared at the orb, transfixed.

I was holding the emo ball my mother had given Arianna to give to me. Knowing she might be killed before I was old enough to remember her, my mother had invested the ball with her love, so that I would know it always. Though I'd carried it on several assignments in the last year, I had remained obsessively protective of it, to the point of using it only as a last resort. I had lost my mother once—I couldn't bear the thought of losing this essence that remained.

"Attack!" Damien ordered.

"No," I countered, pushing energy into the emo ball.

The orb swelled more brightly, causing the nightmare horde to wince and draw back. Born of evil, the creatures had never been in the presence of love before, especially not a love this intense or unconditional. They were as fascinated by it as they were terrified, some part of them sensing the orb's power to undo the wicked coils that held them together.

"Attack!" Damien urged. "Destroy him!"

The creatures lurched forward, as though being shoved by an unseen force. Willing more power into the ball, I shoved back. As light from the emo ball touched the creatures at the front line, their skin began to bubble and hiss steam. They screamed but were powerless to draw away.

I grunted as I pushed even harder through the ball. Though the creatures shrieked and howled, Damien continued to force them forward, determined for the horde to overwhelm me.

Creamy waves lapped around my vision, stronger than earlier.

Need my protection back from the Ark, I thought desperately. *Just long enough to destroy the creatures and finish purifying the necklace.*

With a pair of Words, I dispersed the obscuring and shield invocations that protected them. The members reappeared in the alcove—startled, it seemed, by their sudden freedom. I channeled the released energy into the emo ball, shoving the creatures back ... back ... back...

Blam!

Light burst around my right hand and dissipated. The room dimmed suddenly. The coldness that rushed in carried Damien's laughter. When I heard the tinkling of glass shards hitting the floor, I realized I was no longer holding the emo ball. My heart staggered. My mother's gift...

"A pity," Damien taunted.

I backed from the recovering imps and demon spawn. Beyond them, Quinton stood in front of the alcove. He had recovered his pistol and blown away my mother's emo ball. Fury restored me from my shock.

Thrusting my sword toward him, I shouted, *"Vigore!"*

But one of the charging creatures came between us, dissolving the force invocation. Quinton wasn't fazed. I slashed through the arriving creatures, desperate for another shot at Quinton. But the man was moving now, running low, stooping for something. Silver flashed in his hand as he grabbed the necklace from my casting circle. Then he disappeared down the tunnel I'd entered by.

Shit.

When I tried to chase him, a taloned hand broke through my shield and snagged the back of my coat. It tugged me backwards. I swung my blade wildly as creatures began piling on top of me. A jaw clamped the side of my neck, then another, the penetrating fangs like fire. Pain speared through my wrist as an imp bit down and shook. My sword fell from my grasp.

Have to get these damned things off, I thought desperately as claws tore open my shirt, *have to recover the necklace ...*

I swung my staff, but there were too many of them. And I was losing blood.

Above the carnage, Damien laughed. "Our friendship may have been short, but it wasn't without drama."

Drawing every last ounce of strength, I shouted, *"Respingere!"*

Power detonated from my staff. The room shook, furniture shattering against the walls, but the creatures remained. I collapsed beneath their weight and onto my mother's shattered emo ball, numb to everything except the crashing arrival of Thelonious.

He was the reason I'd expended all of my power.

He was my final hope.

22

I blinked, surprised to find myself in Thelonious's world. In the past I would just black out, remembering nothing until the incubus had had his fill of carousing, or enough of my power had seeped back. But here I was, in his realm of vague shapes and throbbing bass notes. A place I hadn't been since I'd invoked Thelonious for the first time twelve years before, in Romania.

I looked around, but couldn't see his large, corpulent form. Couldn't hear his rich voice. As I listened, I noticed the bass line was off. It sounded irregular, out of tune. And the creamy colors had dulled.

"Hello?" I called. "Thelonious?"

"That Everson?"

I turned to see something taking shape in the dull light. The being was large, like how I remembered the incubus spirit, but his voice had a weak, raspy quality. And he seemed to be limping.

"Been awhile," he said.

"Almost a year," I replied. The last time Thelonious had

visited I'd been pushing too hard on a complex spell in my apartment, determined to reach the needed threshold. Fortunately, the wards had kept him indoors. Tabitha had smartly spent the night on the ledge, though. "So ... what's going on? What am I doing here?"

"This is where you come every time."

"Really? I don't remember ever coming here, except for that first time."

"That's because when we switch, I'm in your head. I've got your memories."

"Why didn't we switch this time?"

Thelonious grunted as he sat down heavily. "Some bad stuff's gone down, brother."

My shoulders sagged with the weight of his words. I wasn't dumb. He was delivering me the news of my own death. I'd intentionally spent my remaining power in the dim hope Thelonious would destroy the demonic creatures so as not to lose me as a vessel. But he hadn't done anything, and here we were.

I stopped. If I was a goner, what was I doing in his realm? *You're still bound to him,* I realized. *This is your eternity.*

I looked around in horror. The incessant bass line alone was going to drive me insane. But spending eternity with a big, jive-talking incubus? No. I had to get the hell out of here.

"You helped me once," I said quickly. "In exchange I acted as your vessel for twelve years. I'm no more use to you now." I tried not to imagine the demon spawn tearing apart my body. "We—or I guess *you* have had some good times. Now I need you to release me."

"What are you talking about, young blood?"

"There's no reason for me to spend eternity here."

"Eternity? Who said anything about eternity?"

"Aren't I ... dead?"

"Not yet. Time don't mean much down here."

"So I'm still..."

"However you left where you were is how you are now."

"Thank God," I breathed. "But why aren't you up there?"

"That's what I'm trying to tell you," he rumbled. "Bad stuff's gone down."

"What bad stuff?"

"Someone's been asking about you. And not just asking. He about broke me, and Thelonious don't break easy."

So that explained the damaged condition of the incubus spirit and his realm. "Someone tortured you to get information on me? Who?"

Thelonious shook his head. "A rough customer is all I can tell you. Never met him before in my life. I mostly keep to myself. No one bothers Thelonious, and Thelonious don't bother no one. Unless we've made a deal, of course." He nodded toward me. "But this customer blows in here unannounced and first thing he does is to rip apart my women."

I remembered the sensual forms that had been attending to Thelonious's various needs the last time I'd been here. A deep loneliness seemed to haunt his realm in their absence.

"No way to treat the ladies," Thelonious went on, "and I told him so. Next thing I know, he's on top of me, and I'm in a world of pain. Was like he was twisting something deep inside me, to the verge of snapping. 'Tell me about Everson Croft,' this cat hissed. And no hard feelings, young blood, but I spilled everything. Down to your measurements. The pain, you see. When I finished, the cat only twisted harder. 'No,' he hissed. 'Tell me what he's been doing recently.' The way he said that word, *recently*. Wish you could've heard it. Sent chills clear up and down me, and I'd like to think I'm a cool customer."

The timing of the interrogation with Damien's appearance in New York probably wasn't a coincidence. But what demon would care about me? Was Damien working for Sathanas, the demon lord I'd banished a couple of years earlier?

"I told him I hadn't seen you in awhile," Thelonious continued. "I didn't know what you'd been doing. Cat didn't like that answer, though. He hurt me, young blood. Hurt me for a long time. First I thought it was 'cause he didn't believe me, but then I saw he was just enjoying himself." He shook his head. "Been a long while since I was made helpless like that."

Despite being captive to our bargain, I found myself pitying Thelonious. The incubus spirit had mortified me many times, had left me in compromising situations, often without pants, but he had never hurt me.

"Do you think it was a demon lord?" I asked.

"Now I don't know about that. But this cat is up there. And if he's intent on getting to you..." Thelonious shook his head slowly. "I hate to say it, but I believe he's going to find a way. Didn't sound like he'd made it into your world, though. Not yet. But he can get to you here. And if he did, you'd *wish* you could spend eternity with me. I should let you get back. Not safe here."

"Yeah, well, I'm not exactly safe up there, either. Can you help me?"

Thelonious's chuckle was a sad rumble. "I helped you one time, that was the deal. I'm in no shape to be making new deals. And even if I could, I'm in no shape to do much of anything with them. Might never be in that kind of shape again. Just brought you down to tell you what's what. You're a good man. Gave me some good times. But I'm broken up. Gonna have to send you back now."

"No, wait! I'm under a pile of demon spawn up there. I expended all my power with the idea you might step in. I-I've got nothing. You send me back, and I'm a dead man."

"No worries," he said, his voice thick with sleepiness now. "Not gonna send you back to the moment you left there. I'll let things roll forward a bit. Send you back a few hours later on."

"What? No, then I'll be dead for sure! How about a few hours earlier?"

"Yeah," Thelonious rumbled as he rose unsteadily. "Few hours later on..."

"No! Wait!"

But Thelonious was already fading away as the creamy waves of his realm lapped over my consciousness.

DARKNESS WRAPPED ME IN A THICK COCOON. I SLOWLY BECAME aware of lying on my back. But I wasn't on the hard floor of the goblin chamber. And demon spawn definitely weren't feasting on me.

I tried to lift a hand to my torso, but pain flared from somewhere deep inside.

I cracked my eyes open to the dim impressions of the end of a bed and a room beyond. To my right, light outlined a door. Voices murmured beyond. Somewhere a door opened and closed. Then the door to my room opened. I squinted away as a silhouette bisected the light.

"Everson?" a woman asked in a whisper.

The door closed behind her, and the bed creaked as she sat on its edge.

"Vega?" I managed from a dry mouth.

Fingers brushed the damp hair from my brow. "Yeah, it's me."

I recognized the room now, the bed. I was in Ricki's apartment.

"How'd I get here?"

"Pierce found you."

"Pierce?"

I tried to sit up, but pain shot through my gut and stole my breath.

"Don't move," she said. "He cast a healing spell, but he said it needs time to work."

Wincing, I settled back onto the mattress. I was underneath several layers of sheets, but my skin felt cool. After another moment, I picked up Pierce's subtle magic. It moved over me as smooth as quicksilver, probing, purging, repairing. Restoring me to wholeness and health.

"He found me in the goblin tunnels?"

"Yeah. About to be torn apart." She sighed. "What in the hell were you doing down there by yourself?"

She'd picked up a large plastic cup from the nightstand and now she held a straw to my lips. I lifted my head and took a sip. The water felt wonderful going down.

"It was a timing thing," I said as I lay back. I told her what had happened after our fight at Becky's apartment building, from Quinton turning up to me leaving Becky's soul-torn body at my place and then disarming the two infernal bags she'd planted. "I'd just finished disarming the second bag when Gretchen told me she had healed Becky. Becky told me the location of the induction ceremony. I wanted to get there before the Ark was restored and Damien could regain his full strength. I tried to reach you, but you were with Pierce." Even in my condition, a jealous burn accompanied the words. "Hoffman must've told you guys where I was, huh?"

"I tried to page you."

"Yeah, I lost the pager somewhere."

"Did you check your voice mail?" she asked.

"Not recently. Oh, you mean earlier." I thought back. I'd only been home twice since Vega and I had parted ways, and both times I'd been in go-go-go mode. "I guess not," I said.

"I left four messages."

"Really?"

"Pierce's work led him to the tunnels too."

"A little late," I muttered, unable to help myself.

"No, actually. He thought it'd be safer to wait until *after* the ceremony and then apprehend them as they were coming out. The messages I left were to fill you in on what was happening and to warn you not to go into the tunnels. Pierce said they were too dangerous."

I had it under control, I thought bitterly. *Just a couple bad breaks.*

"When I called for backup, I was surprised to find out there were already officers at the scene." My eyes had adjusted to the darkness enough that I could see her right eyebrow arch up.

"I coordinated with Hoffman when I couldn't get ahold of you," I explained.

"Hoffman," she muttered. "Son of a bitch knew how to reach me. But calling him probably saved your life. When he told me you'd gone underground, we knew what he meant. Pierce went down and found you under a pile of creatures. He destroyed them and pulled you out."

"What about the Ark?"

"We detained them as they emerged, but Quinton got away."

I remembered him shooting my mother's emo ball and then grabbing the necklace from the casting circle.

"The goblin tunnels are extensive," she said. "He probably found another way out. But Pierce was able to break Damien's hold over the others and get the locations of their bags. Eight in all. I sent teams of officers to collect them. That was a couple hours ago. Pierce just stopped by to say he'd finished neutralizing them. He also wanted to see how you were doing."

"Is he still here?" The English magic-user might have rubbed me in all the wrong ways, not least in just succeeding where I'd failed, but he'd saved my life. I at least owed him a thank you.

"Just left," Vega said. "He's working on tracking down Quinton and the necklace."

I moved the covers aside, struggled against the pain and stiffness, and managed to lift my legs over the side of the bed.

"Hey, what are you doing?"

"There are two infernal bags still out there." I gritted my teeth and pushed myself the rest of the way up, releasing my breath as the pain subsided. "I could be working on finding them."

"Everson..."

"Hey, if I can move, I can help." I had been stripped to my boxers, and my abdomen was covered in bandages. The demon spawn must have really been doing a number on me when Pierce showed up.

"You need to stay here and *rest*," Vega said.

"Where are my things? Was Pierce able to grab my sword

and staff?" Losing my mother's emo ball had been bad enough. I didn't even want to think about being without my father's blade too.

"Yes, but stop," she ordered. "Listen to me."

I'd been peering around the dark room, but now I turned to face her.

"That's not coming from me. That's from your Order."

"The Order put me on bed rest?"

"Yes. And they want Pierce to handle the case from here."

My stomach knotted, but not from pain. "Oh, is that what *Pierce* said?"

"Everson, he found the Ark. He'll find Quinton and the remaining infernal bags."

"Why don't you just come out and say it."

"Say what?"

"That the case would be wrapped up if I hadn't interfered."

"Nothing's your fault. You made as much progress on the case as anyone."

"But that's what this is about, isn't it? The Order didn't pull the decree out of their butts. Pierce told them to kick me off the case."

"It wasn't like that."

"Oh, no? Did he or did he not contact the Order?"

"Yes, but—"

"I rest my case." I spotted my date-night clothes and coat on the dresser and staggered toward them. Someone had leaned my cane against the wall, right beside my shoes. I started to dress.

"Everson, this isn't about you," Vega said sternly.

"That's funny. When I was with Thelonious just now, he told me a story about a demon paying him a visit. The demon ripped apart his harem and tortured him, all for some information on guess who?"

Her brow furrowed. "You?"

"Yup. So I'm guessing this whole thing has just a tiny bit to do with the wizard who can't shoot straight."

"Pierce did mention something about you having a role."

"That's nice. Was he ever going to get around to sharing that with me, or was that for your ears only?"

I winced as I drew my arm through what remained of my shirt sleeves, but there was nothing to button. The front of the shirt was in bloody tatters. Vega moved in front of me, grabbed my shirt collar, and pulled me down until we were eye level.

"Hey—ow!"

Her eyes glinted dangerously. "Listen, jerk. That's what I'm trying to tell you. For some reason, your presence throws off Pierce's divination. He thinks it has to do with your magic. He didn't know you were going to be there tonight. That's why he called to have you sidelined. Not because he doesn't like you, or that this is some kind of pissing contest to him. But so his divination magic will work like it should. When he finds Quinton, he'll neutralize the necklace and track down the remaining infernal bags. That's what's important right now. Preventing more deaths. Then you can do whatever you want to figure out why this demon's interested in you. I'm sure Pierce will help. Until then, you need to heal."

"Fine," I said. "Can I have my shirt back now?"

"Oh, and just in case this has something to do with Pierce and me working together, he's gay."

I paused. "He told you that?"

She yanked me closer. "I almost fucking lost you."

When I saw the pain in her eyes, I sighed. Maybe Pierce

wasn't as Machiavellian as I'd made him out to be. I kissed her forehead and wrapped her in my arms. "I'm sorry," I said.

After the way she'd just handled me, her return hug was surprisingly gentle. She ran her hands beneath my shirt and over my bare back. Pleasant waves, more soothing even than Pierce's healing magic, moved through me.

I let her remove the clothes I'd managed to put on and help me back to bed. I watched her undress in the darkness until she was wearing only a black bra and boy shorts. Her muscles flexed as she climbed in after me.

"Just need a couple hours rest," she murmured, nuzzling her warm body against my side.

"Are you trying to cuddle?"

"Shh. Go to sleep."

But long after Vega's breaths had deepened, I remained staring at the ceiling, going back over the torrent of events from that day and night. Something seemed off, something connected to what Thelonious had told me in his realm, but damned if I could put my finger on what.

At last I rested my head against the top of Vega's and drifted off too.

23

I woke up to an empty bed and light glowing through the cracks of Vega's blinds. I checked my watch and saw that it was a little past one on Sunday. Stretching my arms overhead, I let out a noisy yawn. I'd slept the sleep of the dead, which was fitting, considering how close I'd come.

My transition to sitting was much easier than the night before. Just some vague soreness around my ribs. Legs over the bedside, I peeled the bandages from my torso. A nasty network of scars criss-crossed my stomach, but I could feel Pierce's magic working on them.

I chucked the dressing into the waste basket and stood on surprisingly sound legs. At the dresser, I found a clean-smelling stack of folded clothes that weren't mine. A note sat on top of them.

I had to go back out. Camilla brought over some clean clothes in your size, and your coat's in the dryer (everything from your pockets is on top of the machine—never realized how much you carried). I called the college to tell them you wouldn't be in tomorrow and to cancel your classes.

Call me when you wake up!

Vega left her new number and a heart.

As I folded the note, I thought back to our dinner conversation on Friday. I really had been neglecting a good thing. I showered and then dressed in what turned out to be a pair of white slacks that flared out at the cuffs and a rainbow-colored disco shirt, then went to the kitchen to call Vega. I got her voicemail.

"Hey, Ricki," I said. "I'm up, obviously, and feeling pretty good. I think the new duds have something to do with that. Thanks for taking care of me last night and this morning. I really do appreciate that. I'm going to head back to my apartment here in a minute. Becky's still there, where I think she'll be safest until Quinton is caught and the necklace taken care of." I noticed that instead of saying *until Pierce catches Quinton and takes care of the necklace*, I'd slipped into passive voice. My ego didn't know the contest was over. "I should be there by two or so, but in the meantime I'm going to raid your pantry. Talk soon."

I surprised myself by downing half a box of Raisin Bran, along with a quart of milk, two chopped bananas, and some chocolate chips I'd found in the freezer. While I ate, I tried thinking about what had bothered me last night, but the act of shoveling the dripping cereal into my mouth was too distracting. Healing required a lot of calories, and I'd barely had any for the last two days. Now was eating time. I would have to set aside time for thinking later.

THE INSTANT I STEPPED ACROSS MY APARTMENT THRESHOLD, the tension hit me like a wall of pressure. Tabitha's ears were pinned to her head; Becky was pacing the living room; and Gretchen's door was closed.

"So," I called cheerily. "How's everyone doing?"

"Ugh," Becky said. "You have to let me out of here."

"No one's stopping you," Tabitha muttered.

"Oh, by the way, my cat talks," I said, hitting Tabitha with an exasperated look. We'd had an understanding that she would keep that fact under wraps around non-supernaturals.

"It was a gray area," Tabitha said, anticipating the future argument. "She was demon-possessed. Nice pants."

I glanced down. I'd stuffed the bell-bottom cuffs inside my socks, but they'd worked their way back out and were now flaring beneath the hem of my cinched coat. Good thing she couldn't see my shirt.

"That's been going on *all night*," Becky complained. "Little remarks about my ruined hair, my clothes, my piercings. I'm under enough stress as it is. And then there's your roommate. *God.*"

"What did Gretchen do?"

"What *didn't* she do? Besides the snoring, she slammed both doors every time she got up to use the bathroom. And the last time, she didn't even have the courtesy to turn on the fan. Thought that was bad until she started cooking breakfast —at *five a.m.* The cheese she used in her omelet is the most evil fucking thing I've ever smelled. Someone needs to exorcize *that.*"

I picked up the lingering odor. "Well, I can't argue with you there."

"I can hear you," Gretchen called from my bedroom.

"But," I added, loud enough for Gretchen, "she healed your soul, so be grateful. There are few who could have managed that." I lowered my voice to a whisper. "Look, she's batshit crazy, but you're only going to be here for a little longer. Think about me and Tabitha."

"Is she your mom or something?" Becky asked.

"Gretchen? God, no."

"I heard that too!" Gretchen called.

Becky glared at the wall, her hands balling into fists. "I'm on, like, no sleep."

"Here, have a seat." I sat on the couch and gestured to the reading chair opposite me. "I've got some updates."

Becky walked over wearily and flopped down. "Sorry. On top of everything, I'm going through nicotine withdrawal." Making a face, she dug behind the cushion and pulled out my pager. "Is this yours?"

So that's where the damned thing ended up, I thought, taking it from her.

"Did you find my friends?" she asked.

"I did." I checked the pager, saw all of Vega's calls, then dropped the device into my coat's deepest pocket. "They were down in that underground room you told me about, performing the induction ceremony." I skipped over the blow-by-blow or the fact that I'd nearly bought it. "Four of your friends were caught, their infernal bags tracked down, but Quinton escaped with the necklace. There's a hunt on for him now."

"Still, that's pretty good," she said.

"Yeah, well, I had some help." I swallowed my pride. "A lot of help." I changed the subject. "Hey, you knew about the tunnels. Do you have any idea where Quinton might have gone? Any places he's used in the past to lay low?"

As I watched Becky squint in thought, I remembered what Vega had said about my presence interfering with Pierce's divination magic. The idea still rankled me—like my magic was so bad it was infectious. But if the Order was calling me off, what could I do?

"I don't know about a specific place," she said at last. "But he used to have this old trawler boat docked at Red Hook, in Brooklyn. It belonged to an uncle or something. I'm not sure if it's still there, but I remember him saying once that if things got real bad, we could crash there."

"Sounds like a good hiding spot," I said, getting up.

I'd be lying if I said I wasn't tempted to replenish my spell items and head there myself. That was more or less the way I'd operated for the last twelve years. But I picked up the phone instead.

"Vega," she answered.

"Hey, it's me. Did you get my message?"

"Yeah, but listen, I'm in the middle of something. There's been another attack."

My heart stopped before starting up again. I could hear a commotion of voices and sirens around her.

"Where?"

"Museum of Natural History. Upper West Side. A couple of officers were here yesterday as part of the dragnet, but they didn't find anything. The bag must have been one of Quinton's, well hidden. The attack's over and the bag's been neutralized, but the damage is done."

I was afraid to ask. "How many?"

"At least forty."

"Dammit."

With the Ark broken, I'd thought Damien would be too weak to activate his remaining infernal bags. He must have drawn against the souls he'd claimed. Regardless, we were up to seventy now. And if Thelonious was right about how far up the chain this demon went, Damien was going to need a helluva lot more souls to break through. That meant either his remaining infernal bag was a whopper, or Quinton was forming a new Ark to make more bags.

"How's Pierce doing?" I asked.

"He's getting some impressions. He thinks he'll have something actionable by tonight."

"Well, I don't want to mess up anything," I said, fighting to keep the bitterness out of my voice, "but Becky gave me a location where Quinton might be."

"Where?"

"An old trawler docked in Red Hook. He's talked in the past about crashing there." I paused. "I'd be happy to—"

"What are you going to be doing?" she cut in. She'd known what I'd been about to say, and she didn't want to have to tell me no again. I recognized the kindness and chose not to push it.

"Well, changing clothes for one. Otherwise, eating, resting, probably restocking some spell items and potions." My heart sank as I thought about my mother's emo ball, lost for good. "You know, generally putting myself back together. I'll be here or with my pager. If you need anything, or if I can help in any way, just let me know."

"I will," she said. "I've gotta go."

"Okay. Stay safe."

I hung up feeling about as useful as a chewed-up tennis ball. I took advantage of the empty bathroom to shower and brush my teeth. When I came out, Becky and Tabitha were snipping at each other again. Gretchen banged on the wall and shouted, "Some of us are trying to sleep!"

"Gee, wouldn't want to disturb *that*," Becky shot back.

"Oh, Everson!" Gretchen called. "Order wants you off the case."

"Yeah. Thanks." I had to get out of here.

"Training at five!" Gretchen added.

Whatever.

"Hey, where are you going?" Becky asked when she saw me grabbing my cane.

"To think," I said.

I WALKED OVER TO TWO STORY COFFEE, ORDERED A LARGE Colombian roast, and retired to my favorite corner chair. The West Village coffee house was about half full, but the sounds of conversation and brewing drinks formed a pleasant wall of noise that was conducive to rumination.

As I took a sip and sat back in the soft chair, it occurred to me that I hadn't come here in over a year. With all the extra hours of self-practice, I hadn't had time. Being here now felt a little strange, as if I'd forgotten how to just sit still and think. Indeed, my brain was telling me to read, practice, do affirmations—*something*.

I set the warm coffee cup on my knee, let my eyelids slip to half mast, and tried to settle into the act of thinking. Something was still niggling at the back of my brain, telling me we were all missing something crucial.

I started at the beginning, with the theater attack.

When I'd asked the smoke golem who he was, he'd replied, *You're going to come to know me quite well in the coming days*. And when I asked what he wanted: *In good time, my friend. In good time.*

His voice had been teasing, goading.

Then in Mr. Han's Apothecary: *Careful, wizard. You're putting your nose where it doesn't belong.*

More goading. Like he wanted me to chase him, to nip at his heels.

What about the infernal bag I'd cast a reveal spell on? If the demon was powerful enough to break Thelonious without even trying, would he have allowed me a glimpse of the Ark? Because more than just powerful, the demon sounded intelligent and cunning.

I went back over how I'd discovered the identities of the Ark members. It had started with Becky.

I pictured her placing the infernal bag in the brick wall at the movie house. Revenge, as even she had claimed? Or had Damien compelled her to put the bag there, knowing she'd become a suspect in that first attack? Damien had been possessing her, after all. If it was so important the bags be randomly placed, he should have been able to stop her.

Same thing with Quinton visiting her apartment when the police and I were still there. Coincidence or more manipulation?

Now that I was posing these sorts of questions, I found myself going back even further. Such as why Quinton had made the large purchase of devil's ear at Mr. Han's in the first place—and then paid him to remain silent, ensuring the encounter would stand out in Mr. Han's memory. Last night Thelonious said he had told the demon everything. If Thelonious had access to my memories, he would have known that I'd gone to Mr. Han in the past for info.

Had Damien been planting clues for me to follow?

My rational mind resisted the idea, given how many things would have to have gone exactly right—but who knew how many clues were out there? Damien had only needed us to stumble on so many. And look where the demon had held last night's induction ceremony: in the exact same place as the previous one, even after knowing Becky had talked to me.

Powerful demons weren't that sloppy.

I opened my eyes at the same time my pager went off. Vega.

I carried my coffee outside to the closest payphone and called her.

"Hey," she said. "Just wanted to let you know your lead to Red Hook was a good one. We found evidence that Quinton spent last night on one of the boats and then cleared out quickly. He's probably still in the area. We've set up a perimeter while Pierce works on pinpointing him."

"That's great," I said, but without much conviction.

Vega didn't catch it. "Good work. I'll keep you posted."

Though she was using her detective voice, I could tell she felt bad I'd been sidelined. She wanted to include me some-how, even if just through updates. I almost stopped her to share what I'd been thinking—that Damien had wanted us to find and track down the Ark—but I didn't. One, it was more hunch than hard evidence. And two, I still hadn't figured out why.

While switching my phone and coffee hands, I fumbled the cup. The top popped off, and coffee splashed over the front of my coat.

"Crap."

"What was that?" Vega asked.

"Nothing. Just be careful. Demons are … unpredictable."

"Thanks, Everson. I will."

I remained standing by the phone after we'd hung up, coffee dripping from the hem of my coat. But I wasn't thinking about that. If Damien was leading us down a path of his choosing, he had a reason. Was it misdirection, or was my involvement important to his plans somehow? After all, when he'd tortured Thelonious, it hadn't been for information about Pierce.

Pierce...

Why hadn't his divination magic picked up anything on the duplicity? Or had it, and he was using the excuse of my magic interfering as a reason not to tell anyone? And what had he meant when he'd told Vega that I had a role?

Even though the Order had vetted the man, and even though he'd saved my life last night, I found myself growing suspicious again. I mean, he'd dropped in on the case out of practically nowhere and now seemed determined to control it.

I shook my head. I didn't know what to think. The case felt more tangled now than ever.

I needed my own diviner. Unfortunately, the only one in the city I had ever trusted, Lady Bastet, had been murdered by Lich to keep me from discovering the truth about my mother. The Yellow Pages had a long listing of oracles, sooth-sayers, and diviners, but ninety-nine percent of them were fakes. The challenge would be finding the one percent who weren't.

"Wait a minute," I muttered.

I picked up the phone, dropped in another fifty cents, and called the mayor's office. After going through concentric layers of secretaries and assistants, Budge's voice came on.

"Everson," he said. "What the hell's happening to my city? Your partner's telling me we've got a demon?"

"Well, yeah, but the demon isn't *here* here. He's been working through spell bags and innocent vessels."

"And claiming a helluva lot of New Yorkers! You know about the museum, right?"

"Detective Vega just told me. She thinks they're closing in on the final person under the demon's control."

"And that'll take care of this thing?"

"I think so."

"You *think so*? Unh-uh, Everson. Think doesn't cut it. We could be hosting the World Series next month, not to mention that the developer is already asking for more guarantees."

"Well, I'm not technically on the case."

"What? Of course you are."

I didn't want to get into the whole thing about Pierce's divination magic and the Order's mandate that I sit the rest of this one out. That's not why I'd called him.

"Hey, listen," I said. "I need a favor. Something that might help wrap this up. A year or so ago, you told me about a diviner in Chinatown. Someone you consulted to get background info on your late wife and her daughter."

"Yeah, Jing-Sheng. What about him?"

"Do you know where I can find him?"

"Jing's in an apartment on Grand and Eldridge. He's got a big Yankees sticker on the window. Can't miss it. Been a while since I last saw him, though. And he was already getting on in years."

"Was he good?"

"When you could get him to stop talking baseball."

24

A short subway ride later, and I was in Chinatown. I kept an eye out for Bashi's White Hand enforcers as I navigated the bustling sidewalks. Two blocks from Mr. Han's Apothecary, I found the apartment with the big Yankees sticker on the second-story window.

I climbed a narrow flight of stairs, slid my cane through my coat strap, and knocked on the door. An old Asian woman whose head barely came to my waist answered and squinted up at me.

"Yes, I'm here to consult Jing-Sheng?"

She nodded as if she'd been expecting me. "Yes, Jing here. Twenty dollar for fifteen minute."

The woman, who I assumed to be his wife, apparently handled the business end of their esoteric practice. I liked her efficiency. I opened my wallet, then stopped. "How long is a typical session?"

"Thirty minute."

She took my two twenties and guided me through a neat living room to a closed door. She knocked and said something in rapid Mandarin. As we waited for Jing to answer, I caught myself wondering: If Damien *had* set something up, would he have anticipated this move too?

That was the problem with that line of thinking. The paranoia never ended.

The old woman knocked more sharply. Jing barked back in what sounded like irritation. The old woman smiled up at me and opened the door. Expecting to see a shrine room of some kind, Jing seated at a pillow with tendrils of incense curling up on either side of him, I was surprised to find him seated at a regular desk, wearing a blue and white striped baseball cap backwards.

The old man was hunched over a rectangle of paper, pencil in hand, muttering to himself. A scrying scroll? But when I stepped further into the dim space, I saw it was a stat sheet for a baseball game.

The walls were covered in similar stat sheets, thousands of them. And lines had been drawn over them, connecting a number on one sheet to numbers on others, forming a mind-boggling web. It looked like the work of either a brilliant mind or someone fit for a straitjacket.

The woman closed the door behind me, prompting Jing to look up. Wispy hair fell from beneath his cap to frame a wrinkled, whiskered face. His eyes stared, unblinking, like a pair of black marbles.

"Yes," I said. "The mayor referred me to you. I was wondering if you could help me." On the way here, I'd considered what questions I would ask. With divination, it was best to keep it simple. I needed to know Damien's true identity, one. And then, two, what his ultimate plan was. Were we on the verge of stopping him, or just playing into his hands?

Jing pointed past me. "Get out."

I looked behind me and then back at him. "I'm sorry?"

"Yes, I'm talking to you, stretch," he said with almost no accent. "Get out."

"But I paid for a half hour."

"I don't care. Take your money and go."

"Can I ask why?"

"Black luck."

"Black luck?"

He pointed at the crotch of my coat. "How did that happen?"

I looked down in confusion before remembering the accident at the payphone. "Oh. I, um, spilled my coffee earlier."

"And that?" He switched his aim to a tarry black streak higher up my coat.

"I got caught in the subway doors when I was trying to get on. When I was trying to get off too, actually." That had seemed a little unusual. Almost like a replay of the day before when everything that could go wrong had: the falls, a back-firing invocation, the trouble in the elevator.

"And what's that smell?"

"Oh, an encumbering potion broke in my pocket." Thankfully I hadn't activated it.

Jing opened a desk drawer and took out an old pair of dice that looked like they'd been carved from bone. "Roll," he ordered.

I shook the dice and then dropped them onto his stat sheet.

"Snake eyes," Jing said, eyeing the two ones. "Roll eleven more times."

I did as he said, Jing jotting down the rolls on a scrap of paper.

When I finished, he moved his pencil across the numbers.

"You rolled snake eyes six times. Do you know the statistical probability?"

"Not off the top of my head."

"One in a fuck load."

"What does that mean?"

"Black luck," he repeated.

"Right, I got that part. *Why* do I have black luck?"

"I don't know, but I don't want it in here. Not with the Yankees playing tonight."

"Can we do this in the living room, then?"

"No. We can do it nowhere." He stood and came around his desk. But rather than physically escort me to the door, he made shooing gestures with his hands. He didn't want to touch me.

"Look, I'll leave as soon as you tell me how I got this."

"Leave *now*," he said, making little lunging motions at me. Under different circumstances it would have been comical, given the man's advanced age and that he was shorter than his wife.

"When can I come back?"

"When the black luck is gone."

That wasn't going to work. "I'll pay you double."

He shook his head and then, seeing I wasn't moving, grabbed a Louisville Slugger from beside his desk and rotated it like a batter at the plate. His eyes narrowed toward my head.

"You're not serious," I said.

The swing arrived slowly, but when I tried to skip back, my coat snagged on the corner of his desk. The weak blow thumped against my ear. More frustrated than hurt, I took the end of the bat and twisted it from his hands. He drew back.

"I'm not going to hurt you," I said. "But so help me God, I'll smear my black luck over you and every last stat sheet in here if you don't give me the divination session I paid for."

"I can't," he said. "The black luck would interfere."

I stopped and thought about that. Was that what was messing with Pierce's divination magic? Not my own magic, but the black luck Jing kept referring to?

"Fine. Then how do I get rid of it?"

Jing moved back around his desk, watching me warily. "When did the bad luck start?" he asked.

"Yesterday afternoon. But it went away again until last night."

"That's how black luck works. Come and go, like the tide. But every time it returns, it's stronger than before."

"Could it have anything to do with drinking an expired potion?"

"No, Black luck doesn't come from a potion. It comes from direct magic."

"Demon magic, maybe?"

"Maybe. But yours is from faerie magic."

"Faerie…" My voice trailed off.

Gretchen. When I said I no longer wanted to rely on my luck quotient, she'd had me close my eyes. I hadn't felt anything, but had she tried to cancel my luck quotient and screwed it up? That had been right before I'd prepared the potion, making me think *that* had been the culprit. The falls and mishaps that had followed … Vega's exploding phone…

"I don't believe this," I muttered.

"Whoever put it on you will have to take it off."

"Oh, don't worry," I said. "She's taking it off."

"But it must be fast. It's usually the third time the luck comes back that it kills you."

"Kills me?"

"Statistically speaking. Definitely by the fourth."

Great. I started to set the bat against his desk, but Jing waved his hands frantically.

"No, no, it has the black luck now! You have to take it!"

Thinking of Gretchen, I said, "Good. I might need it."

MY JOURNEY BACK TO THE WEST VILLAGE WAS EVEN MORE fraught than the one to Chinatown. I had just stepped from Jing-Sheng's apartment when a gang of White Hand enforcers spotted me. They chased me for two blocks before I stumbled over a construction barricade in the middle of the street and fell down a manhole. Only a last second force invocation spared me a cracked skull or broken neck. I ducked into a side tunnel as the enforcers began shooting down into the darkness, all of the ricocheting bullets seeming to spark off my shield.

I had no choice but to swallow my phobia and crawl through the tunnels. In the darkness, I was threatened by rats and moaned at by passing soul eaters. I wiped out twice while trying to climb a rebar ladder to the surface. I was replacing the manhole cover when the same gang of enforcers spotted me again. I managed to flag down a cab, but the Waristani driver misunderstood me and started driving *back* toward the enforcers.

A shield invocation followed by a wrestling match for control of the steering wheel eventually got us out of there in one piece, but holy hell. Jing hadn't been kidding about the black luck getting worse with each recurrence.

By the time I stepped over my threshold, I was shaking with anger and adrenaline.

"There you are," Gretchen called from the kitchen. "Did you forget about your training?"

I stalked toward her. She looked up from the stove, where she had something cooking on all four burners. "What in the heck happened to you? You look like something your cat dragged in. Speaking of which, Tabitha ran onto the ledge when I came out to cook. Not sure what that was all about. Oh, and I let Becky use the bedroom. Have to keep the peace around here someho—"

"You," I interrupted. "You happened to me."

"And what's that supposed to mean?"

"Yesterday when you had me close my eyes, what did you do?"

"When I had you close your eyes..." she said, as though thinking back. She slurped something off her thumb.

"During our *training*?" I prompted.

"Oh, right. I neutralized your luck quotient. Like you asked."

"No. You went a little further than that. You gave me black luck."

"Well, gee whiz. You make it sound like we had a romp in the sack without protection."

I was too angry to recoil at the image. "So you knew?"

"Of course I knew." She stirred whatever was bubbling in the big pot. "The fastest way to neutralize a luck quotient is with a dose of black luck. There are other methods, of course, but they're a colossal bore. Not to mention they take a long time. And you were itching to go."

I couldn't believe what I was hearing.

"I almost died just now," I said, my voice trembling with

rage. "Multiple times. I'm on my third cycle of black luck. If this one doesn't kill me, the next one will."

Statistically speaking, I heard Jing saying.

"All right," Gretchen sighed, wiping her hands on the front of her dress and twisting the burners to low. "Let's have a look at you." She came around the kitchen counter and squinted me over. She muttered a few times before shaking her head in a way that said, *Well, I'll be damned.*

"What?"

"I don't know what to tell you, Everson. Wow. I had no idea it would take off like that. You're right. You've got a raging case of black luck. One of the worst I've ever seen."

"You're kidding, right?"

"I'm afraid not."

"Brilliant. Can you take it off me now?"

She blew out her breath, hitting me in the face with a wave of onions and garlic. "It's not that easy."

"What do you mean, 'not that easy'? You put it on me, you're taking it off."

"Oh crap!" she cried and hustled back into the kitchen. She opened the oven, releasing a cloud of smoke. Using an oven mitt, she pulled out a burnt soufflé of some kind, frowned over it, and then wedged it, still smoking, into the crowded sink. "So much for that," she muttered.

I clapped my hands sharply. "Hey!"

"Right, right, the black luck," she said, coming back. "Well, here's the thing. Once it's in your system, it's in your system. I'm talking down to your individual cells. I could try to muck it out, sure, but I wouldn't be able to get it all. And if I can't, there's really no point. You either have black luck or you don't. It's like the plague. Nobody gets a touch of the plague."

"So, what, I'm stuck with this?"

"Well, there are a couple ways we can go about this. The first is that I prepare a bathtub full of stasis potion, and we immerse you in it."

"And that will cure me?"

"No, but it will keep anything from happening to you until the black luck runs its course."

"And how long will that take?"

She shrugged. "A month? Maybe two?"

I stared at her. "I'd have to—to lie in my *bathtub* for two months because of your screw up?" I was so angry, I could hardly get the words out. Definitely a good thing I'd lost Jing's baseball bat in the storm drains.

"I said that was *one* option."

"Forget it. What's the other one?"

"Well, animate forces need energy to sustain themselves, right? Black luck is no different. You starve it, boom, it dies." I opened my mouth, but she beat me to the question. "What does it feed off of? Well, what is black luck? It's the worst of all outcomes in a given moment. Notice I didn't say *every* moment." She muttered as though making an aside, "Though it does come to fill more and more of them until you really *can't* do anything else but die." She shook her head quickly. "The point is that outcomes are subjective. Have you ever heard the saying 'One person's shit is another person's Shinola'?"

"I think you're mixing up sayings."

"Subjective," Gretchen repeated. "So in order to choose the worst outcome, the black luck has to *know* what you consider to be bad. And where does the black luck get that information?"

"The internet."

She slapped my forehead. "Your unconscious doubts and uncertainties."

"Oh great. Let me just call my psychotherapist. He has the perfect couch."

"You're right to be a smartass. That would take years, and you'd definitely be dead by then."

"I'm glad you keep reminding me. So a bath for two months or therapy until a piano falls on my head. Are those really the two options you're giving me?" I held up a hand before she could answer. "Forget it. I'm calling the Order. You never should have been assigned to me, you have no idea what you're doing, you've been a disaster from the moment you got here, and now this." I gave an incredulous laugh. "It's like someone needing heart surgery and being sent a mortician. *Lich* was a better trainer than you."

"They won't recall me," Gretchen said.

"Wanna bet?" I strode toward the phone.

"Anyway, none of the others command fae magic. They can't cure you."

I was about to tell her what she could do with her fae magic when my shoe caught the folded corner of the rug. I fell face first against the phone, then landed on the floor. The phone tumbled over me with a clang. As I thrashed to get up, I became entangled in the phone cable such that one of the loops wrapped my throat and threatened to cut off my air. Gretchen looked on thoughtfully.

By the time I managed to get the phone to my ear, there was no dial tone.

"You pulled the entire apparatus out of the wall," Gretchen observed.

I slammed the phone down as hard as my entangled arm would allow.

"Hold still," she said, waving a hand. A force that could just as easily have strangled me removed the coils of cord from around my body, set the phone back on the counter, and placed me on my feet.

"I'll fix your phone so you can call the Order, but at least let me finish what I was saying."

I looked at the fractured phone jack and wires spilling from the wall and sighed. I started to nod for her to continue, then stopped, afraid that even that bit of head motion could trigger another catastrophe.

"Fine," I said.

"You *could* try to address your doubts and uncertainties, but there's a short cut."

"Which is...?"

"Closing the loops."

"All right. How do I do that?"

"It confuses the black luck, shorts it out."

"How the hell do I do that?" I shouted.

"Sheesh. *Someone* needs a nap. Are there any open obligations hanging over you? You know, things you were asked to do or that you should have taken care of that you haven't."

"Besides wrapping up the case?"

"Yes, but that's out of your hands now. Anything else?"

I looked to make sure she was being serious before thinking back. "Well, there was this woman up in Harlem who summoned some nether creatures. I destroyed four of them, was planning to go back and banish the fifth, but now the Order says they're harmless. So I guess that wouldn't count. Well, except that I lied and told her the others got out and that I'd try to find them—"

Gretchen, who had been squinting at me, snapped her fingers suddenly. "Yes, that's an open loop!"

"Huh? Are you saying that if I go back and level with her, I'll be cured of the black luck?"

"Don't be stupid, that's just one loop. There are..." She squinted at me some more. "Three," she said finally. "Yes, three that need closing."

"What are the other two?"

"You tell me."

"I'm not playing that game again."

She shrugged. "Your choice. But you should probably think it over on your way to Harlem. The third cycle of black luck is winding down, and you'll want to close the loops before the fourth arrives."

"You mean the one that kills me?"

"You might make it to a fifth," she said doubtfully. "But *don't* open any more loops, whatever you do."

"Why three loops?"

"It's one of those crazy fae things." Gretchen snorted a laugh. "Don't you just love them?"

"No," I growled.

25

Twenty minutes later, I was sitting in the back of a cab bound for Harlem, my head on a swivel. At every inter-section, I expected a city bus to run a red light and plow into us. I hadn't even risked changing clothes back at the apart-ment for fear I'd choke on my shirt collar or trip and break a hip. The polyester was starting to itch.

The driver watched me nervously in the rearview mirror as my eyes darted around and I scratched inside my coat like a junkie.

It wasn't until we crossed into the one hundreds that I started to relax a little. It seemed Gretchen was right. The third cycle of black luck was going back out like the tide. But though I'd escaped it in one piece, it had been worse than the first two. I hoped to hell I wouldn't have to deal with a fourth.

At Mae's apartment, I took the stairs to be safe and arrived in front of her battered door. I took a deep breath—I was *not* looking forward to this—and knocked loudly enough for her to hear. As I waited, it seemed impossible that I'd only been here a couple of days earlier. So much had happened since:

demonic attacks, a new wizard in town, Gretchen's arrival, the Ark, getting kicked off the case, and now black luck and *loops* that needed closing.

"You said you wanted a challenge," I muttered.

In fairness, I'd wanted to test myself, to see how far I'd come in the past year. And, yeah, to start becoming the mage my father had been. I'd fallen short, but I wasn't out of the game. Not entirely. While Pierce and Vega tracked down Quinton, I would work on ridding myself of the black luck so I could go back to Jing-Sheng and find out whether my hunch about Damien was in the ballpark.

The knob turned, and Mae's glasses flashed in the cracked-open door. "Oh," she said. "You."

"Can I come in and talk?"

"You didn't find them, did you." It wasn't a question.

"That's sort of what I wanted to talk about."

She grunted and opened the door wide enough for me to enter. As I crossed the threshold, she backed up her walker, then turned and made her way down the hallway toward her kitchen. Buster, who had been hanging back in the shadows, let out a little screech and waved his claws at me. He scuttled backwards, just behind Mae's slippered feet.

In the kitchen, Mae gestured for me to take a seat at the table as she shuffled over to her coffee maker. When Buster climbed the back of her house dress and perched on her shoulder, she hardly seemed to notice. I recognized her silence and general lethargy as depression.

She missed her babies.

"You don't need to make me coffee," I told her.

She let the paper filter fall to the floor as she turned back toward me.

"Mae, listen. I came here to apologize. When I was here the other day, I wasn't entirely truthful with you."

She took the seat opposite me and gave me a tired look that said, *Let's hear it.*

"Since becoming a wizard, my main job has been to track down creatures that don't belong here. Creatures from other dimensions. It's complicated, but small holes can lead to big holes, and the bigger the hole, the bigger the creature that can squeeze through. You've heard of demons. Well, that's how they gain entrance—through breaches. I came to your apartment on Friday because my alarm detected a breach. I didn't know the situation, didn't realize you were keeping them as pets. Like good pets, they tried to protect you."

"So they didn't escape?"

"No," I confessed. "They stayed inside, and I ... well, I banished them."

I expected her to break down or to go for the rolling pin, or both, but instead, a strange light came over her face. And then she did begin to tear up, but not from sadness. Her lips broke into a smile.

"What?" I said.

"If you banished them, they're back where they came from, right? I can just call them up again."

"I incinerated your spell book."

Her smile fractured. "You did *what?*"

"That's the other part of my job: keeping powerful spell books out of the hands of, well, amateurs. You said it yourself —the conjuring spell was supposed to call up a god, right? Instead, you ended up with critters like Buster."

The clawdad wriggled his tendrils and chattered as though sensing he'd just been insulted.

"So that's it, then," Mae said hollowly. "I can't cast anymore."

"On the positive side, I talked to my Order. They said you can keep Buster." Claudius hadn't actually said that, but if they'd been all right with Pierce canceling the alarm, I didn't see the harm.

She scratched Buster's head absently, then folded her hands on the table.

"I should have leveled with you from the get go, Mae. I'm sorry. If I can do—"

"You can," she said, looking up at me.

"Sure, anything. Well, within reason."

"Next time you're called to something, take me with you."

"Come again?"

"When you were last here, we talked about being partners. Well, I want to take you up on that."

"*You* talked about being partners, actually."

"I'm good with these critters. I can help you."

"There's no way I'm putting you in that kind of danger."

"Everson, listen to me and listen good. I'm an old lady in poor health. I've got maybe a year left, two if I'm lucky. Everything I held dear is gone. Well, except for this little guy. I'd rather meet my maker helping people than wasting away in this crappy rent control. I don't care about the danger."

"Mae, I'm sorry, but—"

She rose part way from her chair, the fat on her arms trembling. "You owe me, Croft. And I'm not going to let it go until you say *yes*."

I remembered what Gretchen had said about not opening any more loops. Would denying Mae fall into that category? I couldn't afford to take any chances, and Mae sort of had a point. I showed her my hands.

"All right. But it will be an assignment of my choosing."

She shook her head emphatically. "You'll use that as an excuse to never bring me along."

Crap, she had me. "All right ... the next one."

As I said it, I felt something change, as though a weight I hadn't known I'd been carrying had lifted.

Loop closed?

I stood up before I could do anything to open the loop again. Mae stood with me and gave me a big hug. "God bless you, Everson Croft. I won't let you down. I promise." Sensing I was an ally now, Buster inched across her shoulders to my side and gave my head a shy pat.

"I'll be in touch," I assured Mae.

Only this time I had to mean it.

26

I t was early evening when I left Mae's apartment and emerged onto the street. I looked around as though I might spot the two remaining loops. Obligations hanging over me? There had been Vega's and my talk at dinner the other night about needing to prove my commitment to the relationship. But that felt too big, not something I could close this evening, especially with her working.

I wondered if they'd captured Quinton yet. I checked my pager, but there were no alerts. I walked until I found a payphone and called my voicemail. The one message began with a throat-clearing, followed by, "Ah, yes, I'm trying to get in touch with Everson Croft. This is Winston Snodgrass."

Professor Snodgrass?

"I'm the chairman of his department at Midtown College," the message continued. Apparently he didn't realize I lived alone. "He was supposed to contact me this weekend about something we'd discussed on Friday, and I haven't heard from him. I would like him to call me at his earliest convenience. It's, um, well it's become more urgent."

He left his number, made a sound like he was going to say something more, and then hung up.

I'd blown Snodgrass off so completely on Friday that I had actually forgotten about our conversation. Something about a cable problem upsetting his wife's schedule. An energy expert had attributed the problem to an imbalance of ley energy—which did sound like utter horse crap—and Snodgrass's wife had wanted me to take a look to see if my special skills could fix it.

Snodgrass had even offered to pay me two hundred bucks.

I'd laughed then, but I wasn't laughing now. Because the more I thought about it, the more it seemed to meet the requirements of another open loop: something I'd been asked to do or that I should have taken care of that I hadn't. More than that, it resonated on a gut level. I nodded to myself as I dropped some more change into the phone and punched his number.

"Yes, hello?" he answered.

"Snodgrass, it's Everson. I got your mess—"

"Can you come over?" he asked before I'd even finished.

"That's what I'm calling about. Yeah, I should have some time this evening."

"How about now, then? You can, ah, join us for dinner."

"Okay..." I said, still not used to this side of him.

"Great, let me give you the address." Once I'd jotted it down, he said, "Be here in twenty minutes. No later."

I hung up feeling a little disoriented.

Who was this man?

THE SNODGRASSES LIVED AT THE END OF A ROW OF LARGE townhouses in the one affluent—and highly guarded—neighborhood in the Bronx. As I got out of the cab I could see the halo of Yankee Stadium several blocks away. The main thoroughfares had been crowded with game-night traffic.

I was reaching for the handle of an iron gate when a buzz sounded and the lock clicked open. I passed the gate, walked along a manicured garden, and climbed the steps. Snodgrass met me at the door. He was dressed in a formal blue suit with a crest on the pocket. Throw in his short stature and wet, parted hair, and he looked like a boy being sent off to an English boarding school.

"You made it," he said, a little out of breath. "Here let me take your coat."

"I'll be more comfortable with it on, actually," I said, trying to keep my bellbottoms out of view.

"Is that him?" a loud voice called from farther back in the house.

"Yes, Miriam," Snodgrass called back, his voice meek in comparison.

Was that his wife?

"Well, show him in."

"Here, this way." Snodgrass walked quickly ahead of me.

I followed him down an affluent corridor into a large sitting room with antique furniture, dark oil paintings, and a stone fireplace. A tall woman was there, her white hair in a powerful coif. Pearls hung around the front of her black and tan dress. She was sipping wine from a stem glass, but she put it down upon seeing us and rose from her chair.

"You must be Everson," she said, offering her hand, her wrist bent in the manner of the wealthy.

"I am," I said, taking it. "It's good to meet you."

"And it's so good to finally meet you."

She had the voice of the socially powerful. In fact everything about her was powerful, from her large-boned frame to her bearing. I looked from her to Snodgrass and back. This was the woman he'd called *weak*?

"For heaven's sake, Winston. Offer Everson a seat."

"How about this one?" He waited for his wife's approval before showing me to the chair beside hers.

"And some wine?" she said.

"Oh, ah, would you like white or red, Everson?"

"I'll have what Miriam is having," I replied, which made her smile.

Snodgrass poured the glass at a small bar beside the window, handed it to me, and then took a seat on my other side as if hoping to use me as a shield. I'd never seen him behave so timidly.

"You're not having any?" I asked him.

He opened his mouth, but his wife answered for him. "We had to put a stop to his drinking years ago. Not that he was abusing it, Everson, but he would just become so *emotional*."

"Miriam, I don't think Everson—"

"Fits of crying, even at social engagements. Can you imagine? He had no control over himself."

"Is that so?" I had to fight from grinning.

Snodgrass looked down at his fidgeting hands.

"Oh, I don't allow him to go anywhere where there's going to be alcohol. It's why you don't see him at the faculty functions. Here is fine. He doesn't feel compelled. But out there..." She lowered her voice to a whisper, even though her husband could still hear her. "I think it's the social pressure."

"Probably," I agreed and took another sip.

This was turning out to be more fun than I'd thought.

"So, Everson," Miriam said with a smiling sigh. "I read all about your contributions to the mayor's eradication program last year. So impressive. And to learn you're an associate of Winston's." She shook her head in disbelief. "Well, not only that, but a friend!"

I almost choked on my wine. *Friend?*

"You can imagine my surprise when he told me, especially since I wasn't aware he had any friends at the college. Academics and their petty backbiting." She rolled her eyes at me as though that sort of thing was beneath us. "But Winston tells me you're a professor of ancient mythology?"

"Yes." I paused to cough. "Tenured as of last year, in fact."

"Oh, good. History can be such a dry topic. It's wonderful the students have something more imaginative to engage them. I just love mythology. Those stories endure for a reason, you know."

"I couldn't agree more." I grinned over at Snodgrass, but he was still making every effort to avoid eye contact.

"Miriam," he ventured, "if dinner's still going to be awhile, perhaps Everson can take a look at the problem now?"

"Really, Winston. Is that any way to treat a guest? There will be plenty of time after dinner."

At mention of dinner, my stomach rumbled. I'd had nothing to eat since my one p.m. breakfast at Vega's. Their chef appeared a moment later to announce the meal was ready, and we proceeded into the next room.

The four-course meal was top notch. Miriam talked the whole time, mostly about herself, which was fine. I knew the type: socially gracious but wholly self-absorbed. I was content to eat while she went on about her various causes and societies. For his part, Snodgrass picked at his food and said nothing unless prompted, and then as little as possible.

"So, I understand Winston told you about our cable snafu," Miriam said as I was polishing off dessert: a fat square of tiramisu and an espresso. She snorted. "He tried to fix it himself, which only made the problem worse, I'm afraid. In any case, someone in your line of work suggested the problem involved the ley energy in the vicinity of the cable box."

"I'd be happy to take a look," I said, setting my desert fork down.

"Oh, that would be wonderful. Winston, could you...?" she gestured for him to show me.

He got up and led me through a mudroom and out a back door.

When we were alone, I said, "I have to tell you, Snodgrass, that was delightful."

He ignored the comment and snapped on a floodlight, illuminating the side of the house.

"It's over there," he said, pointing to the cable box.

"I'll get right on it ... *friend*."

He grunted. "Miriam hears what she wants to hear."

"Sure you weren't trying to impress her?"

"How long will this take?"

"As long as it needs to."

But I had to hurry. The visit was already going on an hour plus, and I was only on the second loop. The black luck could roll back in at any moment. Opening my wizard's senses, I squatted in front of the cable box.

"Huh," I said.

"What?"

The line of ley energy, which should normally have been running along the street—path of least resistance—was bending into the Snodgrass's yard, right over the cable box.

Ley energy and electronics usually coexisted more or less peacefully, but warped like this, the line was causing problems.

"*What?*" Snodgrass repeated.

"Shh," I said.

I followed the bulging line along the side yard, through a gate that Snodgrass unlocked, and out into the street. The deviation wasn't huge, and the ley line not particularly strong, but it was strong enough. I wondered how many other households were experiencing glitches with this or that.

Returning to the cable box, I said, "I've found the issue."

"Can you fix it?" Snodgrass asked a little too anxiously.

By now, it was clear what was going on. As high and mighty as Snodgrass acted at the college, he was scared shitless of his wife. That explained his desperation on Friday as well as tonight.

"I think so. Is that your bedroom up there?"

He followed my pointed finger to the second-story window and nodded.

"Okay, I want you to go up and turn on the TV. When the picture clears, let me know."

He nodded again and ran inside.

Poor bastard, I thought and closed my eyes. A moment later, I was aligned with the ley line. I summoned a small force invocation from my cane and walked the line out to the street. I could feel that it didn't want to stay put, though.

Digging into a pocket, I pulled out my tube of copper filings. At the edge of the front garden, I made a hole with the end of my cane and poured some of the filings inside. With a chant, I imbued the copper with just enough energy to repel the ley line. Slowly releasing the force invocation, I stepped back. The ley line remained in the street.

It was still warped, but it no longer ran through the Snod-grass's yard or cable box. When I had more time, I'd come back and figure out the source of the issue. It was Pierce's turf, technically, and I wondered if the wayward line had anything to do with the work he'd been doing in the boroughs.

As I was burying the copper, a knock sounded from the upstairs window. Cast in television glow, Snodgrass was waving and giving me a thumbs up.

I waited to see whether I'd closed a second loop or just wasted the last hour. A moment later, the same feeling of lightness came over me that I'd experienced at Mae's. It had worked.

Hell, yes.

27

"You *must* come again," Miriam said at the open front door, seizing my hand a final time and kissing both of my cheeks. She was overjoyed the cable had been restored—and in time for *their* evening show. Apparently Snodgrass enjoyed the regency romance serial too.

"I'd really like that," I replied. "I had a wonderful time."

"How about next month, then? I'll have Winston give you a date and time."

I smiled past her at my chairman. "Perfect."

Snodgrass mumbled something about yes, that being very nice, but it was getting late. As desperate as he'd been for me to come, he was even more desperate now that I leave.

I bade them goodnight. There was no need to make the man suffer more than he already had. But that didn't mean he was off the hook for the two hundred. As his wife turned, I made the money gesture with the thumb and first two fingers of my right hand. Snodgrass nodded quickly and closed the door. Beyond, I could hear Miriam scolding him for slamming it.

I passed through the gate and was almost to the cab Miriam had called for me when my pager went off. Vega. I directed the driver to the nearest payphone and had him idle while I made the call.

"What's up?" I asked when she answered.

"A couple of updates. Pierce located the final bag and it's been neutralized."

"That's great," I said, meaning it. There had been too many innocent deaths.

"But he's still working on Quinton's location. His painting is telling him Red Hook, and we have the neighborhood surrounded, so it should only be a matter of time before we have him and the necklace. What are you up to?"

"Tying up some loose ends. Don't worry, nothing related to the case." I'd decided to spare her the song and dance about my black luck. It would take too long to explain and she had enough on her plate.

"Is it something you can step away from for a few minutes?"

I hadn't identified a third loop yet, and time was running out. "What do you need?"

"Well, something came up on Pierce's painting that might have to do with you. I think it's what he was talking about yesterday. Anyway, he was wondering if he could discuss it with you."

"That wouldn't be considered *interfering*?" I asked, allowing some bitterness to enter my tone now.

"You said you wanted to help," she reminded me.

Vega was right, and maybe, just maybe, this qualified as a loop.

"Does he want me to call him?"

"He'd prefer to talk to you at his place. He said he could send a car."

I paused, my suspicions from earlier rising inside me. Pierce showing up out of the blue, the way he'd meddled with my alarm system, his claim that my magic was interfering with his divination, reporting me to the Order. And now he wanted to talk at his place one on one? If Damien was running some kind of backdoor play, he would need someone up here to help execute it.

Yeah, but the Order vetted him, I reminded myself.

Then again, the Order had also sent me Gretchen.

"Did you hear me?" Vega prompted.

But damned if this didn't feel like a third loop. And time was running out. Once the next cycle rolled in, my only option would be to run home and soak in a stasis potion, assuming I made it there.

"Ah, sure," I said. "But I've got a cab. Tell Pierce I'll be there in fifteen."

"Thanks, Everson. I know this isn't easy for you."

You have no idea, I thought.

"Let me know what you find," she said.

"I will." I thought about telling Vega to exercise caution with Pierce, but if anything happened to me, she would know where I'd gone. She would exercise that caution as a matter of instinct and training. *Love you,* I almost added. It wasn't a term we'd used yet, but it had never felt more natural to say.

Instead, I said, "Talk to you soon."

Climbing back into the cab, I hit my head on the doorway hard enough to see stars. A lifetime spent getting in and out of cabs, and I'd never given myself a partial concussion like that.

Which suggested the next cycle was rolling in.

I ARRIVED AT PIERCE'S ON FOOT AFTER A CAR REAR-ENDED MY cab at a light. Knowing it could have been worse, I paid the shouting cabbie and walked the remaining two blocks wary of every variable around me, moving or static. I still managed to almost get run over by a garbage truck backing from an alleyway at full speed.

Pierce's assistant met me at the door. I tried to read her cold eyes and set jaw. Displeasure at Pierce? Then I remembered how I'd spoken to her on the phone the last couple of times I'd called.

"Pierce is in the studio," Sora said. "This way."

I managed to keep my feet as I followed her down the corridor, but I did knock down a painting when we turned a corner. She frowned at me over a shoulder.

"Sorry," I mumbled.

At last we descended a staircase and entered a large basement room that had been converted into an art studio. Paintings of all sizes and in various states of completion leaned against the walls. Across from me was an especially long painting on an easel. Pierce was facing it, his back to us, a fist propping his chin. He was wearing a white undershirt that showcased his lean, muscular build. A slender brush dangled from his other hand.

"Mr. Croft is here," Sora announced.

Pierce studied the painting for several more seconds before turning.

"Ah, yes," he said, as though returning to the here and now. "Thank you, Sora. Come in, Everson."

As Sora left us, something told me she wouldn't be returning with tea this time. As I crossed the threshold, I could feel the magic in the room resonating with the healing magic that still lingered in my system. That was another factor I needed to consider in my suspicion toward Pierce. He could have let me die in the goblin tunnels.

"How are you doing?" he asked.

"Much better than last night. Hey, thanks for bailing me out."

He gave a modest smile. "Nothing you wouldn't have done for me. But that's twice now."

"Twice?" When I realized he was referring to the theater, a muscle at the corner of my mouth began to twitch. I hadn't needed saving that night, but Pierce continued before I could point that out.

"Yes, but a pity about last night. Your partner no doubt told you we were en route to intercept the perpetrators as they emerged from the tunnels. Who knows? We might have put this whole thing to bed." He shook his head, then shrugged as if to say, *What's done is done.* But I could see in his cool eyes that he was blaming me for the forty killed at the museum that afternoon—or at least trying to make me feel responsible.

"Funny your paintings didn't have anything to say about that," I shot back.

"Well, like I told the Order, the Himitsu paintings seem to be reacting to your involvement. No hard feelings, I hope."

"Oh, cut the crap."

He tilted his head in a show of puzzlement.

"Look, you saved my life, and I've thanked you. We're past that now. Why don't you tell me what's really going on?"

"I'm not sure what you're referring to."

"Right," I scoffed. "Mr. Innocent. You cancel my wards, you go to the mayor's meeting in my place—to 'help' me." I air-quoted the word. "You edge me out of the investigation. You call the Order. Why? And don't give me any more of your high-bred horseshit."

I thought I caught a tensing in Pierce's neck. He nodded once, set down his paintbrush on the easel, and showed his hands, which were smudged with blue paint. "I assure you, Everson, everything I've done has been with either your or the city's best interest in mind."

"My best interest. Really."

"All right." He leveled his gaze at me. "I didn't want to have to come out and say it, but since you're so insistent ... You've done an admirable job in the city, Everson. But you're in over your head."

"This coming from a guy whose ley lines are all over the frigging map."

"I don't know what you mean. The jobs I canceled were either unnecessary or beyond your skills. I attended the meeting because I could assure the mayor of success whereas you could only make uninformed promises. When it became clear my Himitsu paintings were reacting to your magic, I had no choice but to call the Order. Your involvement was interfering, prolonging what should have been a one-day ordeal. I know you don't see it that way, but how could you? I perceive where you can't. It's that old sphere and circle analogy. It—"

Before I could stop myself, I stepped forward and threw a right cross. The black luck must have been as fed up as I was because there were no mishaps. My fist caught him solidly in the jaw. Pierce blinked and staggered back two steps before landing hard on the seat of his pants.

"I'd like to see a circle do that," I snarled.

Pierce stared at me for several moments, then brought the

back of his hand to his mouth. There was a little blood on his lower lip.

If this *had* been the third loop, I'd just effed it up royally. But I'd gotten something else I'd wanted: an assurance that Pierce wasn't a danger to Vega or the city. His rationale for why he'd been working against me made more sense than him working for Damien.

That was before he removed his extensible wand from his back pocket. I fumbled to raise my cane, but he only touched the tip of the wand to his mouth. Faint white energy swirled around the swelling wound.

"Well," he said mildly, replacing the wand. "Have you gotten that out of your system?"

I considered his question, my heart pumping hard and strong. "Yeah," I decided. "I have."

Pierce looked at my offered hand before accepting it. Something in his grip told me he could have flipped and pinned me, but he let me help him up, again without mishap.

"I wish you had let me finish," he said as he straightened his shirt. "I was going to commend you on the fact that your investigation led you to the same conclusions as my divinations. I was also going to confess that, despite my earlier misgivings, I need your help."

"Oh?" I said lamely.

Pierce turned to the painting on the easel.

"This is the work I've been divining from," he said. "Do you recognize it?"

I tilted my head sideways. The painting had been rendered in dark blue paint with lighter lines running here and there. With the adrenaline of my punch still pumping through my system, it took me a moment to recognize the shapes. "That's Manhattan and the five boroughs."

"That's right." Though Pierce's lip had healed, his tone had changed. He was talking to me like a peer. "I saw the Ark first, and then the converging of the Ark here, underground." He indicated the southeast corner of Central Park. "The focus has shifted here, to south Brooklyn, where Quinton is hiding with the necklace. The city is safe until I learn his precise location. Quinton can't risk emerging to create a new group, not with so many police down there. It's really only a matter of time. But something's bothering me."

"You think Damien has another play," I said.

He looked over at me in surprise. "Why do you say that?"

"As much as I appreciate the earlier compliment about my investigative skills, that's the problem, isn't it? That, what, two days after Damien's first attack we're on the verge of putting him out of business? Hell, it might have been one day if I hadn't boned things up," I allowed. "Whatever Damien's doing has been in the planning a long time. This feels sloppy. I think we're seeing what he wants us to see. Chasing what he wants us to chase."

Pierce nodded. "That's been a growing concern of mine as well. And there have been intimations of what you're saying in my painting, though they come and go. I've not yet been able to interpret them. The strongest images are no longer here, but they had to do with you."

"How so?"

"I explained mirror events to you."

"Right, past patterns repeating in the future."

"Well, we're dealing with one now. How, I'm not certain yet. But what the painting depicted for a moment were two items belonging to you. Your coin amulet and your ring."

I remembered Pierce's eyes touching on them at our first meeting, and I became conscious of their weight and grip now. "They were both gifts from my grandfather," I said. "He gave me the necklace first, and then I found the ring among his things after he died."

"They hold enchantments, yes?"

"Right, powerful protective enchantments. The ring contains the binding power of an ancient pact between wizards and vampires: the Brasov Pact. The coin wields more general protection." I paused. "My grandfather also instilled the coin with the power of the Brasov Pact. As a backup."

"A backup," Pierce said, turning to consult the painting.

A bolt of understanding hit me. "There's another cursed item out there."

Pierce remained silent, but the more I thought about it, the more sense it made. Damien's manipulation of Quinton and the Ark, the sensational attacks, the too-obvious clues. It had all been meant to divert attention from a second item, which was presently working on another person or group, only much more quietly. And with a more devastating finale, I concluded.

"Yes, very likely," Pierce murmured at last.

"Are you going to be able to divine what the item is? Or where?"

When Pierce spun from the painting, I realized too late he was holding his wand. White energy flared from the tip, transforming his grimacing face into a frightening mask of light and shadows.

I threw my cane up and shouted, *"Protezione!"*

But whatever reprieve I'd gotten from the black luck was spent. Instead of enclosing me, my own orb of light plowed into me, knocking me down and breaking apart in a light shower. Pierce's attack shot past me and detonated in the doorway to the basement room.

I managed to right my cane and shout a force invocation, but I was aiming with the wrong end. Before I could take it back, the blast caught me under the chin and sent me sliding the length of the studio. A stack of paintings broke my trajectory and clattered over me.

Woozy and in a world of hurt, I struggled to push the paintings off me, but I only managed to punch myself in the face. *I am so dead.*

But by the time I wriggled free, Pierce had lowered his wand. He wasn't even looking at me. I turned to where his assistant had fallen onto her back in the doorway, smoke pluming around her. A gun lay beyond her outstretched hand.

"I believe you and I are onto something," Pierce said.

28

"Wait." I struggled to my feet. "She was working for Damien?"

"And I hired her six months ago, which suggests the extent of his planning. She's been altering my paintings to keep me fixated on the Ark. To ensure we wouldn't learn the larger plan."

"Altered the paintings? But how would Damien have even known..." The question trailed off as I remembered that Thelonious had told the demon "everything." The incubus had access to my memories when he took over my body. And the last time that had happened, months before, the Order had already told me a little about Pierce and his Himitsu paintings.

"Sora was a student of Himitsu," he said, confirming my suspicion. "Damien used her knowledge to keep me in the dark." He walked over and looked down at her, stern lines across his brow.

"She was possessed?"

"No, I would have sensed that. More likely someone

under Damien's control paid her off. I had no idea until I felt her outside the door just now." Using his magic, he wrapped her in a blanket he must have translocated from upstairs.

I'd never heard Pierce admit a shortcoming, and I wasn't sure what to say.

"It wasn't your magic interfering; it was her." He turned toward me. "My apologies, Everson. I'll let the Order know."

I nodded, still at a loss. Pierce returned to the painting, took up the brush, and began to work. Wispy, transparent magic moved around the bristles. I couldn't see what he was doing—he wasn't using paint—but he was touching the brush here and there, making patterns that looked like small sigils before they dissipated. He did this for several minutes, not saying anything.

At last he stood back. "I've managed to restore some of what Sora altered, and yes, a second pattern has emerged. Up here." He gestured to the upper half of Manhattan. "But it will take time for the information to resolve into something we can act on. Hours, perhaps."

"We might not have hours," I pointed out.

"Fortunately, I know where Quinton is now." On the painting, he indicated a location in Red Hook. "Once I have the necklace, I'll be able to locate any other item or items the demon cursed. But we have to act now." He grabbed his shirt from the back of a chair and was halfway to the door before he realized I wasn't following. His eyebrows went up in question.

Coming here hadn't had the same result as my visits to Mae and Snodgrass. I hadn't felt the same lightening effect. I hadn't felt anything. "I've got a little curse problem," I said.

"Curse?"

"Black luck. It's sort of a long story, but I'm not going to be able to help." Hell, I was going to be lucky to last the cycle.

Pierce's eyes shifted, and I sensed him examining my aura. At last he nodded. "You have so much going on, I missed it earlier." He drew his wand and aimed it at me. Though he said nothing, I felt a wave of energy growing around me, forming a gentle layer of protection. "That will blunt its effects while I'm away. Combined with my wards, you should be safe until my return." He raised a stern finger. "But don't go anywhere, or the protection will lose all effectiveness."

It was a relief knowing I wasn't going to die in the next hour, but now I felt like a hopeless waste of space. "Thanks," I said. "I'm sorry I can't do a damn thing to help you."

"You just did," Pierce said, his eyes cutting to the painting. "There will be plenty more opportunities for future collaboration. Indeed, once we get your magic sorted, you and I are going to be a force in this city."

The year before, one of my students gave me a page-turner of a book about a supernatural duo fighting the good fight on the streets of New York—*Montague and Strong*. I almost made a comparison but wasn't sure Pierce would get the reference. When he grinned, my face flushed with an odd sense of satisfaction. Apparently straight men were no less susceptible to his charm than women. Pierce had turned out to be a good guy.

"Be careful," I said.

He nodded and disappeared through the doorway. A moment later, I felt a subtle wave of pressure, telling me he had translocated.

Just hope he's right about the necklace, I thought, turning back to the painting.

Now that Damien knew we were on to him, he would be putting the pedal to the metal. And that meant executing the plan he'd taken pains to keep veiled. I looked at the part of the city Pierce had indicated with a broad sweep of his hand. The wards hadn't picked up anything in the upper half of Manhattan, which suggested there had been no breaches into our world.

I turned from the painting and began to pace the length of the studio. That I was able to do so without tripping over my feet or choking on my own breath told me Pierce's magic was having the desired effect.

"What do demons value over everything, even depravity?" I asked aloud.

"Power," I answered.

"And how do they amass power?"

"By claiming souls."

I thought about the Ark and their infernal bags. The activated bags had claimed seventy souls. Though devastating, the number was little more than an appetizer for a high-level demon. No, Damien wanted *thousands* of souls. That meant a giant infernal bag...

"And a large concentration of people," I finished.

I rushed back to the painting and, head angled sideways, looked at the top half. Yankee Stadium was up there. Game six of the American League Championship was starting in—I checked my watch—just over an hour. With the city subsidizing ticket prices, the attendance would be north of fifty thousand. The NYPD had surely searched the stadium already, but they had done the same at the museum, and look what happened that afternoon.

As my heart slammed in my chest, I reminded myself that this was all guess work. Once Pierce tapped into the necklace, we'd know for sure. Plus, the Order's wards weren't sensing anything around the stadium. I'd just checked when I was at the Snodgrass's place.

"Wait a second..." I muttered.

I pulled the pencil from my pocket notepad.

Yankee Stadium is here, I thought, making a point on the painting. *The Snodgrass's house is a few blocks down this way ... and the ley line was warped in this direction.* I sketched the line out. It bent away from the stadium. I extended the line into a large circle, then working inward, drew concentric circles until I arrived at the epicenter: Yankee Stadium.

"Son of a bitch."

Damien had pushed the ley lines away from the stadium, not unlike what I'd done at the Snodgrass's, but on a larger scale and requiring a lot more power. The point? To create a dead zone in the stadium the wards wouldn't detect. But the zone had created a ripple effect, altering the ley lines for blocks—including the line that ran along the Snodgrass's street.

The stadium *was* Damien's play.

But how in the hell to get ahold of Pierce?

Vega, I thought.

I ran up the stairs to Pierce's office and picked up his desk phone. It was a modern model, but the spell he'd cast seemed not only to have tempered the black luck but controlled my aura as well.

I dialed her number. Straight to voice mail.

"Ricki, listen, it's me. Pierce just left for Red Hook, he knows where Quinton is. But the demon's play is Yankee Stadium. He's after the crowd. Pierce needs to get up there ASAP. I'd go myself but, well..." I thought about Pierce's warning that I not leave the house. "I've been cursed," I finished lamely. "In the meantime I need you to evacuate the stadium. I repeat, evacuate the stadium."

I tried Hoffman and then the Homicide Department and got voicemails at both as well. I left messages, asking them to compile a list of everyone who worked on the crews in Lower Manhattan and then cross-check it against current Yankee employees and contractors. If Quinton had found his cursed artifact in the debris downtown, there was a chance Damien's other vessel had too.

I then tried the mayor's office but was told he was unavailable. I called my apartment. I knew what Gretchen had said about not wanting to get involved, but I couldn't believe she was serious. Not in a situation like this. Tabitha answered.

"Put Gretchen on," I said.

"She left about ten minutes ago."

"Where?"

"She doesn't talk to me, remember? But I did catch her saying something about the faerie realm."

"*What?*"

"She seemed determined to find some decent entertainment this evening."

I blew out my breath. "All right," I said. "I've gotta go."

I hung up and called the Order. When Claudius answered, I filled him in as quickly as I could. By now the urgency of the situation was pounding my head and making a fist of my stomach.

"I see," Claudius said once I'd finished. "I'll let Arianna and the others know right away. They're occupied in other tasks and other realms, obviously, but perhaps one of them can be there by morning."

"It will be too late by morning!"

"Oh?"

"Claudius, listen to me. If we don't clear that stadium and defuse whatever the demon's planted, he's going to claim thousands of lives. With that kind of power, he'll emerge and claim thousands more."

"Yes, yes, we'll see what we can do."

I recalled what Gretchen had said about Claudius being senile. I'd thought it was a stretch at the time, but now I wasn't so sure.

"Call them," I said and hung up.

Not knowing what else to do, I punched three numbers.

"Nine-one-one, what's your emergency?"

"There's a bomb at Yankee Stadium."

"Oh, really?" the operator said in a bored voice.

"I'm serious. You need to get everyone out."

"Can I have your name?" she asked.

"My name? Who cares about my name? Did you hear what I said?"

"Yeah, and do you know how many bomb threats we get every time the Yankees take the field? It's not exactly original. You're the fourth caller tonight."

"You aren't going to do anything?" I asked, incredulous.

"A crew was there this afternoon, dogs and everything. They didn't find squat."

"Evacuate. *Now.*"

She hung up.

I slammed down the phone and paced a frantic circle in the office. Pierce was down in Red Hook. I couldn't reach Vega, Hoffman, or the mayor. Gretchen was literally in la-la land. The powerful members of the Order were hours out. I couldn't get the police to clear the stadium. And if I attempted to leave Pierce's house, the black luck would have me by the throat. I wouldn't make it two blocks, much less all the way to Yankee Stadium, before dropping dead.

But you have to try. You're all the city has.

I walked to the front door, opened it, and teetered on the threshold. I had barely survived the last cycle. I wasn't going to survive this one. I thought about Vega. How bad was this going to hurt her?

Then I thought about my parents, who had sacrificed their lives in service to the Order. I drew my father's blade from my cane and gazed at its runes. What would he have done?

I snorted. Did I even have to ask?

Sheathing the blade, I stepped over the threshold.

29

As I made my way down the walkway, I felt Pierce's protection thin. By the time I reached the sidewalk, it was gone. A cab was coming, which seemed unusually lucky under the circumstances. But as I waved it down, a black muscle car tore around a corner from the other direction and slewed into the cab's lane. The cab driver reacted, jerking the steering wheel. In a burst of sparks, he jumped the curb as the muscle car swerved away, bass thumping.

"*Vigore!*" I shouted.

The force invocation caught the cab's front fender and, feet from me, heaved the vehicle back onto the street.

I released my breath. The invocation had actually worked.

I jogged over to where the cab had jounced to a stop and climbed into the back seat. The driver was gripping the steering wheel in both hands and muttering a prayer of thanks.

"Yankee Stadium," I said. "As fast as you can get me there."

As the words left my mouth, something happened. The

sensation that had come over me following my visits to Mae and Snodgrass returned, only this time it was a complete lifting.

Holy crap.

By committing to this course, I'd just closed the third loop. My black luck was gone.

I waved my arms wildly around my head to make certain. Sure enough, I didn't punch myself. Then I cast a small shield invocation. It manifested without a hitch. I was back in business.

But the cab wasn't moving.

I looked at the driver's ID card. "Hey, Kumar? This is sort of an emergency."

The driver lifted his head from the wheel and looked in the rearview mirror. Damn, I knew him. It was the Bangladeshi driver the Blue Wolf and I had all but hijacked last summer. I dipped my head into my jacket collar and looked away. To my surprise, we began rolling forward. He hadn't recognized me. I wondered if the black luck had been setting up a situation where, even if the cab hadn't maimed or killed me, the driver would have refused to drive me.

Damned fae magic.

"An extra hundred if you can get me to the stadium in the next fifteen minutes."

"Don't want to miss baseball?" he asked.

"Something like that."

As the cab sped north onto Broadway, I relaxed enough to center myself. I was still carrying a few spell items from earlier, but I was banking on my one remaining potion. The important thing now was to ensure that both my mental prism and mental acuity were operating at full capacity. I may have been rid of the black luck, but I had forfeited my luck quotient. I wouldn't be able to depend on it. This was going to be all Everson.

It wasn't until we hit the one hundreds that I remembered my promise to Mae.

Fuck.

"Mae!" I shouted, pounding her door with the side of my fist. "It's Everson Croft!"

Doors began to open up and down the hallway, and grumbling tenants peered out. I pulled out my NYPD card and flashed it to both sides while pounding the door again.

"Mae!"

Back in the cab I had almost said "screw it" and gone straight to the stadium, but Gretchen's warning kept pinging in my head: *Don't open any more loops, whatever you do.* She hadn't said what the consequences would be, but they weren't hard to imagine. Such as the black luck crashing back at the worst possible time.

I was about to pound again when the door opened and Mae squinted out at me. She was wearing a night robe and shower cap through which I could see a creamy hair treatment.

"Everson?" she said. "What are you doing here at this hour?"

"This hour? It's not even eight thirty."

"Well, I'm in bed every night at eight sharp. My body wakes me up at four a.m. no matter what, so—"

"That's great," I interrupted. "But we've gotta go."

Her eyes squinted at me another moment before popping wide in understanding. "Are you saying...?"

I nodded. "We've got an assignment. A big one."

"All right, well hold on," she stammered, shuffling her walker in a half circle. "Let me change out of this and rinse my hair real quick. Then I've gotta put on some special shoes for my bunions. If I can remember where they are..."

"No, Mae, it has to be now. Fifty-thousand lives are in jeopardy."

She turned back to face me. "Fifty *thousand*? Lord Almighty. Okay, just need to grab one thing."

Before I could stop her, she slammed the door, and I heard her shuffle away. I shifted from foot to foot as I checked my watch. The stadium was at full capacity now. How long would it take for Damien to activate whatever he'd planted there? The door opened again, and Mae emerged holding a small pet carrier. Buster's tendrils writhed through the wire mesh door.

"You're taking him?"

"I can't leave him here all by himself," Mae said, as if that should have been obvious. "He's just a baby."

Buster squealed once.

There was no time to argue. I took the carrier so she could manage her walker. While the elevator rattled us down, I gave her a quick account of what was happening. Outside, she climbed into the cab, and I set the pet carrier on her lap. I then folded her walker and threw it into the front seat beside Kumar.

When we were all in, Kumar took off again. He hadn't wanted to stop at Mae's until I told him it wouldn't count toward the fifteen minutes. To earn his hundred, he had four minutes left to get us to the stadium.

Apartments and row houses shot past my window. Not wanting to repeat my mistake from the goblin tunnels, I pulled out my remaining potion and my travel bag. I found the small lighter at the bag's bottom and thumbed the wheel. Incanting, I waved the flame beneath the clay tube. Kumar was too focused on weaving through traffic at a high rate of speed to notice what I was doing, but Mae made several noises of interest as she watched. When I felt the potion activate, I killed the lighter and slid the warm potion into my coat's inside pocket.

"What is that?" Mae asked.

"The most powerful potion I've ever mixed," I replied, unable to hide my pride. It was the one I'd been working on for the last year, determined to get right. "When I drink it, stand back."

I was preparing to elaborate when we shot onto the Macombs Dam Bridge connecting Upper Manhattan and the Bronx. Beyond the steel trusses, I could see Yankee Stadium glowing like a beacon. I could even hear the din of fan noise. It didn't sound like panic yet. A large number of police cruisers were parked around the stadium, lights flashing.

Kumar aimed for them and pressed the gas until the needle trembled past eighty. The stadium seemed to rush up on us.

"Whoa, s-slow down there," I stammered. "Slow down!"

Kumar slammed the brakes, and we slewed sideways between a pair of squad cars and up onto the sidewalk. Buster let out a shriek and crouched low, claws over his face. The tires peeled as we rocked to a stop just shy of a row of bollards. Kumar turned and flashed a victorious smile.

"Fourteen minute, fifty-six second."

"Good Lord," Mae said, a hand to her chest.

"Yeah, I would've spotted you those few extra seconds," I told Kumar, pulling out the fare plus one hundred and slapping the stack into his palm. I got out, took the carrier from Mae, and prepared her walker.

A pair of police officers hustled over, and I pulled out my NYPD card. "It's all right," I said. "I told the driver to do that."

The first officer to arrive took my ID and looked it over. "Are you the one who left a message about an imminent attack?" she asked.

"It got through?" I looked around. "Why the hell isn't the stadium evacuating?"

"Because every exit is sealed," Detective Hoffman said, walking up from the other side. "We can't open them, not even with the rams."

I turned to face him. "Is Vega here?"

"She's down in Red Hook with your pal. I happened to be up this way when I got your message. I alerted every car in the area. There are more on the way. Hey, you were right about the suspects at Central Park," he said, explaining why he would ever listen to me in the first place.

"Alert the crowd, and I'll start opening the gates," I said quickly.

"Open the gates first," he demanded. "'Cause if you can't, we're gonna have the mother of all panics on our hands. People are gonna get trampled and crushed to death. Maybe for nothing."

I'd been prepared to argue, but he was right. I ran up to the glass doors at Gate 4. Familiar dark magic writhed around the doorframes, like hundreds of snakes. I uttered a Word to dissolve the locking spell, but no power moved through me. When I tried again, the result was the same.

...the hell?

Then I remembered how I'd hit on Yankee Stadium to begin with. Damien had altered the ley lines, voiding the stadium of energy. Without ley energy to channel, I couldn't cast here, not even to find and undo whatever magic he'd used to force out the ley lines in the first place.

That left the potion I'd activated in the cab and the enchanted items I carried: my ring, coin pendant, and sword. The ring only worked against vampires, though, and I'd already used the pendant against Damien, at the packing plant. According to Arianna, my father had buried enchantments in the sword, but I didn't know what they were, and none had activated yet.

I drew the sword anyway and inserted its tip between the glass doors in front of me. The runes in the blades glowed white. The binding magic responded by wriggling uncomfortably. Deep in the stadium something rumbled. I withdrew the blade quickly and watched the binding magic resume its writhing course. The rumbling subsided.

Damn, I thought, backing away.

"Any luck?" Hoffman asked.

"The doors aren't just locked, they're armed," I said. "The second they're breached, whatever Damien planted inside will activate." I still suspected a giant infernal bag. Why it hadn't gone off yet, I didn't know. Maybe Damien was still imbuing it for maximum effectiveness.

"We've got choppers on the way," Hoffman said. "They're gonna pick up the mayor, players, and some other VIP. I can have one of them land out here and give you a lift in."

"What about the fans?" I asked.

"There's more than fifty thousand, Croft." The disapproval must have shown on my face because he said, "Look, we've got the fire department arriving too. There are some gaps between the bleachers and stands that their ladders can reach, but that's not gonna be much quicker than airlifting everyone. We're talking hours. Until then, they're trapped. What I'm trying to say is that if you're sure something's happening, it's gonna be up to you to stop it."

"And me," Mae said, clacking up on her walker, the pet carrier swinging from the right handle.

Hoffman squinted at her in confusion. But before he could ask who she was, the thumping of rotary blades sounded above the whine of approaching fire engines. Hoffman spoke into his radio while waving at the lead chopper and pointing to the intersection in front of the stadium.

The chopper descended, while the rest of the fleet disappeared over the stadium's bowl. The decibel level in the stadium rose a notch, the fans no doubt believing the arriving helicopters to be part of the pre-game show.

"You know how to work one of these?" Hoffman shouted above the noise of the helicopter. He was holding out a small two-way radio with a shoulder microphone. "It's set to receive. Hold down this button when you want to talk."

I was about to tell him I was more likely to blow the radio up when I remembered I was in a dead zone. My aura was at minimum strength, meaning electronics would be safe around me.

"I've got a team working on the employee cross-check you requested," he said. "I'll let you know if they learn anything."

"Thanks," I shouted back as he clipped the shoulder mic to my collar.

"Just don't fuck this up."

Hoffman clapped my shoulder hard enough to send me in the direction of the chopper. Mae was right beside me, head bowed as her shower cap and gown flapped in the rotor wash.

"Maybe you should stay outside," I told her. "You know ... secure the perimeter."

She frowned at me. "Don't try and ditch me with some bullshit. I heard everything you said. The action's on the inside, so that's where I'm gonna be. Even though I'm scared to death of flying."

"All the more reason," I said in a final attempt to get her to stay.

She rolled her eyes and continued tapping her walker toward the helicopter. A police officer in SWAT gear emerged, opened the side door, and helped Mae inside. I climbed in after her and buckled us both in.

"So you're the A-team," the pilot said, peering over his shoulder.

"That's right," Mae said proudly before I could answer. "Everson Croft and Mae Johnson."

The pilot shrugged as if that meant nothing to him. When the other officer was back inside, he lifted off. Vertigo hit me as the squad cars and crowds of officers shrank beneath us and the steep wall of the stadium rushed up in front. Soon, we were over the stadium's steel frieze, and I got my first look at the crowd of people. Fifty thousand sounded like a lot, but to see them all packed in one place—and knowing they were in the clutches of a powerful demon—made me feel faint.

As we descended past the upper bowl, the wall of noise hit us full on. The fans were still cheering the arrival of the helicopters. Two had touched down near the home dugout, and I could see security escorting Budge and his entourage from the dugout toward the waiting choppers.

Unable to resist the opportunity for attention, Budge stopped to wave at the crowd with both arms. When the feed showed him on the giant screen above center field, the crowd responded with a surge of noise. He was still popular, some-how. Or maybe the crowd was just primed for a playoff game that, unbeknownst to them, had been cancelled. Next to leave the dugout were a line of men in street clothes, hoodies hiding their faces—the players.

The feed quickly switched to a woman in a white sequin gown standing behind home plate with a microphone and color guard. She peered around with a fixed smile, awaiting her cue to begin the national anthem.

As we continued to drop toward the outfield, I glanced over at Mae. She had squeezed her eyes shut and was hugging the pet carrier with both arms. I couldn't help but admire her determination. Frightened or not, she was dead set on helping. But was putting her in harm's way the right move? Before I could answer, we were touching down.

"This is your stop," the pilot said over his shoulder.

I got out and helped Mae down. As we stepped onto the manicured grass, I peered around. I'd never attended a game in the new Yankee Stadium, and the place was huge. Where was I going to start the search for the infernal bag? A half dozen security guards jogged up to us.

"NYPD says you're looking for something?" the man in the lead said.

I nodded, meeting his eyes to center myself. "A big sack," I said, not knowing for sure. I was guesstimating based on what I'd encountered so far. "Might be leather, but it's going to be stuffed. I need you to look anywhere one could be stashed. The restaurants, stores, concessions."

"What's your frequency?" the man asked.

"Huh?" Then I realized he meant my radio.

I showed him the unit and he nodded. "We'll call if we find anything."

As his team fanned out, I noticed Mae's pet carrier rocking. Inside, Buster was running around in circles.

"What's a matter, baby?" Mae asked him.

The first screams of terror landed like needles in my brain, but they weren't coming from the cage. I spun toward right field, trying to make sense of the commotion in the stands. The screams had originated from inside the concourse, but now they were emerging onto the main level of grandstand seating. People were fleeing something. The stadium's pitch lowered to a din of murmurs as people started to take notice before it rose again suddenly.

Like an agitated storm of wasps, imps began blowing in from the concourse. I watched helplessly as a spiny imp seized a large man's neck in its jaws and, in a spray of gore, ripped out his soul.

"Lord Almighty," Mae said beside me.

30

I drew out the potion I'd prepared in the cab, yanked off the cap with my teeth, and drank it down. The potion would take several minutes to work, but with the carnage spreading, I couldn't just stand there. I drew my sword from my staff. Before I could make a move toward the stands, Mae grabbed my arm.

"If those things don't kill you, the crowd will," she hollered.

In their terror, fans were climbing over one another to escape the imps. The first fan leapt from the grandstand into the rows beneath him. Others followed. I couldn't blame them. The imps were bigger and uglier than the ones from the other infernal bags—and more deadly. I watched their teeth and talons tear out more souls and toss the bodies off like rinds.

"I have to do something," I shouted and shook her loose.

The imps were swarming into the adjacent stands now. A few spotted me and flew toward the field. I was running at full speed by the time they reached me. I cleaved the first one in half at the torso, then thrust the blade up through the heart of another coming in overhead. With a violent rip, I took out half its chest and left wing. It fell to the ground with a shriek.

I kept my legs and blade in motion as the potion mixed with my chemistry. I couldn't banish the creatures, but I could keep the ones I crippled from attacking anyone until I found the bag that had spawned them.

C'mon, dammit, I thought toward the potion. *Start working.*

In my peripheral vision, I could see the rest of the stadium stampeding into the concourses. It was only a matter of minutes before they would reach the outer gates and find them sealed—Hoffman's nightmare scenario.

I maimed two more imps and climbed into the stands at the foul line. For now, the fleeing crowd was giving me a path to the concourses inside. Then it would be a matter of following the imps back to their source.

But loud shrieks from behind made me turn. Imps were blowing into the left field stands now, turning the fans back out. And the storm was only growing thicker. The imps were going to wipe out the entire stadium.

"Stop this nonsense!" a familiar voice boomed over the sound system.

I turned and spotted Mae behind home plate. She had recovered the microphone from where the national anthem singer had dropped it when she fled along with the color guard.

"Leave those people alone!" Her voice reverberated around the stadium.

The hell is she doing?

But something was happening. The imps were rotating their heads at the sound of her voice. I spotted a hideous speckled creature, its talons in the hair of a screaming woman, its other hand reared back for the kill, hesitate long enough for the victim to disentangle herself and scramble away.

"You heard me!" Mae shouted. "Get off those nice people, and get down to the field!"

Slowly, the imps began releasing their victims. They flew, hopped, and crawled toward the outfield, several passing within feet of me. I couldn't believe it. When the first ones arrived onto the grass, their heads and shoulders sulked a little, as if expecting punishment.

Mae walked toward them in her shower cap and gown, using her thighs to advance her walker. Buster's carrier swung from the right handle while the microphone cord trailed out behind. It was one of the most absurd things I'd ever seen ... except that the creatures were listening to her.

"You want me to come up there and pop you?" she shouted at the laggards. "All of you down here with the others! Now!" The microphone picked up Buster's squealed exclamation.

The imps arrived in hordes until the last of them had left the bloodied stands where hundreds of fans had fallen victim. Soon the outfield was packed with creatures. The scene looked like a nightmare Lollapalooza. When Mae arrived at the edge of the grass, she stopped and glared across their numbers. The stadium lights reflected from her thick glasses in menacing flashes. I didn't know where her abilities had come from, but Mae had a gift.

"Now you're going to sit there, head between your legs," she ordered. "And I don't want to hear another peep out of you."

The imps chattered among themselves, glowing eyes

seeming to ask each other what they should do. I'd been climbing as I watched, but now I paused, terrified they were going to recover their malice and swarm Mae. But starting at the front, they began to descend, falling to haunches and spiked tails in a wave. When they were all seated, they fell silent—and I released my breath.

Mae's gaze found me, the lone person in the lower seats. "They're not going anywhere," she assured me. "Find that bag."

I nodded quickly and ran through the exit and up a ramp until I was in the Great Hall. The large concourse was a thick river of packed bodies. I looked around. I hadn't heard back from security, and without the imps to backtrack along, I didn't know where to go. Their attack had ended, but I could feel a low vibrating, and it wasn't coming from the moving crowd. The vibrating shook my eardrums. A powerful, dark energy was building in the stadium.

"*Croft,*" Hoffman's voice sounded from my radio. "*How's it going in there?*"

"We've neutralized the first attack, but I feel a second one coming."

"*Go to the Yankees museum,*" he said.

"Why? What's there?"

"*That cross check you wanted us to run? Got a hit. A guy who's been working at the museum for the last five years was picking up weekends at the site last fall. Name's Jimmy Land. Late 40s, short, balding.*"

"I love you, man," I said. "Where's the museum?"

"*Lower level of Gate 6, near the right foul pole. And I'll forget you said that first part.*"

"Fair enough."

I repeated the directions to myself. I wasn't far from the

museum, but the traffic in the Great Hall had come to a grinding halt as the crowds arriving from different directions created a logjam. The din of the panicked crowd filled the seven-story concourse. I was turning to run back into the stands to find another route to the museum when my potion began to take effect.

I'd been feeling electric for the last minute, and now golden light pulsed from my body. I rose into the air as the light grew from my legs. The same light swelled around my torso, extended from my arms, pulsed around my fists, and formed a protective dome over my head. By the time the golden light was in place, I was encased in a massive, magical battle suit.

Strength and confidence coursed through me. I sheathed my sword and slid the cane through my belt. *I* was the weapon now. With a triumphant shout, I leapt into the air and flew over the packed crowd.

"Stay calm," I called. "The creatures have been contained. We'll have you out shortly."

I felt like a superhero, but the panicked fans who looked up had seen enough flying things for one night. They tried to shove away from me, some thrashing violently. Children screamed.

Okay, bad idea.

Before I could get anyone killed, I rose higher. I sailed past the giant banners of current and past Yankee greats and dove into a stairwell. When I came out at the lower level, I spotted the entrance to the museum and flew inside. A number of fans had taken refuge behind the displays, and I made sure to land before addressing them. Thanks to the suit, I was still two feet above the floor.

"I need everyone to clear out," I said. "You're not safe in here."

When no one moved, I swung my armored fist into a display case. The glass shattered spectacularly. One of Babe Ruth's bats clattered to the floor. Even to a lifelong Mets fan, the destruction felt like sacrilege, but it got the desired result. When the people had left, I looked around.

"Where are you?" I muttered at the hidden infernal bag.

The museum was an open affair designed to accommodate large numbers of people. There were no obvious hiding places in or around the displays. In the back, I spotted an open door with a sign reading Authorized Personnel Only.

I stepped into what turned out to be a dark stairwell. With the battle suit, I had no fear of descending. At the bottom, I arrived at another open door. I found a large, climate-controlled storage room inside. The packed room was filled with sulfurous smoke, but vents along the ceiling were drawing it out. The glow from my suit highlighted rows of labeled storage containers.

I moved down them until I was at the back, where a pair of especially large containers had been blown open. Inside, I found two large infernal bags—the sources of the imps. Spells had likely concealed them when the police performed their earlier search. Using my enhanced hands, I tore the bags apart, the suit's energy dispersing the dark magic that held the creatures together.

Smoke, black powder, and evil billowed around me. I heard a collective shriek go up in the field and then fall silent just as suddenly.

The imps were destroyed.

Exhaling, I looked over the remnants of the bags. Damien must have had his vessel bring the ingredients in a little at a time, never enough to draw attention. Over the course of months, it would have added up until Damien had exactly what he needed. Then, using the same vessel, he had activated them.

I tried to call Hoffman to see if the doors had opened, but the radio was blowing static, no doubt because of the magical battle suit. I could still feel the vibrating, though, deep in my inner ears. It was the same sensation I'd felt when Damien had animated and taken possession of his smoke golems. Only now it was more potent. There was another infernal bag somewhere.

Footsteps entered the room. I spun as a flashlight beam shot through the dark and hit me in the face.

"Who are you?" a tight voice demanded. "What are you doing down here?"

I squinted past the light, one arm raised, to find a short, balding man with a round face peering back at me.

"Jimmy Land?" I asked.

"How do you know my name?"

He was the man the cross-check had turned up. He must have been drawn to Damien's other cursed item, the one Pierce had foreseen in his painting. If I could find and exorcize it, I could break its hold over him.

Then he could tell me where the infernal bag was.

"S-stay there," Jimmy stammered as I strode toward him, gold energy humming around me. I expected to find a weapon in his other hand, but he wasn't armed. When he turned to run, I stretched my enhanced arm forward and grabbed him by the back of his blue work shirt. He shouted and tried to hit my hand with the flashlight, but it thudded harmlessly against the suit.

"You found something in Lower Manhattan," I said, dragging him back. "Something that talked to you. I want it."

"I-I don't have it anymore!"

"What was it?"

"A ring."

I thought about how Pierce had glimpsed my necklace and ring in his own painting. It looked like we were dealing with a mirror event in more ways than one. I took Jimmy's hand and aimed the flashlight toward the ruined infernal bags. "Did you make those?"

"Yes, b-but only because Damien told me to. I didn't know what they'd do!"

I squinted at him. He wasn't talking like a possessed man. Without my wizard's senses, though, I couldn't tell for sure. I looked at his fingers. No rings. Why would Damien have released him?

The man struggled in my grip.

"Hey, hold still!" I rearranged my hands so I was clamping his shoulders. With the suit, it was effortless. The gold light shone from the sweat beading over his bald head. "Where's the other bag?"

"I don't know."

But I could still feel the dark energy vibrating in my ears, becoming almost painful. I shook him. "Where is it?"

"I don't know! I swear!"

I thought of the Ark. "Who else did Damien induct?"

"J-just one other person."

"Do they work at the stadium?"

"No, I didn't know her. I'd never seen her before. Damien told me where to go. What to do. Some kind of ceremony. That was six months ago. I never went back."

"Everson?" Mae called from upstairs. "Are you in here?"

"Stay there, Mae!"

The man had cocked his head at the sound of her voice. Now his eyes widened. "Mae?"

"You know her?"

"Black woman with a walker?"

I nodded slowly, my blood turning cold.

"Th-that's her," he whispered. *"That's the woman."*

"Everson?" she called again.

31

I stood there, Jimmy in my grip, my eyes canting up toward the sound of Mae's voice. My mind scrambled to make sense of what Jimmy had just told me. He'd inducted Mae? She was a part of this?

There's no way.

I thought back over our two meetings, how Mae had convinced me to bring her tonight. Her control over the nether creatures had seemed a natural gift, but was there a darker explanation? Was Damien using her as a vessel too? One way or another, I needed to get to the bottom of this.

"C'mon," I said, tugging Jimmy toward the door.

He struggled, but with the power of the magical suit, I hardly noticed. I pulled him up the stairs until we were emerging into the museum. I found Mae shuffling on her walker, Buster in the carrier. She had been peering around the displays, but now she turned toward us.

"There you are," she said, letting out her breath. "The creatures in the ball field exploded. Made a godawful mess, but they're gone."

"What are you doing here?" I asked.

"Seeing if you needed my help."

I pulled Jimmy to the front of me. "Do you know this man?"

She squinted at him from behind her glasses, then shook her head. "Can't say that I do."

"He didn't come to your apartment a few months ago?"

"Everson, I can count on one hand the number of visitors I've had in the last year, and, no, he wasn't one of them."

"It's her," Jimmy insisted in a whisper.

She cocked her head at him crossly. "I'm *who?*"

"The ring!" He pointed. "That's Damien's ring!"

Mae looked from the man to her left hand in confusion.

"Stay there," I told Jimmy and walked up to Mae. If she had been inducted, if she was presently possessed, Damien could have altered her memory, compelled her to do things without her understanding why she was doing them—without her even thinking to question them. Which meant her present show of confusion could have been as genuine as it appeared. But I still didn't understand the play. What advantage did Mae's presence give the demon?

"Where did you get this?" I asked, pointing to the tarnished gold band. It looked common, but so too had the necklace.

"Where do you think? It's my wedding band."

"Are you sure?"

She narrowed her eyes at me. "I'm not senile, Everson."

Above us, I could hear the cries of the tens of thousands of trapped fans.

"I need you to take it off and give it to me," I said.

"This ring hasn't been off my finger in more than twenty years."

When I reached for it, Mae drew her hand back. The vibrating I'd been feeling deep in my ears broke open, and threads of sulfurous smoke whirled around us. *Wait,* I thought. *Is* Mae *the final bag? Is Damien's power stored inside her? Did I just deliver the bomb to the stadium?*

It made sick demonic sense.

Mae shouted when I seized her wrist and pried her finger away from her palm.

"I know you don't understand what I'm doing," I said. "But the ring's not what you think it is."

I twisted off the gold band, then using my body to block Mae, pulled the vial of copper filings from my pocket and sprinkled out a hasty circle. I dropped the ring inside and began reciting the exorcism from memory. I jockeyed to keep Mae from coming around me to reclaim the band. She grunted and butted her walker against me. Buster chattered excitedly inside the carrier.

I spoke the exorcism as quickly as I could, while the smoke whipped around in thicker and thicker bands.

"Everson!" Mae yelled.

I ignored her until I realized she was no longer trying to get to the ring.

"Everson! The man! The man!"

I'd lost track of Jimmy, but when I looked up, I found him standing in front of the wall that featured hundreds of auto-graphed Yankees baseballs. His eyes had turned a fierce red —and he was grinning. My eyes dropped to the silver ring glinting from his left ring finger. Dark flames licked through the smoke. I could feel its heat biting through my suit.

Jimmy was the final bag. The infernal energy was coming from him.

I aimed an open hand and fired. A shaft of gold energy

shot from my palm and exploded into Jimmy. As he staggered back, I lowered my head and charged. The shoulder of my battle suit caught Jimmy in the center of his chest. The collision of magic produced an electric jolt. Sparks burst around us. We crashed into the Ball Wall, shattering the protective glass. Baseballs, some of them priceless, tumbled over us and rolled off in every direction. By the time we hit the floor, my hands were around his throat.

Jimmy is just a vessel, I reminded myself. *Damien is casting through him.*

And the demon's focus object was the ring. I needed to get it off his finger. Needed to exorcise it. With no one to control through his cursed objects, Damien would lose his power here.

But when I grabbed Jimmy's hand, he punched me with his other fist. The blow that caught me in the chin felt like a cannonball. I was blown off him and sent through two displays. Glass, jersey-clad dummies, and pieces of seat from the original Yankee Stadium exploded around me.

I came to a rest against the far wall and blinked my vision straight.

He shouldn't have been able to do that. Not with the potion protecting me.

By the time I rose, Jimmy was already on his feet. He strode toward me, dark laughter shaking his body. I pawed for my cane, but I'd lost it. When Jimmy spoke, I heard Damien's voice.

"You surprised me, Everson. You're more tenacious than I gave you credit for. It almost cost me. My ruse was a clumsy one, I admit. Telling you the old woman was under my control. Claiming she had the ring. But it fooled you long enough for me to adapt to your potion."

I looked down at the energy humming around my body. I remembered the minutes I'd spent handling Jimmy, exposing Damien to the potion's power.

No, I thought.

"That's right," Damien said. "I'm immune to it now, like your other spells and invocations. That was part of the point of the piddling infernal bags. To either lead you down a wayward path that would end in your death—the route your partner took, the poor thing..."

For a moment I thought he was talking about Vega, and my heart stopped before resuming with such force that I felt it in the pit of my gut. But then I realized he meant Pierce.

"You're lying," I said.

"*Or,*" Damien continued with a grin, "to deprive you of your power. And here we are." He opened his hands as the fiery smoke cycloned around him, flames gashing my battle suit like a sandblaster. "You've nothing left that can hurt me. And *I* have fifty thousand souls waiting to be claimed." His grin broadened until it looked like it was going to split his face. "Do you know what I'll be able to do with them? The kind of power I'll be able to command?"

He was right. I had already used my enchanted items against him as well as the potion. A handful of spell items still bulged in my pockets, but without ley energy to push through them, they were useless.

"Who the fuck are you?" I growled as he arrived in front of me.

"Well, you know what they say, Everson: a picture is worth a thousand words. You'll soon see for yourself. And then we can discuss your options. Namely whether you want to join the others souls as slaves in the Below, or if you would prefer to serve me here on Earth."

"How about none of the above?"

Before he could respond, I put my personal training to use, jabbing him twice with my left hand. The shots snapped his head back. I followed with a right hook that should have taken his head off. But when Damien's face rotated back to face me, he was smiling.

I only realized he'd struck me when I found myself rolling over the wreckage of the museum. The coppery taste of blood filled my mouth. By the time I stopped, my magical suit was sputtering. I tried to stand, but I staggered and fell to one knee, my head a mass of cobwebs.

Damien laughed and spread his arms like a fallen angel. The storm around him grew more fierce, and I could hear fresh screams in the concourse.

"If I can't stop you, the Order will," I promised.

"The Order?" Damien laughed. "Do you mean those doddering magic-users? Do you know how easy it was for me to evade them? No, Everson. The only challenge will be deciding how to use them once I've brought them to their knees."

He leaned his head back, eyes fluttering. Wisps of light joined the spiraling smoke, but coming from the other direction. Shit, the claiming had begun. Each time a soul rushed into him, Damien shuddered in ecstasy. The storm emanating from him grew larger, more violent.

I peered around for Mae, but I couldn't see her.

Grimacing, I crawled toward Damien. I had to get the ring from him, had to exorcize it. Though I wasn't the object of his attack, it took every bit of my trembling strength to advance against the force and heat. Caught up in the claiming, Damien wasn't looking at me. I hoped to use that to my advantage.

When I was beneath him, I reached for his hand. His foot landed hard on my throat, cutting off my air.

"Oh, good," he said. "I would have hated for you to miss this."

I struggled, but it was futile. He had me pinned. I managed to turn my head enough to draw air. More likely, Damien had *let me* turn my head enough to draw air. Because with each soul he absorbed, his strength and presence swelled. Soon, his demonic form would erupt through Jimmy's body, and I'd know who I was dealing with. That was what he wanted me to witness. And by then it would be too late for me to do anything. More souls rushed into him with increasing speed.

"*Vigore!*" I tried, straining a hand toward his ring.

Nothing moved through me. I wished now that I hadn't sacrificed my luck quotient.

No, I thought resolutely. *Getting you to doubt yourself is a demon's stock-in-trade. The Order's not as weak as Damien is making you believe. Arianna sent you Gretchen for a reason.*

I thought back to our training, how Gretchen had applied the black luck. I then considered the three loops I'd had to jump through in order to remove it. Those acts weren't arbitrary, I decided.

I thought of the last loop in particular, the one that had involved the mirror event Pierce had picked up in the painting: the pendant and the ring. Fresh understanding broke through me.

As though sensing the conclusion I had reached, Damien's red eyes met mine. He scowled and mashed harder on my neck until my air was cut off again. As souls continued to pour inside him, I grasped his ankle and tried to speak, but I couldn't form the Word.

Something scurried into my peripheral vision.

For an instant the storm broke. "Dammit!" Damien cried.

Buster was out of his carrier. He'd come up behind Damien and snapped a claw into his Achilles' tendon—not something the demon was immune to, apparently. Raw air rushed into my lungs as the pressure lifted from my neck. Buster dangled from Damien's leg for a moment before dropping and trying to scuttle away. But Damien aimed a hand at him.

And I aimed Grandpa's ring at Damien. *"Balaur!"* I shouted.

The power of the enchantment erupted from the embossed face of the rearing dragon and slammed into Damien. He screamed as his body erupted into bright flames. I pushed myself back, keeping the ring leveled at him.

"No!" he screamed. "No, damn you!"

I hit him with another dose. He ran around blindly as fresh fire billowed from his body. He flailed his arms, trying to find me. But he never came close. And he was slowing, his cries falling to mumbles.

At last, he collapsed to his knees, then face down. The infernal storm broke apart, as though the portal to his realm had been slammed shut. The room fell strangely silent, the ringing fading from my ears.

I watched for several more minutes as the fire consumed Damien. Buster joined me, peering out from behind my legs. When something moved off to our right, the clawdad and I both turned.

"Goodness gracious," Mae huffed, pushing herself up from behind a ruined display. She dusted herself off, then righted her walker and tapped it toward us. "Everyone all right?" she asked.

I coughed to clear my throat. "Yeah. How about you?"

"Buster and I took a hard fall, but I'm no worse for the wear." Halfway to us, she stopped and stooped for the open carrier. Buster scurried up her gown and perched on her shoulder.

"Well, Buster just saved my butt."

"You did?" Mae said to him, chuckling and scratching his head.

Buster chattered something and wriggled his tendrils. When Mae arrived beside me, she looked at where Damien's vessel continued to burn. I hadn't wanted Jimmy to die, but I'd had no choice.

"What in the hell did you do to him?" she asked.

I looked down at my right fist. "There's a power in this ring that my grandfather also stored in my coin necklace, as a backup. Turns out he also placed the power of the necklace in the ring. But enchantments react with the metals they're stored inside, altering the effect somewhat. Damien adapted to the enchantment in the iron coin, but he wasn't prepared for the same enchantment coming from the silver ring."

That's what I'd been counting on, anyway: not luck, but the culmination of my study and experience to arrive at that conclusion.

Mae sighed and shook her head. "I've got a lot to learn about magic."

I went over and retrieved her wedding band from the floor. "Speaking of rings, I'm really sorry about that." I handed it to her. "I should have known better than to listen to him."

"Man did sound seven shades of shady," Mae agreed, pushing her wedding band back onto her finger.

I looked around until I spotted my cane. It was lying

beside Babe Ruth's baseball bat. I retrieved the cane and was sliding it back into my belt when the mic affixed to my shoulder crackled.

"Hey, Croft, you still with us?"

"I'm here, Hoffman. How's it looking up there?"

"The doors just came open. We're working on getting everyone out."

I pumped a fist before asking, "How are we looking casualty-wise?"

"Too early to tell, but we've got thousands streaming out and it looks like thousands more coming from the concourse. So I'd say limited. Did you find what you were looking for?"

I glanced over at Jimmy's body. "Yeah, I did."

"All right, good."

"Hey, Hoffman?"

"What is it?" he asked suspiciously.

"You helped save a lot of lives tonight."

He grunted. *"I could probably say the same about you."*

I recalled what the demon had said about Red Hook being a trap.

"Have you heard from your partner recently?"

"No. I'll see what I can find out."

"Please do," I replied urgently.

"See you when you come up, Croft."

32

By the time Mae and I reached the main concourse, police and emergency personnel were already inside. The dead we passed had been covered, but it wasn't hard to imagine their shriveled corpses. As Mae averted her eyes, I reminded her—and myself—that it could have been so much worse.

We emerged from the stadium to a throng of activity. Emergency vehicles were parked everywhere, red lights flashing. The news trucks had arrived too, and I recognized Courtney from Channel Four. Before the blonde anchor could spot us, I steered Mae away.

I craned my neck in search of Hoffman. With the crisis over, I was thinking more and more about what Damien had said about the false trail he'd planted with the Ark and how he'd designed it to end in death.

That was the route your partner took, the poor thing.

My heart pounded sickly in my chest. He was a demon. Surely he'd been lying.

I was about to radio Hoffman when someone called my

name. I turned to find Vega limping through the crowd. Her face was blackened with soot and she'd been gashed above her right eyebrow. I ran to her, legs weak with relief. Arriving in front of her, I held her arms.

"Are you all right?"

She nodded solemnly. "And you?"

"Yeah. I'm fine."

Her large eyes searched mine for another moment, then she slipped her arms around my waist and pressed her body against me. I held the back of her head to my chest and absorbed her solidity and warmth. I could feel the amulet pulsing beneath her shirt. It had kept her safe. Vega and I remained like that for the next minute, deaf to the chaos around us.

"What happened?" I asked at last.

"Quinton was hiding in a basement. Pierce went after him, but there was an explosion. The windows shattered for blocks. When we got inside, the suspect was in pieces, and Pierce was dead."

I swallowed hard on a tide of grief. Just as Damien had intimated, not only had he meant to lead us to Red Hook, he had intended to kill us when we arrived—apparently by using Quinton as a high-powered infernal bomb. His painting altered, Pierce hadn't seen the ambush coming.

"I was able to recover this." Vega stepped back and pulled a Ziploc bag from her pocket. Inside, I could see the silver necklace. She had packed it in salt, just like I'd taught her.

"Good work," I said, accepting the bag. I placed it in a coat pocket near the salt-filled bag that held the ring. I would give them to a high-level member of the Order when one arrived.

"So it's done?" she asked.

I looked over at Yankee Stadium. The Order would be able to tell me for sure, but I nodded. The enchantment in Grandpa's ring had blasted Damien back to his realm and slammed the door in his wake. The demon had been hurt. He would need time to recover. In the meantime, the cursed items would be sterilized and the channels he'd arrived by filled in.

"Everson?" I turned to find Mae tapping her way up to us. "I don't mean to interrupt your reunion with this pretty thing, but it's past my and Buster's bedtime, and I'm getting a little chilly."

"Oh, Mae, this is Detective Vega."

"Pleased to meet you," Mae said.

"And this is Mae Johnson. My partner."

Vega cocked an eyebrow at me as she shook Mae's hand.

"I'll explain later," I said, guiding her a few steps away. "Listen, I know we're going to be tied up for a few days with all of this, but how about stealing a few hours at Prospect Park this weekend? You, me, and Tony."

Vega's eyes glistened above her weary smile. "I'd like that."

I leaned down and kissed her. Screw the PDA agreement. Judging by the force of her return kiss, Vega felt the same. When we separated, I brushed a strand of hair from her gashed brow and held her sooty cheek.

"Talk soon," I said.

"Talk soon," she agreed, and returned to work.

———

A POLICE OFFICER GAVE MAE AND ME A LIFT BACK TO HER apartment. I escorted her inside and up to her unit. "Well,

Everson," she said, accepting the carrier. "You sure know how to show an old gal a good time."

"I've still got it," I quipped, making her laugh. "In all seriousness, Mae, what happened tonight ... I couldn't have done it without you. I mean that. Those imps would have eaten the stadium alive."

"And don't forget about Buster." She held up the carrier.

"Of course not." And to think I'd nearly banished the nether creature that would spare me from Damien. I poked a finger through the mesh door to scratch his head, but Buster backed away and snapped a claw at me.

Mae chuckled. "He's getting a little cranky. We made a good team tonight, though, didn't we?"

"Damn good."

I thought about what Arianna had said about my future team finding me one by one. I'd be lying if I said I had pictured someone like Mae, but here we were, on the back end of a mission accomplished.

"Hey," I said before she could disappear into her apartment. "Would it be all right if I called on you in the future?"

"I'll beat you over the head if you don't. But to be honest, I'll have to take things on a case-by-case basis. I'm a little old for this city-saving stuff. Older than I realized. Tonight taught me that."

"It takes a different kind of endurance," I agreed. "Heck, *I* still get tired. You might feel differently about it in the morning."

"Which for me is only a few hours away. Night, Everson."

"Goodnight, Mae." I kissed her cheek and then closed the door firmly behind her.

I didn't want Buster to get out.

For the rest of the week, the city was abuzz with the "Massacre at Yankee Stadium." Just over five hundred fans lost their lives that night. Way too many, but I found consolation in knowing that if Damien had carried out his full plan, it would have been a hundred times that.

Plenty of cameras and phones had caught the imp attack, but as often happened when extra-planar beings with their extra-planar auras took form in our world, the images were blobby. With the blobbiness, rumors began to spread that the attack had never happened, that it had all been a staged event. Websites and online videos sprang up ascribing various motives to city and federal officials. Never mind the parade of eyewitnesses or interviews with the victims' families. That was all part of the conspiracy too, the doubters claimed. The doubts became even more widespread when witnesses described a man encased in golden light flying around the concourses.

Probably just as well.

But in fairness to the doubters, I suspected Mayor Lowder and his team of planting some of the early rumors to keep the developers from backing out. Right now, Budge needed to preserve the redevelopment projects more than he needed credibility with the public.

Naturally, the NYPD was busy that week. I only got to talk to Vega here and there. The period was busy for me as well. Arianna from the Order arrived the morning following the attack. I gave her the ring and necklace to inspect. Before neutralizing them, she scanned the city for other artifacts bearing the same energy signature, but she found no trace of

Damien's presence. Neither could she determine the prove-
nance of the common items.

She did find something, though. In the charred remains
of Jimmy Land, a small hole snaked from his core. "As if
something had burrowed out," she said. With the five
hundred souls Damien claimed that night, a germ of the
demon's essence may have taken root in our world, she
explained. But Arianna doubted it had been able to maintain
itself once out. Most likely it evaporated within moments.
And indeed, a search had turned up nothing.

As perhaps further evidence that the demon was history,
Becky's inheritance fell into jeopardy when the state of Cali-
fornia determined that her grandparents' will was a forgery.
Similarly, the member of the Ark who had won the state
lottery was scammed out of her winnings. And the member
Becky had called "the second coming of Jimi Hendrix" fell off
the stage at the end of a late-night show, shattering his guitar
and the bones in both hands. Suspect to begin with, demon
deals needed a demonic presence to sustain them.

No more demon, no more deal.

Arianna spent two days sealing the hole back to his realm.
When she returned, I sensed there had been more to
Damien's plan than she was telling me, but only because she
had questions of her own that needed answering first.

On her last day, Arianna performed Pierce's final rites. We
held them at his house, just the two of us and Pierce's
wrapped body. To think Damien had claimed someone as
powerful as Pierce sobered me. I remembered Pierce's final
words to me: "You and I are going to be a force in this city."
That hit me right in the feelings. He went up in a transparent
blue flame that reminded me of a Himitsu painting, simple
and yet beautifully layered.

I was thankful I'd made my peace with him.

Arianna ended her visit by giving me some updates on the Order's work. The damage around our world was more extensive than first thought, hence the scarcity of Elder members. The good news was that the Order had located more magic-users, and several had begun their training. In the near term, the Order would be depending on our scattered numbers more than ever.

"And my team?" I asked.

"They'll come," she assured me.

Gretchen Wagonhurst returned from the faerie realm that Friday with a haircut and a fae tan, which was to say her skin was a shade lighter. Sort of an esoteric joke. She made no mention of the case and seemed to have forgotten all about my black luck. Instead, she announced she was moving into Pierce's house, something she'd apparently worked out with the Order. I can't say I was sad to see her go.

But as I watched her pack, I remembered her whole spiel on our first day of training about not being a mentor:

You know, the wise hag who gives you cryptic clues that sound like nonsense until the final act when you're staring death in the face, and then—whammo!— a flashbulb goes off, all those clues make perfect sense, and you save the day.

But that was more or less what she *had* done, though it had been far from clear at the time. The black luck she'd given me had compelled me to go out to close the loops—actions that had turned out to be key in finding and repelling Damien. I thought back over them.

The third loop had involved the mirror event Pierce had picked up in the painting: the pendant and the ring. That led to the insight that Damien had another play. The second loop alerted me that the ley lines were off; I later pinpointed

Yankee Stadium as the epicenter of the disturbance. And the first loop led to me bringing Mae along, someone who could control nether creatures.

"Thank you," I told Gretchen.

She blinked over at me. "For what?"

"Helping me. You made sure I had everything I needed to solve the case."

She finished stuffing her clothes into the suitcase. "I told you I'm not that kind of teacher."

"Sure you're not."

"If you learned anything, though, I hope it's that your luck quotient is only a handicap if you have to depend on it. Your magic's always talking to you. It's a matter of learning to listen. That's how you become your best magic-user."

I nodded in understanding. "Kind of like seeing the world as a Himitsu painting."

"I don't know what you're talking about, but sure. Practice, practice, practice will only get you so far. It can actually have a stunting effect after a point. Professionally *and* personally."

"That's why you took my *Magical Me* book."

"That trashed thing? You can have it back if you want."

I followed her cocked head toward the divan. The taped-up book was being used as a leveler again, the leg planted smack in the middle of Jocko Wraithe's plastic grin. Gretchen was right. There was faking it, and then there was making it. For the past year, I'd been doing too much of the first. The weekend had shown me that. I left the book where it was.

When Gretchen hefted her several suitcases, I offered to help, but she tottered past me. "We should probably set up some kind of training schedule," she said. "I don't work weekends or the first, second, and fourth Mondays of the month. I'm away most Fridays too, more so now. And Thursdays can be iffy, especially in months ending in *r* or *y*. I'll give you a call."

"Sounds good," I said. "Hey, I take back what I said earlier."

"What? About Lich being a better trainer than me, or that I'm batshit crazy?"

"You heard that too, huh?" I blushed as I hustled around her to open the door. "Look, I'm glad you're my mentor."

"Well, I still think you're going to be a project. But as long as you do exactly what I tell you..." She left it at that, breaking wind as she heaved herself into the corridor. I quickly shut the door.

"Is she gone?"

I turned to find Tabitha entering through the cat door in the window.

"Mostly," I replied, grimacing and waving a hand in front of my face.

Tabitha hopped onto the divan and plopped down with a sigh. "I know I complain a lot, darling, but I rather enjoy it being just the two of us. It will be nice having things back to normal."

I nodded vaguely, even though I was sure things were going to be far from normal for awhile. Especially if doing *exactly* what Gretchen told me was anything like last weekend.

"Oh, and I'd just *die* for one of your meals tonight," Tabitha added as she settled into the depression on her perch. I looked from Tabitha to the wrecked kitchen. I'd have to clean it up sooner or later, I reasoned. Plus I was craving some home-cooked food myself.

"How does a nice filet mignon sound?"

33

The next day was one of those perfect late-September Saturdays, the air dry and clean but not yet cold, with the first fallen leaves beginning to swirl around the sidewalks. Vega, Tony, and I left the sidewalk near where we'd parked and joined a path that circled the playing fields at Prospect Park.

I took Vega's hand in mine. Her son surprised me by running around and clasping my other hand.

"So was that the best pizza you ever had or what?" he asked, referring to our lunch stop. It had been a chain restaurant with a big cartoon mouse for a mascot. I could still taste the freezer burn on the crust.

"It's, ah, officially in my top twenty," I hedged.

"Hey, what's this?" he asked, releasing my hand to reach into my coat pocket.

"Tony," Vega scolded. "Don't grab. *Ask*."

"He did, technically," I pointed out, which got me one of Vega's deadpan looks. But when she saw the misty ball he was holding, her expression changed to one of surprise, then curiosity.

"Is that...?"

"Yeah," I said.

"What is it?" Tony persisted.

"It's called an emo ball," I said. "It holds one of the most precious gifts in the world: the love of a mother for her son. An emo ball is the next best thing to having the living, breathing artifact." As the mist shifted, the light inside glowed over Tony's wonderstruck face.

"Whoa," he said.

"Never take that love for granted," I added.

"I thought it was destroyed," Vega whispered.

"The object was, but not its Form." I recalled the joy I'd felt when Arianna had produced the ball from her skirt. It contained the same warmth and vitality I'd remembered— maybe more so for believing I had lost it for good. "Arianna reminded me that my mother created the ball in a thought realm. As such, it can be reproduced here. Not by me, though. Not yet, anyway."

Tony handed the ball back carefully. Ahead, a group of young kids were playing a pick-up game of soccer at one end of a field. Tony turned to his mother, eyes large and expectant.

"Go ahead," she said before he could ask.

Tony took off, his curly hair fluttering in the wind.

"Well," I said when Vega and I were alone, "we survived the week." I regretted the word choice the second it left my mouth. We'd both come too damn close to that *not* being the case.

I started to stammer, but she spoke first. "I know what you

meant. It helped having this to look forward to." She squeezed my hand.

"Absolutely," I agreed, smiling at her.

"But I want you to tell me what's wrong."

"The two of us together? How could anything be wrong?"

She stopped and faced me. "Your eyes, Croft."

"Damn. That obvious?"

She nodded.

I considered how much to tell her, but I decided that if I was serious about this, us, it had to be everything. I inhaled and blew out my breath.

"I told you about Pierce's painting, the necklace and the ring?" I waited for her to nod. "It revealed a few things: that Damien had another play, that it involved an actual ring, like mine. But when I faced him, I had a third insight. If Damien was locked in a mirror event, as Pierce put it, then maybe I was locked in one as well. I had destroyed the vampire Arnaud by using the power Grandpa had secretly stored in the pendant. But what if Grandpa had done the reverse? What if I could conquer *this* opponent by calling up the power of the pendant with the ring?" I paused. "It worked ... but maybe not in the way I thought."

"What do you mean?"

"Well, enchantments can deviate somewhat depending on what metal they're stored in. I reasoned that while Damien had adapted to the enchantment in the pendant, he'd have no defense against the same enchantment in the ring."

"Different metals," Vega said.

"Yeah, or different enchantments."

Her brow furrowed in confusion. "Explain."

"I'm worried it was the Brasov Pact that lit Damien up."

"But lit up is lit up, right?"

"Yeah, but if the Brasov Pact did the lighting, it would mean the demon had vampire in him. And judging by where the cursed artifacts were found, not to mention Damien's familiarity with me, I have a nasty feeling I know which one."

"Wait, you think Damien was…"

I lowered my eyes and nodded. "Arnaud Thorne."

"How? You destroyed him."

"Yes and no. Vampires are descendants of the earliest demons. When a vampire is destroyed, he's cast down to whatever infernal pit his strain came from. The pits are horrible places. Take the worst torture chamber you can imagine, then multiply the pain and sadism by a hundred. Or better yet, don't." I grimaced as I remembered some of the descriptions I'd read that week. "Even a vampire as powerful as Arnaud is nothing to the demons that rule down there. They delight in the torture and humiliation they can visit on their weaker kin. Ultimately, the vampire is made a slave, or else his essence is pulverized and put to other evil purposes."

"So how could Damien have been Arnaud?"

"Because when I destroyed Arnaud, he was bonded to an ancient shadow fiend. I didn't think about it at the time, but that might have afforded him some power down there. Enough, maybe, to have become something else."

"Like what?"

"A demon."

Vega fell silent long enough for me to become aware of the excited shouts from the soccer field. Tony had just scored a goal. The same child Arnaud had abducted the year before.

"Even if it was Arnaud," Vega said quietly, "you sent him back, right?"

I remembered the hole Arianna had described in the

burnt corpse of Damien's vessel. A hole large enough for the germ of the demon to have emerged. She hadn't found anything, but...

"Everson?" Vega prompted.

"Arianna thinks so, yeah. But just in case, I want you to have this."

I removed the amulet from around Vega's neck and replaced it with my coin pendant.

"I can't accept this," she said. "It belonged to your grandfather."

I pressed the coin softly to her sternum. "It holds the power of the Brasov Pact. It'll keep you safe."

She looked down at my hand, then over at the soccer fields. At last she folded her hand around mine, and we resumed walking.

"Do you think this will ever end?" she asked after a long silence.

I knew she wasn't just talking about Damien or Arnaud now, but all of it. "I don't know," I answered honestly. "All we can do is keep fighting. Keep pushing back. Just look around. Today the kids have the playing fields. Tomorrow it might be the woods. Someday, the entire city."

"And we'll never know if we give up."

"That's right." I peeked over at her. "Or forget to love."

Vega snorted. "I give you an opening to drop the L word, and *that's* your move?"

Face warming with embarrassment, I waved my hands. "All right, yeah, that was pretty awful. Let me try again."

"Forget it, Croft. You whiffed."

"Hey, that was only strike one. I get two more chances."

"Nope." She smirked. "My game, my rules."

"I'm calling foul."

"Call it all you want."

"Well, I love you. So there."

"I love you too. But it still doesn't count."

I sighed in pretend exasperation. "Well, will it count in the morning?"

She gave me a sidelong look. "It might."

"Cool," I said, taking her hand again. "I can live with that."

We rounded the end of the field behind the soccer net just as Tony kicked in another goal.

34

The East River

That night, while the city slept, a small creature slipped from the dark waters and scrambled, shivering, over the rocks of a wooded island. Moonlight glistened from his gray, wrinkled skin.

At the tree line, he stopped and rose onto bony hind legs. His eyes were pale and bulbous, and in his still-developing vision, a mass of lights blurred to the south.

Manhattan, he tried to say, but the name came out a gargled whisper.

The creature swore and fell to his claw-like hands. So close to wielding the power he'd earned, so close to commanding it all. But here he was—a naked little being, hiding from the world.

Because of *Everson Croft,* he seethed, fresh hatred burning through him.

But you were reborn, he reminded himself in a gentler voice. *You're here.* His plan had afforded him that, at least. And he had started out small before. He had grown, developed, amassed power...

He could do it again.

Something rustled in the grass to his right. The creature turned and pounced without thought. The rat was large, more than half his size. He thrust his face into the rodent's dank-smelling neck, drawn to the pulsating jugular. Needle-like canines punched into the warm vessel. He sucked hungrily, delighting in the rat's struggle, in its weakening shrieks and kicks.

When it was over, the creature rose from the dead rat and wiped the hair and blood from his mouth. Fresh vitality pumped through him. Maybe it was his ambition, but he felt a little larger. And when he peered south again, the mass of lights seemed slightly sharper in his vision.

Tonight, this wretched island, he thought. *One day soon, the entire city.*

Falling back to all fours, he scurried into the trees.

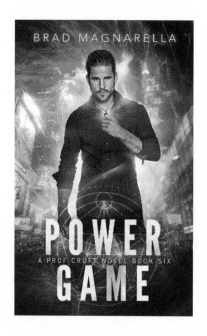

Power Game
(Prof Croft, Book 6)

AUTHOR'S NOTES

In the month or so after *Black Luck* was published, I received several messages from readers saying Mae is now one of their favorite supporting characters and can they have more of her, please? The funny thing is she was never supposed to have happened.

In my original notes for the chapter, I wrote that Everson would perform a routine banishment, largely so we could observe his improvements in the year or so since *Death Mage* and understand that he wants to be more like his father. But as I was writing the scene, I got to thinking...

What if we pitched Everson a curveball? What if the "victim" could somehow control the conjured creatures and was raising them as pets? What kind of person would that be? Maternal, strong-willed, a touch off kilter (at one point I had her garnishing the pet food with her own blood before deciding that was too much), prior experience with animals preferred. Enter retired veterinarian and nether whisperer Mae Johnson.

It excites more than disturbs me when a character writes herself into a story, especially one as fun as Mae. And we got Buster out of the deal too. So to the readers who were asking, yes—expect to see more Mae.

The character of Pierce Dalton was much more premeditated. With Everson having insecurities around his magic-use as well as his relationship with Vega, I wanted to bring in someone who would needle both. Pierce, with his good looks, unflappable English manners, and mastery of magic, was the ticket. I also liked that his brand of magic was radically different from Everson's, the made-up *Himitsu* being an Eastern form of *pigmentomancy*, or divination from colors.

Speaking of new characters, Everson finally has the mentor Arianna promised him. And disgusting or not, Gretchen *did* shove him up the next rung of the ladder, even if it meant pumping him full of black luck.

Which begs the questions: Is she really the best match for him, or is the Order that short staffed? And will Everson ultimately survive her training? For now I'm just glad he seems to be over his self-help phase. If affirmations and tofu/wheat-germ shakes had become a regular part of the story, I'm not sure how much longer I could've stuck with him. Tabitha agrees.

The book began with some questions surrounding Everson and Vega's relationship and ended with them swapping L words. Everson also gifted her his grandfather's coin pendant —no small token. Will they go further, or will the pressure of their deepening commitment prove too much?

I'm almost as intrigued by what could be the start of a budding bromance between Everson and Detective Hoffman. Talk about characters surprising me. Geez.

Finally, the creature at book's end. Arnaud? Not Arnaud? That question and many others will be answered in the next book. But given that the creature destroyed a very powerful mage in Pierce tells you he's no slouch.

Everson better watch his ass.

All right, time to acknowledge those who made the fifth installment in the *Prof Croft* series possible. To mark the beginning of the second quadrilogy, the design team at damonza.com went with a fresh color scheme for the cover, as well as a new wardrobe for Croft, and I love it. Thanks, guys. Thanks also to my beta and advanced readers, who included Beverly Collie, Mark Denman, and Erin Halbmaier, for their editorial feedback. And hugs to Sharlene Magnarella for final proofing. As always, any errors that remain are this author's alone.

I also want to acknowledge James Patrick Cronin, the very talented voice actor who brings the books in the Croftverse to life on the audio editions. Those books, including samples, can be found at Audible.com.

Last but not least, thank you, awesome reader, for seeing Prof Croft through yet another adventure.

Until the next one...

Best Wishes,
Brad Magnarella

P.S. Be sure to check out my website to learn more about the Croftverse, download a pair of free prequels, and find out what's coming! That's all at bradmagnarella.com

CROFTVERSE CATALOGUE

PROF CROFT PREQUELS

Book of Souls

Siren Call

MAIN SERIES

Demon Moon

Blood Deal

Purge City

Death Mage

Black Luck

Power Game

Druid Bond

Night Rune

Shadow Duel

Shadow Deep

Godly Wars

Angel Doom

SPIN-OFFS

Croft & Tabby

Croft & Wesson

BLUE WOLF

Blue Curse

Blue Shadow

Blue Howl

Blue Venom

Blue Blood

Blue Storm

SPIN-OFF

Legion Files

———

For the entire chronology go to bradmagnarella.com

ABOUT THE AUTHOR

Brad Magnarella writes urban fantasy for the same reason most read it...

To explore worlds where magic crackles from fingertips, vampires and shifters walk city streets, cats talk (some excessively), and good prevails against all odds. It's shamelessly fun.

His two main series, Prof Croft and Blue Wolf, make up the growing Croftverse, with over a quarter-million books sold to date and an Independent Audiobook Award nomination.

Hopelessly nomadic, Brad can be found in a rented room overseas or hiking America's backcountry.

Or just go to www.bradmagnarella.com

Made in the USA
Middletown, DE
05 March 2023

26258514R00187